The Unfortunate Debutante

The Unfortunate Debutante

Laura Beers

Phase Publishing, LLC
Seattle

Phase Publishing, LLC first paperback edition
October 2019

ISBN 978-1-943048-96-0
Library of Congress Control Number 2019914542

Cataloging-in-Publication Data on file.

More Romance from Phase Publishing

by
Laura Beers
Saving Shadow
A Peculiar Courtship
To Love a Spy
A Tangled Ruse
A Deceptive Bargain
The Baron's Daughter

by
Rebecca Connolly
An Arrangement of Sorts
The Lady and the Gent
The Merry Lives of Spinsters

by
Emily Daniels
Devlin's Daughter
Lucia's Lament
A Song for a Soldier

by
Grace Donovan
Saint's Ride

Prologue
England, 1813

Miss Emma Pearson's black dress billowed around her legs as she stood at the edge of her parents' graves. She could not stop the tears that flowed down her cheeks. She was alone now. There was no one to protect her from the harsh realities of being a young woman with little income. Her dreams vanished the moment she buried her father.

Her eyes shifted towards the plot of land next to her father's. The headstone read *David Ernest Pearson*. The Marquess of Downshire had been gracious enough to send her brother's body back to be buried in their ancestral cemetery and even sent along a marble headstone with David's birth and death dates carved into the stone. David had been an agent of the Crown and was killed while on assignment in Scotland. A sob escaped her lips because his death hurt the most. He had been her best friend, her confidante. What was she going to do without her brother? How was she going to survive?

After her mother died five years ago, Emma was sent off to boarding school, and she'd only just returned when her father had unexpectedly fallen ill. Her father was a constable, but he also owned a general store in the small village of Totternhoe. To her, he seemed unbreakable, and her heart had become saddened as she watched him withering away.

She swiped at the tears on her cheeks. Crying wouldn't accomplish anything. She had to pick up the pieces of her shattered life and begin anew. Somehow, she was going to survive this and become stronger because of it. But first, even though it would do no good, she was going to allow herself the privilege of crying.

Walking through the tall grass mingled with red poppy flowers gently blowing in the wind, Emma put her hands down and ran her fingers through the soft, green blades. Her two-level, thatched roof cottage came into view, and she forced herself to smile. She could count her blessings amidst her trials and hope she could eventually find joy again. At least she had a home to live in.

As she drew closer, Emma saw a tall, broad-shouldered man with dark hair and stern features knocking at her door. He was finely dressed, as was the beautiful, blonde-haired woman standing next to him.

She wiped away the last of the tears from her cheeks as she increased her stride. "May I help you?" she asked, stopping a few yards away.

"Is this the home of Constable Pearson?" the man inquired.

Emma forced down the lump in her throat. "I am sorry to be the bearer of sad tidings, but my father passed away over a week ago." She glanced mournfully over her shoulder. "I have just come from visiting my parents' graves."

His eyes searched hers knowingly. "Are you Emma, by chance?"

"I am," she replied. "Were you friends of my father's?"

"No, we were friends of your brother, David," he responded with a shake of his head.

A genuine smile came to her lips. "Please, do come in." She brushed past them and opened the door, leaving it open.

"May I offer you some refreshment? I know we have tea, but I am not sure where it was left," she shared over her shoulder.

"Why is that?" the woman asked in a polite voice as she followed her into the dirty kitchen.

"After my father died, our housekeeper left because I didn't know how I was going to pay her wages," she admitted reluctantly as she searched through nearly empty drawers.

"She left you?" the man asked with a frown.

Emma froze, and her eyes grew wide at his tone. Perhaps she had been too hasty in letting these strangers into her home. After a moment, her gaze transferred to the woman, and she found herself relaxing at the kindness visible in her eyes.

"I do have some money, but she urged me to keep it since she had already found suitable work in the village," Emma explained.

"My apologies for my tone," he expressed. "My wife has stated, on more than one occasion, that I can come across as boorish."

Good, he's married, she thought, as she continued her search. "I'm afraid I did not catch your names."

"I am Luke, and this is my wife, Rachel," he informed her, smiling, as he sat down on a wobbly, wooden chair.

Emma wanted to giggle as she saw Luke struggle to remain seated on the rickety chair.

"And what of your family? Do you plan to live with them?" Rachel inquired, the concern evident in her voice.

Turning around with a jar of tea leaves in her hand, Emma shook her head sadly. "I am afraid I have no other relations to speak of." She placed the jar onto the table, her voice becoming strained. "I am very much alone in this world, and I must accept my fate."

Blinking away her emotions, she removed her straw bonnet and placed it on the cluttered table. "How did you know my brother?" she asked as she started to heat the water over the hearth.

Rachel sat down near Luke as she explained, "David was assigned to protect me…"

Her words were stilled as the kitchen door was thrown open, and Peter Lockhart walked into the kitchen, oblivious to the fact that she had guests.

"Emma, there you are…" His voice trailed off when he noticed she was not alone. "And who are your guests?"

She shook her head and pressed her lips together. "Really, Peter," she admonished, "you can't just barge into my home."

He huffed indignantly. "I can if you are my betrothed."

"I never consented to marry you," she responded, frowning. Why did he insist that they were engaged?

"We shall see," was all he said.

Luke rose, and his commanding presence dominated the small room. "Are you engaged to this man?" His tone was abrupt.

Emma frowned as Peter advanced closer to Luke, then stopped. His mouth tightened, and his eyes sparked with annoyance. "You do not need to concern yourself with Miss Pearson's welfare."

Luke scoffed and turned his attention back to her, dismissing the man. "We were hoping to speak to you privately."

"You may speak freely in front of Peter. He was my father's solicitor," Emma said as she walked over to a chair.

Peter grabbed a chair and repositioned it close to her. "I am now *your* solicitor, dearest."

Emma glanced disapprovingly at the closeness of the chairs but didn't say anything. Peter was handsome enough, with his chiseled jaw, brown hair, and broad shoulders, but his words were always too smooth, too rehearsed. It had been that way since they were kids.

Luke adjusted his waistcoat as he slowly sat down. "As we stated before, we were friends with David, and we owed him money, in addition to a great personal debt."

"How much money?" Peter asked eagerly.

Ignoring his question, Rachel smiled at Emma. "David was assigned to protect me when I was in Scotland…"

Emma cut her off as realization washed over her. "You're Lady Rachel," she blurted out. She turned towards Luke, her eyes wide in amazement. "And you are Lord Downshire… or John, as my brother called you." At their puzzled expressions, she revealed, "David always wrote to me when he was on assignment, and he predicted you two would eventually marry." She grew sad and pensive. "He considered both of you his friends."

Tears welled up in Rachel's eyes as she shared, "I also considered him a friend, but it was my fault he was killed." She swiped at the tears streaming down her face. "David tried to warn me about going down to the shoreline that night, but I was stubborn and refused to listen. I was attacked and he…" Her words hitched as a sob escaped her lips.

Leaning forward in her chair, Emma reached for her hand, her voice full of compassion. "You must not blame yourself for David's death. He had a tendency to help damsels in distress." She smiled, her eyes growing reflective. "He always looked after people, even if you ordered him not to."

Luke grinned knowingly. "It sounds as if you have firsthand experience."

"Heavens, yes." Emma laughed for the first time in weeks. "My older brother was relentless in his protection of me, but over time, I grew to understand that was how he showed he loved me." Her lips tightened, and tears welled in her eyes. "Excuse me," she whimpered, "I just miss him so much."

Peter reached over and patted her leg. "There, there," he said, solicitously. "You must remember, it is not proper for a lady to show emotion in public."

Emma diverted her gaze towards her lap but not before she saw Rachel frown with displeasure at Peter's inappropriate display of affection.

"Now, about the money you owe Miss Emma," Peter prodded.

"We do owe you £5,000, or…" Luke stopped and turned to look at his wife. Something passed between them, but she couldn't decipher what it was exactly. He turned his focus back towards Emma and continued. "Or, you can become my ward."

Her mouth parted in surprise, and she found herself speechless at his offer.

Huffing, Peter shook his head. "Miss Emma is sixteen years old and does not need a guardian. She is old enough to marry and begin having children."

Luke's eyes grew hard in response to Peter's words, but his expression softened as his gaze returned to Emma. "If you become my ward, Rachel and I will grant you every luxury that we can bestow upon you. We will continue your education, clothe you in the finest gowns, and prepare you for a life in Society, if you so desire," he said, his voice kind and encouraging. "You will not lack for anything, including love and family."

Her mind began reeling with the possibilities. Could this be truly happening to her? If she became the Marquess of Downshire's ward, she would be presented to Society. She would mingle with aristocrats.

Peter turned towards Emma. "You are a constable's daughter. The ton will never accept you. It will only lead to more heartache."

In response, Luke's firm voice drew Emma's attention. "As my ward, you will be entitled to a dowry of £25,000, and I give you my word that you will be embraced by the ton wholeheartedly."

Emma's eyes grew wide as she stared at Luke incredulously. "I would be an heiress," she finally managed to say.

"You would be far more than just an heiress," Rachel assured her. "You would be free to make your own choices, to fall in love, and choose your own husband."

Leaning even closer to Emma, Peter's voice grew hushed, urgent. "Do not be fooled by them. He wants you for his mistress."

"How dare you make such an offensive accusation!" Luke shouted, jumping up so fast that he knocked his chair over.

Rachel put her hand on her husband's sleeve, stilling his outrage. "Emma, you must believe that we only have your best interest at heart, nothing more."

"Why would you be so generous?" she asked curiously.

Luke picked up his chair and sat down. He reached for Rachel's hand, his eyes lingering on her face before turning back towards Emma. "Because David was my friend. He taught me how to speak to Rachel and kept my secret, which allowed me more time to woo her." He gave a half-hearted smile as his voice hitched. "He also saved my life, but more importantly, he saved my wife's life. He gave his life to give me mine. Without Rachel..." His voice trailed off as a tear rolled down his face. "To repay my debt, I vow to protect you as he would have, to ensure you are happy and cared for."

Emma could hear the sincerity in his voice, and she knew his offer was genuine. "Thank you. I would like to accept your offer and become your ward," she responded, smiling.

"No, Emma!" Peter shouted. "We are to be wed."

She shook her head in response. "No, Peter. I already told you, you're like a brother to me. I could never marry you."

"Don't do this," he urged. "I love you."

Emma shifted in her seat, knowing she was making the right choice. Peter had offered for her multiple times, but she had always politely turned him down. For some reason, he had always assumed they would end up together, but that had never been a part of her plan.

"And I love you, too... as a brother," she informed him.

"You will regret this, make no mistake of that," Peter assured her as he stood up. He tugged down on his waistcoat before he stormed out of the room, slamming the door shut behind him.

Emma nearly jumped at the loud slam of the door. She slowly

turned her apologetic gaze back to them. "He means well," she said in a hesitant tone.

Luke rose from his seat and assisted Rachel. "We're traveling back to our estate in Scotland. Would you like to accompany us? Or we can send back our coach, giving you time to pack up your home?"

Emma's eyes roamed wistfully around the kitchen. There was nothing for her here anymore. "If you are not opposed, I would like to accompany you now. I find that my loneliness makes my heart ache."

Rachel reached out and embraced Emma. Leaning back, she reminded her, "You will never be alone again. You are now a part of our family."

A smile lit up her face, and Emma felt her eyes sparkle with renewed happiness. "Thank you," she responded appreciatively.

"It is I who should be thanking you," Luke maintained, stepping closer. "If you had refused my offer to become my ward, we would have been forced to abduct you." He shrugged, his eyes full of merriment. "It makes life easier when a ward comes along willingly."

Emma laughed as she started walking towards the stairs. "If you will give me a few moments, I will pack my trunks. It won't be long."

As she walked up the steps of the narrow staircase to the second level, Emma thought her heart was going to burst with excitement. She was going to become the ward of the Marquess of Downshire, the heir to the Duke of Remington. How her life had changed in mere moments. She was going to socialize with the members of the ton.

Another, more important thought occurred to her. She wasn't going to be alone anymore. She was going to be a part of their family. Perhaps her dream of being a writer wasn't so farfetched. After all, nothing would be beyond her reach now.

This may be the greatest thing that had ever happened to a constable's daughter, she mused.

Chapter One
England, 1815

Emma was a notorious dreamer. She dreamed improbable dreams, and her mind was often far away, in another time. But even her wildest imaginations could not have prepared her for the good fortune that had befallen her. She was in the most remarkable circumstance for a constable's daughter.

At sixteen, she had become the ward of the Marquess of Downshire. She went from living the life of a country miss to one of grandeur and opulence. The simple cotton gowns she had worn in her youth were replaced with the finest silk, her brown hair was now adorned with ribbons, and the coral necklace around her neck was worth more than her family's cottage and land in Totternhoe.

Rachel, the Marchioness of Downshire, leaned closer and whispered, "You are staring at Lord Brisbane."

"Am I? I must have been woolgathering," she replied, diverting her gaze to Rachel.

"Dear heavens," Lady Downshire said, bringing her teacup down to her lap, "I thought we had sufficiently stopped your tendency to reverie. I fear that you may require additional tutoring."

Emma shook her head, causing her ringlets to swish back and forth. "No more training. I will behave."

"See that you do," Rachel responded with mirth in her eyes.

Sitting in the elaborate drawing room of Caddington Manor, Emma couldn't believe that four gentlemen were already vying for her attention, especially since they had only been in London for a fortnight. Two were titled men, but the other two were also men of considerable worth. At least, that is what her guardian had informed her.

One man kept drawing her attention, and it was not because of his appearance or countenance. She couldn't seem to take her eyes off the crumbs on Lord Brisbane's moustache. He looked rather ridiculous, and yet, he somehow managed to retain a sad dignity, making her suspect that he was not a man of great confidence.

"Miss Pearson," Mr. Southhampton, the brother of Earl Fitzroy, began, "please say that you will save me a dance at your ball tomorrow."

She gave him a gracious smile. "I would be honored, Mr. Southampton."

"I shall look forward to it," he replied with a flirtatious wink.

Hoping no one witnessed his bold move, Emma took a moment to consider Mr. Southampton. With his blond hair and sharp features, he was a handsome man, but not enough to tempt her. His words seemed too smooth. Perhaps she should refuse him rather than encourage him by allowing him to dance with her.

Lord Brisbane cleared his throat, and Emma found herself leaning forward to see if the crumbs would finally break free from the confines of his neatly groomed, hairy lip.

"Would you care to go riding with me tomorrow, Miss Pearson?" he asked as the crumbs continued to hold strong to the hairs.

Emma could see the line of sweat forming on Lord Brisbane's brow, and she couldn't help but notice that Mr. Southampton and Mr. Ramsbury were both hiding smirks behind their teacups. It was clear that they expected her to let him down gently. Poor Lord Brisbane, she thought. She had no interest in the man, but she didn't dare embarrass him in front of his peers.

"I would be honored, Lord Brisbane."

He let out a relieved sigh, causing the crumbs to take flight. "That pleases me immensely."

Sitting alone on the upholstered settee, the solemn-faced Lord Haddington appeared content to observe as he sipped his tea. Emma directed her next comment to him.

"Have you read any interesting books, Lord Haddington?"

He gave her a complacent smile. "I'm afraid none that you would understand, my dear," he replied in a condescending tone.

What an insufferable man, she thought. "Truly? You have piqued my interest, Lord Haddington," she stated in a steady voice.

Lord Haddington huffed in a way that implied he was just indulging her. "I just finished *Critique of Practical Reason* by Immanuel Kant."

Ah, she knew that book! Placing her teacup on the table, Emma recited, " 'Two things fill the mind with ever new and increasing admiration and reverence, the more often and more steadily one reflects on them: the starry heavens above me and the moral law within me.' "

Lord Haddington stared at her with a stunned expression on his face. After a moment, he asked, "You have read Kant?"

"I have," she responded, savoring the moment, "and I found it quite enjoyable. Did you not?" She offered him a sweet smile.

"I did, but I did not memorize it like you apparently have," Lord Haddington commented.

Attempting to keep the amusement out of her voice, she stated, "I suppose his work just spoke to me."

Mr. Ramsbury placed his teacup onto the table. "May I be so bold as to ask for the supper dance, Miss Pearson?"

"You forget yourself, sir," Lord Downshire declared from the doorway. "As Miss Pearson's guardian, I will have the privilege of arranging her supper dance."

All the men in the room rose when the tall, dark-haired marquess walked into the room. Emma had to admit that her guardian was a man of great strength and confidence. His intense stares may have frightened many people... well, most people, but he had never given her cause to fear him. From the moment she'd met Luke, he had treated her as family, showering love upon her.

Mr. Ramsbury bowed. "My apologies, my lord."

Ignoring his response, and the other men's presence, Luke strode up to his wife and kissed her cheek. "How are you, my dear?"

Rachel smiled lovingly up at him. "I am well."

Without removing his gaze from Rachel, he proclaimed, "Miss Emma is no longer receiving callers for today. You are all dismissed."

Emma brought her gloved hand up to her lips to hide her

growing smile as she watched all the men awkwardly file out of the room. Once the last man left the drawing room, she rose, walked over to the window, and watched as the men started walking down the pavement.

"You must really stop glowering at all my potential suitors," Emma stated in a mock chiding voice.

"Those men were not worthy of your notice," Luke proclaimed, placing his hand around his wife's waist. "I did you a favor." He paused, before smirking. "You're welcome, by the way."

She let out a puff of air. "You don't think any man is worthy of my notice."

"That's not true," he acknowledged. "I would be happy to arrange a marriage between you and the Duke of Dudley's eldest son, Lord Stuart."

Emma arched an eyebrow. "The Marquess of Stuart would be interested in marrying me, an untitled country miss?"

"I have no doubt," Luke remarked eagerly.

An image of a pallid, slightly podgy man came to her mind as she thought of her offered suitor. She shuddered. "I shall pass."

"Good choice, Emma," Rachel said, earning a disapproving look from Luke. "By the end of the Season, you shall have your pick of suitors."

"I detest the Season," Luke whispered to his wife.

Rachel laughed as she placed her hand on Luke's chest. "You have made that abundantly clear, but we had to come to Town for Emma."

Turning his attention back towards Emma, he offered, "I will give you £10,000 if we can forego the Season and return back to Scotland tomorrow."

Emma shook her head. "You're lowering your price. Previously, you offered me £20,000 to remain in Scotland for the Season."

"£30,000 then," Luke attempted hopefully.

"You cannot deny Emma the opportunity to have a Season," Rachel said.

"She already had one last year," he pointed out.

Walking over to the tray of biscuits, Emma picked one up. "If you recall, you refused to let me dance with any gentlemen, refused

11

to hold a ball in my honor, and refused to let me read any books from your library."

Luke gave her a baffled look. "I issued no such order. You are always free to read."

"That's so kind of you, my master," she teased, dropping into a curtsy. "I just assumed that would be forbidden, as well."

Letting out a deep sigh, he replied, "You just turned nineteen last week. You were much too young to entertain suitors last year. Frankly, you're still too young to even consider marriage. It would be preferable if we departed for Scotland tomorrow."

"Oh, hush," Rachel said in a light tone. "We went through great lengths to prepare Emma for the Season. For the past two years, she has endured a barrage of tutoring on social etiquette, drawing, needlework, dancing, riding, and learning the pianoforte. Will you please stop trying to pressure her to go back to Scotland?"

The image of Mr. Hawkins shouting at her to look livelier as she danced caused Emma to shudder. "Mr. Hawkins was the most unpleasant dance instructor."

"I agree completely," Rachel responded, smiling. "He felt you were a lost cause." She grew serious. "But you must try not to bait all the gentlemen. Poor Lord Harrington was about to have a fit when you quoted Kant."

"You quoted Kant?" Luke shook his head. "We have been over this... multiple times. A lady of your station is to avoid..."

She spoke over him. "...topics such as literature, politics, morality, and anything that is remotely interesting. Instead, we are supposed to focus on our accomplishments and other polite topics."

"I fear that our ward is not pleased," Rachel teased.

A knock at the door interrupted their conversation. The butler stood on the other side with a silver tray in his hand. "We received a letter for a Mr. David Blackmore," Mr. Munro announced with his usual stoic expression.

"That's for me." Ignoring Luke and Rachel's curious looks, Emma walked over and picked up the letter from the tray. "Thank you, Munro."

Ripping open the envelope, she read the letter and let out a joyous cry. "My article has been accepted, and they have included two one-pound notes as payment," she announced, rushing over to Rachel to show her the letter. "And the editor of The Morning Post would like me to submit additional articles for their consideration."

Rachel read the paper, handed the note off to her husband, and embraced her. "I am so pleased. What wonderful news."

"I'm at a loss for words," Luke declared, his eyes scanning the note. "Why would you submit an article to the newspaper?"

Emma stepped out of Rachel's arms. "I sent in an article detailing the unscrupulous eviction of thousands of tenants in the Highlands at the hand of Lady Sutherland. Those poor families were forced into communities, where they were expected to learn a new way of life, and I wrote about the injustice of it all."

"It's the Countess of Sutherland's land, Emma," Luke countered. "It's more profitable to let the land to sheep farmers than the current renters. It was a simple business move."

Emma lifted her brow. "Because of the countess's desire to replace Highlanders with sheep, riots have become commonplace, and an elderly woman was even murdered when they came to evict her family."

"In Scotland, it is a normal practice to destroy the roof timbers of a cleared house by fire to prevent the reoccupation by the evicted party."

Accepting the missive back from Luke, Emma countered, "Just because something is common practice, doesn't make it right. The people need to understand the struggles the Highlanders are facing."

Luke turned towards Rachel, his disapproval evident on his features. "Will you kindly explain to Emma that it is wholly inappropriate for her to write articles for the newspapers? Not only is she a lady, but she is my ward. It would cause a scandal if anyone ever found out."

Rachel grinned. "I'm confident that Emma just heard you."

"No one will find out," Emma rushed to assure him. "I am writing under a pseudonym and using my mother's maiden name."

Luke frowned. "Do you require more pin money?"

Shaking her head, she replied, "I do not require any additional funds. You have been more than generous."

"Then explain to me why you submitted an article to The

Morning Post?" Luke asked.

Emma met his gaze as she attempted to find the right words. "I want to be more than what Society expects me to be."

Luke grunted as he turned towards Rachel. "This is your fault. You let Emma read your book, and now she wants to be a writer like you."

"I see nothing wrong with that," Rachel declared. "As long as she is writing under a false name, there is no harm in her writing articles. Is there?"

"Thank you," Emma mouthed.

Turning his gaze towards the ceiling, Luke said, "I see that I am outnumbered... again. I cannot wait until Matthew is old enough to start siding with me."

"Considering he is only four months old, that might take a while," Rachel joked as she wrapped her arms around her husband.

Luke brought his adoring gaze down to his wife and smiled.

Emma sighed at the love so evident between Luke and Rachel and knew it was time to grant them privacy.

"I will go to my room and practice my needlework," she said, walking over to the door and closing it behind her.

As she walked along the tiled floor of the expansive entrance hall, Emma admired the ivory walls, the gold accents, and the tapestries that hung along the wall. It had been a little over two years since she had been plucked out of her modest home, but still she regularly pinched herself to confirm she wasn't daydreaming.

This was her life, and what a grand life it was.

Emma tilted her face towards the warmth of the sun as her grey gelding strolled leisurely through Hyde Park. It's such a beautiful day, she thought. Due to an earlier rain shower, the path was muddy, and the trees alongside the road glistened. A few gentlemen riders rode past them, tipping their hats in acknowledgement, and offering pleasantries.

She found her ride to be most enjoyable, so much so that she hardly gave Lord Brisbane any attention. He kept babbling incessantly about the most tedious subjects, and she wished he would stop speaking. Perhaps she should kick her horse into a run and leave him far behind. She sighed. No, that wouldn't be socially acceptable, and she really didn't want another lecture from Luke about ladylike decorum. He was exceptionally astute in the ways of women, after all.

With a glance over her shoulder, Emma confirmed that the three liveried footmen Luke had assigned to watch her were trailing her. They were far enough back to grant privacy, but close enough to ensure propriety. She was confident that they would be able to match her horse's stride.

Lord Brisbane broke through her musings. "Are you in agreement, then?" he asked in an eager voice.

Drat! Now she would have to admit that she wasn't listening to him. Or she could make up a ludicrous excuse and see how he would respond.

"I am afraid my bonnet strings were too tight, and I missed your question," she said, reaching up and untying the straw bonnet's strings from under her chin.

His face softened, drawing attention to his black, slick-backed hair. "I understand, my dear. Bonnets can be tricky."

Emma wanted him to elaborate on how bonnets could be tricky, but she decided not to ask the question. For she was fearful that he would actually have an answer, and she just wanted this outing to be over with.

"Back to my original sentiments," Lord Brisbane began, "I would be remiss if I didn't reveal my intentions towards you."

"Your intentions?" she repeated back in surprise. When had the conversation turned to his intentions? She really should have been paying attention.

He reined in his horse, and she reluctantly followed suit.

"It is time that I marry, and I believe you are a suitable choice."

"Suitable?" She attempted to keep her face expressionless. He found her '*suitable*'? While she was debating whether she should be insulted or relieved by that comment, he continued.

"Aye," he replied, oblivious to her annoyance. "You are beautiful, engaging, and the ward of the Marquess of Downshire.

Furthermore, you are young and vigorous enough to supply me with heirs."

Emma's lips parted in disbelief. She didn't know where to start with this insulting proposal.

Mistaking her silence for acceptance, Lord Brisbane pressed, "With your generous dowry, I will be able to fix up my country estate in Liverpool and…"

"No," came her sharp reply.

Brushing off her answer with a wave of his hand, he said, "I haven't spoken to Lord Downshire, but I am confident he will agree that I am a good match for you."

Her horse pawed at the ground as if sensing her irritation. The moment he stopped speaking, she declared, "I will not now, *not ever*, marry you, Lord Brisbane."

It was his turn to looked surprised. "I beg your pardon?"

"We hardly know each other, but I can tell that we would not suit."

"Then may I ask why you agreed to this outing? I would hope that you understand the implications of being seen together in Hyde Park."

Emma pursed her lips. No good deed goes unpunished, she thought. "Frankly, I was attempting to be polite." She paused, then added, "And I always enjoy riding through Hyde Park."

He frowned, or did he smile? She really couldn't tell with his moustache. "Well, I never," he declared in a haughty voice. "I daresay you will not do better than marrying an earl, despite being the ward of Lord Downshire."

Adjusting the reins in her gloved hands, she gave him a tight smile. "I do not aspire for a title, Lord Brisbane. My only aspiration is to marry a man that will love me above all else."

"You are a foolish girl. Love is for the weak-minded, not for the aristocracy. Surely you've been told that."

"I have, but I do not accept it."

Shifting his gaze over her shoulder, his next comment caught her off-guard. "Then you are destined to be a spinster and will become a strain on your guardian's household."

How dare he speak to me like that, she thought. She had many choice words that she would like to say to that arrogant man, but she bit those back, instead saying, "You, sir, are an ignoramus."

Not waiting for his haughty response, she kicked her horse into a run. However, rather than her gelding racing away as she had intended, it reared up, and upended her. She landed in a heap on the muddied road and looked up in time to see the horse stepping backwards... right towards her. Reacting quickly, she rolled to the side, and landed in a deep hole, filled with mucky, muddy water.

Emma closed her eyes in mortification, hoping that no one had just witnessed her misfortune. However, when she opened them, she saw several women with their mouths agape and a few gentlemen rushing over to assist her. She rose swiftly and wiped her muddied gloves onto her mud-coated, dark-blue riding habit. That was counterproductive, she thought to herself, as she removed the ruined gloves.

She heard a man clear his voice from behind her. "This couldn't get any worse," she muttered under her breath as she reluctantly turned around and saw Lord Brisbane extending a white handkerchief towards her.

He looked appalled as his eyes roamed over her person.

"Thank you," she said, accepting it.

Before she finished wiping the mud off her face, a footman from Caddington Manor approached her, holding her horse's lead. "Miss Pearson, please allow me to help you mount your horse."

"I would greatly appreciate that," she murmured as she came to stand next to her gelding.

The footman assisted her onto her saddle. "It might be best if we walk back to Caddington Manor, Miss Pearson. I have never known this gelding to upend someone before. It makes me wonder if there is a burr somewhere under his saddle." He glanced back at his horse and lowered his voice. "I would have offered the use of my horse, but it would have required me to change saddles, and I assumed you wouldn't want to wait for that."

Keeping her head held up, her eyes darted over his shoulders at the growing crowd. The mud smeared on her person and clothing was starting to dry and stiffen, giving her an almost uncontrollable desire to race her horse back home. But the footman made valid points.

"You presumed correctly," she agreed.

As she urged her horse forward, Emma realized that Lord Brisbane had already mounted his horse and was trotting away from her. Good riddance! She attempted to ignore the gawking gazes of the riders that passed her along the road. She also managed not to act on the impulse of huffing in exasperation. She was not a public spectacle!

When she finally reined in her horse in front of Caddington Manor, she dismounted and walked up the stairs towards the main door. The butler opened the door and stepped aside as she entered.

Munro cast her a concerned look. "Are you all right, miss?"

"I was thrown off my horse and landed in the mud," she admitted weakly.

Closing the main door, he responded, "I can see that, but are you injured? Should I call for a doctor?"

"Only my pride," she remarked with a shake of her head.

"Pride is easier to mend than a broken bone," the butler said, attempting to reassure her. "I will order a bath for you."

She gave him a grateful smile. "Thank you. Do you know where Lady Downshire is?"

"In the nursery, miss," he hesitated, before revealing, "along with Lord Downshire."

With a tense smile, she replied, "It is better to get this over with."

"Over with?"

"Lord Downshire's lecture about…" she ran her hand over her mud coated riding habit, "this."

Munro gave her an understanding smile. "I wish you luck."

Feeling dread wash over her, she walked up the two flights of stairs and slowed her steps when she heard Luke and Rachel speaking to Matthew in loving tones. What a disappointment I've turned out to be, she thought. She had ruined her Season before it had even started.

Stepping into the doorway, Emma expected Luke to start shouting, and he did, but not the way she had anticipated.

"Emma, are you all right?" he asked, striding towards her. He placed his hands on her shoulders and crouched lower to look at her.

"Are you all right? Are you injured?"

Tears started forming in her eyes at the depth of compassion she saw staring back at her, but Luke gave her a stern look.

"No crying," he demanded. "Tell me exactly what happened."

Blinking back her tears, she admitted, "My horse upended me, and I landed in a mud puddle."

Luke's eyes narrowed as he stepped back. "I will fire all of the groomsmen. It's no less than they deserve. After all, it was wholly irresponsible of them to provide you with a horse you were unable to handle."

"It's not their fault," she objected, shaking her head. "I've ridden that gelding before, and he's a gentle horse. He reacted poorly when I kicked him into a run."

Coming to stand next to Luke, Rachel was holding baby Matthew in her arms. "Are you injured?" she asked with sympathy in her voice.

"No." Again, she shook her head. "But, unfortunately, this occurred in Hyde Park and quite a few people witnessed it. My Season is ruined! I'm ready to return to Scotland. We can try again next year."

Emma saw something pass between Luke and Rachel, but she couldn't decipher it. After a moment, Luke declared, "We aren't going anywhere. You are my ward, and I vowed that you will be adored by the ton. It shall be done."

"How is that possible?" she asked. "My reputation is my greatest possession, and I just ruined it by rolling in the mud."

Handing Matthew off to Luke, Rachel wrapped her up in a loving embrace, despite her being coated in mud. "You're wrong. Your greatest possession is your family, and we protect each other... including reputations."

"But..."

Luke spoke over her. "No buts. We'll sort this out. You're under my protection, Emma, and that means a great deal."

Rachel smiled kindly at her. "Go take a bath and rest. We shall talk later. Besides, tonight is your ball, and everything will be made right after that."

"Thank you," she replied with a full heart.

With a final parting glance at Luke and Rachel, Emma headed

towards her bedchamber. She had expected Luke to rail on her, but instead, he had shown her kindness. Perhaps he was right. Maybe her Season wasn't ruined after all?

If that was true, why did she have the feeling that this Season was going to be anything but ordinary?

Chapter Two

After a wonderful soak, Emma felt rested and found herself becoming anxious as she prepared for the ball being held in her honor. She sat on her dressing room chair as her cheerful lady's maid styled her hair into an elaborate chignon, adorning it with small flowers and curls framing her face.

"You look beautiful, miss," Peggy said, taking a step towards the dressing table and picking up a small tin. "Would you like some rouge for your cheeks?"

"Yes, please."

After applying the rouge, her red-headed lady's maid stepped back. "You're quite fortunate that you don't need to add color to your lips. They are such a naturally vivid crimson."

Emma took a moment to look at her reflection in the mirror. With her oval face, creamy white skin, dark brown hair, and green eyes, she was pretty enough, but certainly not exceptional. She had noticed that she stood out amongst the blonde-haired beauties at the social gatherings and suspected many people found her to be a rather peculiar-looking girl. Her brother often told her that she was beautiful, but she had always cast his compliments aside, not daring to believe them.

Thinking of David caused her mood to turn melancholy. She had been given this life at the expense of her brother. Her brother had been assigned to guard Rachel when she was forced to flee to Scotland. During that time, David had sent many letters home detailing his assignment and had predicted that Luke and Rachel would eventually fall in love and be married. She smiled at that thought.

But so much secrecy still shrouded David's death. Neither Luke nor Rachel would share the full details behind his death. She only was privy to knowing he died saving Rachel from four despicable men on the shores overlooking her uncle's estate. Luke had shown her the cave where the attack happened, but she never had the strength to venture inside. The image of her brother's body sprawled out on the cave's floor always gave her pause. Perhaps it would change when they confided the rest of the story to her.

"Are you all right, miss?" Peggy asked with a worried frown.

"I am," she replied. "I'm afraid I was just woolgathering again."

Peggy grinned as she walked over to the gown laid out on the bed. "Are you ready to put on your gown?"

"Very much so," Emma said, rising.

A short time later, she was dressed in the most beautiful muslin gown, with a net overlay of the palest pink, and Peggy was fastening all the ornate buttons that ran down the back.

"If you don't mind me saying, Miss Cosette did a wonderful job designing your ballgown," her lady's maid commented.

Holding out the sides of her skirts, Emma admired the elaborately embroidered pattern of flowers, and she couldn't even comprehend the time that went into making this dress. "Miss Cosette is very talented."

Peggy had just finished the last button when a knock came at the door. She opened it, revealing Rachel and Luke on the other side. Then, she curtsied and exited the room quietly.

"You look beautiful, Emma," Rachel gushed as she approached her. "Your dress is exquisite."

Taking a moment to admire Rachel's green high waisted gown, with puffy sleeves, she replied, "You look quite fetching yourself."

Rachel smiled at her. "It doesn't matter what I look like tonight. You are the belle of the ball, and all eyes will be on you."

"You are going to make Emma more nervous than she already is," Luke chastised her lightly.

With humor in her voice, Rachel instructed her, "You have trained for this moment for two years. Keep your head held high and enjoy the evening. But for heaven's sake, don't drink more than one glass of champagne, avoid the usual subjects, and do not dance more than one dance with any gentleman."

A playful smile came to her lips. "No counsel on my fan?"

"No fan!" Luke and Rachel shouted in unison.

Emma laughed. "I am not sure why I find it so complicated to learn how to communicate with my fan."

"Fans can be a nuisance," Rachel declared. "The common fan language is known to both genders, and specific fan movements are a way to convey messages about emotions and love."

Emma walked over to the dressing table and picked up her ornate lace fan. She shut it fully and opened it slowly. "I believe this indicates that I would like to get more acquainted."

Rachel sighed in exasperation. "Not at all. You just gave a promise of marriage."

"What?" Emma asked, dropping the fan back onto the table. "In the country, we used them to fan our faces and to protect us from insects. Furthermore, my boarding school never had a class on fans."

Luke chuckled. "I'm grateful that no courses on fans were ever taught at Eton and Oxford."

Clasping her hands in front of her, Emma straightened her shoulders. "I won't let either one of you down. I will be on my best behavior."

"We know you will," Rachel said with a tender smile.

Reaching into his black jacket pocket, Luke pulled out an amethyst rivière necklace. "Rachel and I wanted to give you something to celebrate this special occasion." He walked up to her, showed her the necklace, and asked, "May I?"

Emma turned around, and Luke fastened the necklace around her neck. She fingered the purple stones tenderly as she turned back to face them. "It's spectacular. I will return it after the ball."

"No, you misunderstood," Rachel said, her smile growing. "This is our gift to you."

Emma started shaking her head profusely. "It's too much. You've already given me so much."

Placing his arm around Rachel's shoulder, Luke responded, "You have been a delightful addition to our family, Emma. We wanted to give you something that would reflect how much we have enjoyed these past two years with you."

"Thank you," she said, attempting to stop the tears threatening to form in her eyes. "If you hadn't taken me in when you did, my life would have been dramatically different."

"It was the least we could do," Luke remarked in a terse voice, but she swore she saw him blinking back tears. He started leading his wife towards the door. "It is time for us to make our appearance at the ball."

As they stepped into the hall, Luke informed her, "Just so you know, I rescinded Lord Brisbane's invitation. With any luck, you will never have to see that despicable man again."

"I pity the girl that marries him," she muttered.

Rachel looked over at her and smiled. "That may have been your first proposal, but I have no doubt you will receive many others. I suffered through the most awful proposals. Most of the men were just interested in my fortune and lacked the sense to attempt to woo me first."

"I believe my proposal was rather forthright and inventive," Luke remarked smugly.

"It's true," Rachel admitted, "but there was some groveling, too."

Luke shrugged one shoulder. "There usually is when a man is trying to convince the woman that he loves to marry him."

They stepped into the hall leading to the side door of the ballroom. Two footmen were standing watch by the set of doors, waiting for them to approach.

The doors were opened, their names were announced, and everyone turned to watch their entrance. The domed room was flooded with light from mirrored wall sconces and three massive crystal chandeliers, each with hundreds of lit candles. She saw the dance floor was chalked with the Marquess of Downshire's crest. A full orchestra was warming up in one corner of the long, rectangular room.

Most of the guests were stationed near the white and gold walls, and a few women were already sitting on the chairs, fanning their faces.

Emma's eyes scanned the crowd, hoping to see a friendly face, when she saw the Marquess and Marchioness of Lansdowne break through the crowd and approach them.

"I am so pleased to see you," Emma admitted as they stopped in front of her.

Eliza smiled knowingly at her. "That bad?"

"I'm just fearful I will make a fool of myself," Emma replied honestly.

Benedict chuckled. "You have nothing to fear. From what I heard, Luke has left nothing to chance, and he has already filled your dance card."

"It's true," she answered. "I am dancing with you during the cotillion."

"My brother can be rather..." Eliza's voice trailed off, before saying, "cautious. After what happened in Hyde Park..."

"Luke told you about Hyde Park?" she asked, speaking over her.

Adrien, the Earl of Camden, spoke up from behind her. "Everyone knows about Hyde Park."

She groaned. "I am ruined."

Dressed in a rose-colored gown, the blonde beauty, Lady Camden, stepped up next to her. "Hardly. My first husband was a villainous man who made many enemies, and the ton still embraced me," Kate shared.

"But you were the daughter of a duke," she pointed out. "I'm just a ward."

Eliza wore a look of amusement on her features. "Trust me, being Luke's ward means something. With your beauty and connections, you are the envy of the ton."

A servant passed by with a tray holding several ornate glasses. He stopped in front of her and extended the tray to her. "Champagne, Miss Pearson?"

She put her hand up to refuse it, but Benedict accepted it and handed it to her. "You should drink this. It will calm your nerves."

Accepting the glass, Emma sighed. "I am only allowed one glass of champagne for the evening."

"Have you ever had champagne before?" Kate asked curiously.

She shook her head. "Never. Luke ordered me not to. He says that alcohol can lower your inhibitions."

"Women should never drink to excess," Eliza warned, "but an occasional glass of champagne at a ball is permissible."

Emma brought the glass to her mouth and took a large sip, not anticipating that she wouldn't enjoy it. She made herself remain still for a moment before starting to cough. And cough. "It is bubbly, but very bitter."

"Bitter?" Adrien questioned, looking at her in surprise. "Do you mean sour?"

"Champagne can be an acquired taste," Eliza pointed out.

The room grew quiet, and Emma saw Luke standing in the middle of the dance floor. "It will now be my honor to dance the opening set with my ward, Miss Emma Pearson."

"Oh, bother," Emma muttered under her breath as Kate took the glass from her hands.

She saw the crowds parting as Luke approached her and bowed. "Miss Pearson," he said, extending his hand towards her, "may I have this dance?"

"I would be honored, Lord Downshire," she replied with a curtsy.

As he started leading her towards the dance floor, she started feeling light-headed. It must just be nerves, she thought to herself. The room was filled with people, and they were all watching her. Luke gave her a reassuring smile as they stepped into the middle of the dance floor and the music began.

At first, Emma and Luke executed the minuet flawlessly. Their steps were in sync, and they were achieving an air of unaffected ease and nonchalance. They approached and withdrew from each other with grace, and she was grateful that Rachel had made them spend hours practicing together.

However, as the dance progressed, Emma found it increasingly difficult to focus on the intricate steps. Now, as they approached each other, she had to strain her eyes to focus on Luke. Something was wrong. She felt odd, weak. The room felt overly warm, and her steps began to falter.

"Are you all right, Emma?" Luke's concerned voice asked from somewhere far away.

"Yes," she managed to force the word out as she continued to dance.

The music began to change, indicating that the first set was over, and she would now choose another partner to finish the dance. It had already been decided that Luke's younger brother, Lord Jonathon Beckett, would dance with her.

Emma began searching the crowd for Lord Jonathon, but all the faces were blurry and unrecognizable. She closed her eyes tightly and opened them again. Only this time, she felt the sudden urge to fall into a deep sleep. Just as she felt herself falling to the ground, she was scooped up into Luke's arms. Then, everything went black.

Emma returned to the conscious world in a cloud of pain. Her head ached something fierce, and the bright light in her room was making her regret the decision to open her eyes. What's happened, she wondered, as she brought her hand up to her forehead.

"You're awake," her lady's maid said in a cheerful voice next to the bed.

"Do I have to be?" she questioned, closing her eyes again. "Would you mind closing the drapes?"

Peggy immediately jumped up to do her bidding and closed the two sets of drapes, darkening the room. "How are you feeling?"

"Awful," she remarked. "What happened?"

Coming to stand next to the bed, Peggy gave her a curious look. "You don't remember?"

She winced as she attempted to conjure up the memory. "I remember being at the ball, but the events are hazy after I drank the champagne."

"You fainted during the minuet with Lord Downshire," Peggy revealed.

"I fainted?" she asked, knowing that sounded nothing like her. She had never fainted before.

Reaching behind her, Peggy adjusted the pillows under her head. "Fortunately, Lord Downshire saw you were going to faint and caught you up in his arms. He immediately brought you to your room and called for a doctor."

The pain in her head was starting to subside when she went to sit up. "I need to go speak to Lord Downshire."

"Lord and Lady Downshire specifically requested that you remain in bed until the doctor returns later this evening," Peggy informed her.

Emma moved her feet over the side of the bed and rose. "I'm not an invalid. Where are Lord and Lady Downshire now?"

"In the study," Peggy revealed. "But—"

"No buts, Peggy," she insisted. "Will you help me dress or shall I wear my nightgown?"

Her lady's maid frowned before reluctantly walking over to the wardrobe and removing a simple white cotton gown. "I daresay Lord Downshire will be angry with you for being out of your bed," she muttered.

Once Emma was dressed, and her hair was pulled back into a loose chignon, she headed towards the study on the first floor. She was within a few feet when she heard male voices drifting out of the opened door. She stopped at the door and peered in. Luke was pacing near the window, and Rachel was sitting on the settee holding Matthew. Lord Camden, Lord Jonathon, and Lord Lansdowne were sitting on armchairs, each with a snifter in their hands.

She knocked on the door and everyone turned towards her. The men quickly rose and were watching her with stern expressions.

"Emma," Rachel exclaimed in a relieved tone. "You're finally awake."

Taking a few tentative steps into the room, Emma stopped and diverted her gaze. "I am," she replied, hesitantly. "I wanted to apologize for my behavior last evening…"

"You have nothing to apologize for," Luke declared as he stopped pacing. "There's no easy way to say this, so I will just tell you." He paused, looking over at Rachel. "Last night, your champagne was spiked with laudanum."

"Laudanum," she repeated. "I don't understand. Who would do such a thing?"

Walking over to the drink cart, Luke poured himself a drink before answering. "After you fainted, we summoned the doctor, and he explained you had digested a large dose of laudanum. He cited your irregular heartbeat and your dilated pupils as proof." He brought the drink to his lips. "And based upon the timing of your fainting, we traced it back to the glass of champagne."

Benedict spoke up. "You spoke of the champagne being bitter, and at the time, none of us recognized that as a perceived threat. Champagne can be considered sour to some but never bitter. Whereas laudanum is inherently bitter."

Emma couldn't seem to wrap her brain around what they were telling her. "I don't understand. Why would someone want to poison me?" she asked as she walked over to Rachel and sat down.

The men all sat down as Adrien shared, "Jonathon and I took it upon ourselves to speak to the lead groom, and we confirmed that a burr was found in the blanket under your saddle."

Emma nodded. That made sense. "That would explain why the gelding upended me."

"Yes," Lord Camden answered, "and a man, fitting the general description of the servant from last night, was seen spotted near your gelding yesterday. When the groomsmen confronted him, the man used the vague excuse that he was Lord Brisbane's groom, and he went ahead to ensure your horse was already saddled."

Baby Matthew made a lunge towards her, and Emma eagerly wrapped him up in her arms. "Why would someone go through all the trouble of spiking my drink with laudanum and placing a burr under my horse's saddle?"

Lord Jonathon sat forward in his seat. "My guess is to ruin your Season."

"If that's the case, then they succeeded," she remarked. "I daresay I won't be able to show my face amongst the ton anytime soon."

"Nonsense," Rachel declared. "We're already working on a plan to ensure you have a successful Season."

"How?" Emma asked in disbelief, removing a lock of her hair from Matthew's fist. "I fell into a muddy hole in the middle of Hyde Park, and I fainted during the opening set of my own ball. I have no doubt that the flibbertigibbets in Society are having a field day with this."

Adrien rose from his seat and went to refill his drink. "Is there anyone that you can think of who may wish to do you harm?"

"No one," she replied honestly.

"I can," Luke stated, placing his drink down on the tray and walking over to his desk. "His name is Peter Lockhart."

"It couldn't possibly be Peter," Emma said with a shake of her head.

Lord Camden glanced between them with a pointed look. "Who is Peter?"

"He was my father's solicitor, and a friend of the family," she said, turning Matthew in her arms and sitting him down on her lap.

"He had it in his head that he was going to marry Emma," Luke revealed, removing a stack of letters from a drawer and placing them on top of the desk. "He has written to her every month for the past two years."

"He has?" Emma asked in a surprised tone. "But I haven't received any of his letters."

Walking over to Adrien, Luke extended him the stack of letters bound by string. "Of course not. I ensured they were intercepted before they reached you."

"For what purpose?" she inquired, her voice rising in irritation.

Luke's expression grew serious, and his tone matched it when he spoke. "Peter is a bloody nuisance. He has filed multiple lawsuits to contest my guardianship over you. He even sued me for breach of promise because he claimed your father granted him permission to wed you."

"My father did no such thing," Emma argued.

"Exactly," Luke stated. "We were protecting you."

Emma turned her gaze towards Rachel. "You knew about Peter?"

Rachel nodded. "I did. He's not a good man, Emma."

A terrible feeling of guilt swept over her. What a horrible burden she was to Luke and Rachel. "I am sorry. I had no idea that Peter was harassing you."

Placing a hand on her shoulder, Rachel regarded her with kindness in her eyes. "And that is why we didn't tell you. We didn't want to distress you in any way."

"But I have been nothing but a burden to you," Emma replied, attempting to control her growing emotions.

"That is utter nonsense. Get that thought out of your head immediately," Luke declared. "My solicitors have been handling these trivial matters."

Emma felt oddly comforted by Luke's authoritative manner. She had learned that Luke spoke his mind and rarely became sentimental, but now she could hear the emotion fluctuate in his voice.

"For what purpose would Peter want to ruin my Season?" she questioned as Lord Camden distributed some of the notes to Jonathon and Benedict.

"If I had to guess, Peter didn't have access to you in Scotland, and you are within his grasp here in London," Jonathon remarked.

"This is ludicrous," Emma replied. "I grew up with Peter, and he was like a brother to me. He is not capable of what you are accusing him of."

All the men in the room cast worried glances at each other. Finally, Luke cleared his throat. "If someone intends to harm Emma," he said, "we need to ensure her protection. It might be best if we brought in the Bow Street Runners."

Lord Jonathon grunted. "There must be another way. Bow Street Runners are incompetent at best."

"Do you know where Mr. Lockhart is?" Benedict asked.

"I do not, but I know he maintains an office in the village of Totternhoe," Luke shared, glancing between the men. "Would Uncle Charles be willing to open an investigation into Peter Lockhart?"

Tucking the stack of letters into his jacket pocket, Jonathon replied, "I'll see what can be done. Perhaps we can assign an agent to protect Emma."

A slow, satisfied smile grew on Adrien's lips. "No need. I can recommend a Bow Street Runner."

"No. Not him," Jonathon contended, shooting him a warning look. "Anyone but him."

"Who?" Luke asked with a lifted brow.

Benedict wore a look of amusement. "He did get shot saving Emmett's life."

"He deserved it," Jonathon muttered under his breath.

Luke crossed his arms over his chest. "I'm afraid I am not following this conversation. Is this Bow Street Runner trustworthy?"

"Yes," the three men said in unison, but then Jonathon added, "He is just a dunderhead."

"Well, then," Luke replied, uncrossing his arms, "how do I get in contact with him?"

Benedict directed his gaze at Jonathon. "You don't, but we will."

Chapter Three

Simeon Martin found he rather detested most people. It was an unfortunate discovery on his part, but perhaps it was a good thing. These past few years had hardened him, making him sullen. People tended to steer clear of him, allowing him to work his cases alone as a Bow Street Runner. It was easier that way, and much simpler. He answered to no one, except for the Bow Street magistrate. More importantly, he wasn't responsible for anyone besides himself.

Now, he sat in the darkened corner of the crowded Bottomless Pit Pub, observing the ruffians sitting at the table across from him. He had been tracking a group of rebels garnering strength after the Corn Laws were passed by Parliament. Little was known about this Anti-Corn Law ring, but after spending a small fortune on bribes, he was able to identify one of the members. Mr. Carew Boyle.

Mr. Boyle was of average height, a little on the thin side, with dark hair that fell to his shoulders, and he worked at a shop down the street. The suspect was sitting with three other men, all of whom were becoming increasingly inebriated.

The aging barmaid sashayed up to the table. "Can I get ye another drink, love?"

"Not at the moment," he replied dismissively as he slid a few coins in her direction, hoping to satisfy her.

She deposited the coins into her ample bosom and left without saying another word.

He didn't blame her for checking up on him. After all, he'd been sitting at this table for more than two hours watching these men toss back drink after drink of this cheap ale.

Simeon's plan had been simple. He would follow Boyle until he led him to the group of rebels. Then he could assess the threat. He needed to see if the group was organized, or if they were a bunch of unmotivated complainers. Not that he blamed them for their anger. He had been outraged when the Corn Laws had passed, despite his vote against it. Regardless, it mattered not. He rarely attended Parliament. He didn't belong there.

He shoved his drink to the side, causing it to slosh over the top. He was a blasted viscount. What a terrible consolation prize! Prince George had honored him by giving him the title of Viscount of Wentworth after his role in bringing down the smuggling ring in Gravesend. He became Lord Wentworth while Dr. Emmett Maddix claimed Martha Haskett's heart.

His first love; his *only* love.

Simeon had spent the past year trying to forget her, but how could he forget someone that he had fought so valiantly to find? Unfortunately, once he finally found her, she had already given her heart to Emmett. It didn't matter that he had wealth, power, and now a title. He wasn't content. He was still trying to find a new purpose for his life.

The door was wrenched opened, and the last ray of light shone on the wall. Two familiar faces ducked under the low frame and stepped into the room, but he felt no desire to make his presence known. He was on an assignment, and he did not have time to chit-chat with Lord Jonathon Beckett or Benedict, the Marquess of Lansdowne. Nor did he want to.

Lord Lansdowne, dressed plainly tonight, scanned over the room until he spotted him. Simeon acknowledged him with a tip of his head, but he made no move to call him over. Rather than take the hint, they headed straight for him.

Once they approached the table, he politely acknowledged them. "Beckett. Lansdowne."

"May we join you, Wentworth?" Benedict asked.

Reaching for his tankard, Simeon replied, "I'm on assignment at the moment."

Jonathon knowingly glanced over his shoulder at the table where Mr. Boyle was sitting. "We'll help you. Which one is your suspect?"

He scoffed, loudly. "I am quite familiar with your *help*. I experienced it firsthand in Gravesend, and, if you recall, your horribly executed plan got me shot."

Benedict let out a laugh. "None of the agents managed to get themselves shot. Just the Bow Street Runner. Ironic, isn't it?"

The barmaid bustled over to their table and asked, "Can I get you blokes some ale?"

"They were just leaving," Simeon declared.

Sliding into the seat across from him, Beckett smiled up at the barmaid. "Pardon my friend's boorish manners. We would like two tankards and bread, if you have it."

"We sure do, love," the barmaid responded, smiling. "We just baked a whole new batch."

Watching her walk away, Simeon asked in a dry tone, "What do you want?"

"Just wanted to catch up with an old friend," Benedict said, sitting next to Beckett.

Simeon took a sip of his drink. "We aren't friends, and I apologize if I gave the appearance of such."

Sitting back in his seat, Lansdowne regarded him for a long moment. "You seem different, Wentworth." He snapped his fingers as if making a discovery. "If I have to guess, I would say you appear more bitter than the last time I saw you."

Simon cast him a look of annoyance. "I am. Happy?" He tipped his head towards the door. "Now leave."

"But we haven't gotten our drinks yet," Beckett said with a shake of his head. "Walking away now would be inconsiderate."

Boyle and his friend started laughing loudly and clapping each other on their backs. Simeon's plan had just gotten more complicated. He highly doubted that Boyle would lead him to the other rebels if he was too drunk to do more than stagger.

"We have a job for you," Benedict said unexpectedly.

"Not interested," came his quick reply.

Beckett placed his forearms on the table and leaned forward. "The pay is generous."

"Find another Bow Street Runner."

The barmaid walked up with two tankards of ale and a tray of bread. She placed them in the middle of the table and hurried off.

Lansdowne reached for the bread and broke off a piece. "A young woman is in trouble."

The refusal was on the tip of his tongue, but he couldn't find the strength to say it. Blazes! How could he deny their request if a woman was in trouble?

He lifted his brow. "Why ask me?"

Beckett slid the tankard in front of him. "Frankly, because you are the only Bow Street Runner that we can trust. Plus, you are adequate at your job."

"I assure you that I am more than adequate," he contended, while ironically feeling a source of pride at Jonathon's words.

Shrugging, Beckett replied, "We shall see."

"Someone is going to great lengths to sabotage Miss Emma Pearson's Season," Benedict explained. "A burr…"

Simeon spoke over him. "Who is Miss Pearson?"

"She is the ward of my brother, Lord Downshire," Beckett shared.

He let out a low, approving whistle. "The ward of the Marquess of Downshire. That's an impressive guardian to have."

Lansdowne continued. "As I was saying, a burr was placed under her saddle, resulting in her being upended in Hyde Park. Then, later that evening, her glass of champagne was laced with laudanum, causing her to pass out during the opening set of the ball."

"Both could be labeled as accidents. Burrs are not uncommon, and she might not have been the intended target of the laudanum. How do you know someone meant to do Miss Pearson harm?" he questioned.

While lowering his tankard, Jonathon answered, "If not for both incidences occurring so closely together, it might have been dismissed as a coincidence. However, the servant that had handed Miss Pearson her drink was also seen milling around the stables under false pretenses."

"Again, why me?" he asked. "Surely, any agent could be tasked with keeping her safe."

"That's true, but we aren't sure what we are up against," Beckett replied. "We need someone that we can trust to ensure Miss Pearson's protection while we continue to investigate. Besides, this falls under the Bow Street Runners' jurisdiction."

Reluctantly, Simeon had to admit that Beckett had a point. The Home Office dealt more with foreign threats. "Do you have any suspects?"

Benedict tossed back his drink and placed it on the table. "We do. Mr. Peter Lockhart. He mistakenly believed that Miss Pearson and he were to be wed. Apparently, he did not take kindly to her becoming Lord Downshire's ward."

Reaching for the bread, Simeon asked, "Has he made any threats?"

"Not yet," Beckett said, reaching into his jacket pocket and pulling out a large stack of notes. "But he's written every month for the past two years."

Beckett placed the pile in front of him.

"Have you read these?" Simeon asked.

"We have," Lansdowne confirmed. "Other than sappy declarations of love, Lockhart says little else."

"Perhaps he's just a spurned lover and not the perpetrator," he suggested.

Jonathon nodded. "There's a chance, but my brother believes Lockhart is behind this."

"Unfortunately, I am working a case right now," he said with a sigh. "I'll find another Bow Street Runner to—"

Lansdowne spoke over him. "It has to be you."

Simeon diverted his gaze away from the agent's gaze. He didn't want this assignment. "I assure you that there are other, more competent—"

Beckett cut him off. "Please," he stated in a firm voice. "Miss Emma Pearson is family, and we protect our own."

Hearing that plea come off Beckett's lips caused his resolve to crumble. How could he deny their request now? He sighed. "Fine. I will meet with Lord Downshire tomorrow to discuss the case, but I won't make any promises."

Both men broke out in wide, relieved smiles. Simeon almost smiled back at them... almost, but then he saw Mr. Boyle heading towards the door. He rose from his chair.

"I trust that you two can make it out of the rookeries alive?" he jested.

Without waiting for a response, he headed out the main door and pulled up the collar on his worn brown jacket. He watched as Boyle staggered back and forth on the cobblestone street, skirting piles of animal dung, and singing a jolly tune.

Simeon dealt with the scum of Society, and yet, he found that preferable to guarding a spoiled debutante. What had he gotten himself into?

"Don't die, don't die, don't die..." Emma kept muttering under her breath over and over. Her white-knuckled fingers were gripping the edges of the bricks as she attempted to climb down the back of Eliza's townhouse. It was still early, but the sun had risen brightly over the Lansdownes's well-manicured garden.

Gritting her teeth, Emma ignored the sweat rolling down the sides of her face and the pain in her tired fingers. She was dressed in a white shirt, fitted tan trousers, and ankle boots. Moving her foot, she was having a hard time finding a foothold on the brick wall. Perhaps she wasn't ready for this step.

No, I can do this, she thought, strengthening her resolve. After all, she had scaled up the wall to a second level window... multiple times, but she had wanted to challenge herself by climbing down from the third level. Attempting to stay calm, she replayed Eliza's instructions in her head; *Stay as close as possible to the wall and position your boots in the space between the bricks.*

Eliza's unconcerned voice came from the ground. "I'm impressed that you haven't fallen, but you are taking entirely too long."

The jovial voice of her friend, Lady Easton, came from next to her. "Ignore her," she encouraged as she moved closer. "Eliza can scurry up a wall faster than any rats I've seen."

"I can hear you, Josette," Eliza said in a light tone.

Josette laughed down at Lady Lansdowne. "I'm just offering encouragement to my friend." She turned towards her, appearing completely calm and oriented. "Look for bricks that are jutting out vertically and find your foothold. Make sure you check the bricks before placing your weight on them. A loose brick could cause you to tumble off the wall."

Emma lowered her right foot until she found a brick that jutted out.

"Good," her friend praised. "Now find a handhold."

Tentatively, she began finding the nearest holds, alternating her feet and hands. "It's much simpler climbing *up* the wall," she remarked, blowing out a puff of air.

"That it is." Keeping pace with her, Josette stated, "Once you get the hang of it, then it really is quite simple."

Once she was within a few feet of the ground, Emma dropped down, and was met with Eliza's clapping.

"Well done," the Marchioness of Lansdowne said. "Was I correct that it is much easier in fitted trousers?"

"It was," Emma agreed as she wiped the sweat off her brow with her shirt sleeve. "I will have to thank Miss Cosette for the fitted clothing the next time I am in her shop."

Placing a hand to her barely discernable protruding belly, Eliza said, "I won't be climbing many walls until my babe comes."

"If I recall correctly, Benedict forbade you from climbing walls this morning," Josette remarked.

Eliza grinned. "Benedict tends to be a bit overprotective."

"A bit?" Josette questioned.

Directing her next comment to Emma, Eliza asked, "Are you ready for your next lesson, or would you like to take a break?"

"Break, please," Emma declared loudly.

Eliza laughed. "Fair enough. Let's have some breakfast first."

They walked over to a table where a buffet was set up and each picked up a plate. After Emma served herself, she walked over to a round table and accepted the proffered chair from the footman. He placed a napkin on her lap and filled her teacup.

"Thank you," she acknowledged as she reached for her fork.

Sitting down next to her, Eliza asked, "How are your fingers?"

Emma looked down at her red, blistered fingers. "They hurt." She glanced between Eliza and Josette. "How do you both make it look so easy?"

Reaching for her teacup, Josette gave her a mischievous smile. "The more you practice, the more it becomes second nature. Besides, every self-respecting lady should know how to climb down a wall."

Emma arched an eyebrow. "For some strange reason, my boarding school curriculum did not offer a class in climbing down walls."

"Pity," Josette said before taking a long sip. "It's quite a useful skill."

Taking a moment to admire her friend, Emma couldn't believe the transformation in Josette since she'd married Lord Morgan. She seemed freer, happier, and the sadness that had lurked in her eyes had been replaced with joy.

"I'm surprised that Morgan is letting you out of his sight," Emma teased.

Josette let out a soft, airy laugh. "We arrived home late last night from our wedding tour, and he tried to persuade me to skip training this morning with Eliza." She brought her fingers to her lips. "He was quite persuasive, I must admit."

"How disconcerting," Eliza chided in a mocking tone.

Josette brought her hands down to her lap. "But, in the end, I convinced Morgan to join me."

Glancing around the veranda, Emma said, "I didn't realize Morgan came along. Where is he?"

"He followed Benedict up to the nursery to play with Caroline," Josette shared.

Eliza picked up a newspaper resting next to her plate. "Have you had a chance to read the newspaper, Emma?" she asked with a pointed look.

"No." She shook her head. "Luke refused my request to see it." Pushing her food haphazardly around the plate with her fork, she inquired, "What does it say?"

Opening the paper up to the Society page, Eliza read, " 'Miss Pearson was so inebriated that she passed out during the opening set with her guardian, Lord Downshire.' "

Emma's fork stilled. "Everyone thinks I was inebriated?"

"Not to worry," Eliza declared, folding the newspaper back to the first page.

Emma frowned. "How can you say that? My reputation is in tatters, and I have embarrassed my family."

"You did no such thing," Eliza contended. "Besides, the ton is a fickle lot. Once a new scandal comes to light, your accidents will become a forgotten memory."

Josette wiped the sides of her mouth with her napkin. "There was a time when the Society papers dubbed me 'Black Josette' due to the timing of the unfortunate deaths of my family members."

"Truly?" Emma asked, knowing Society now adored Lady Easton.

"It's true," Josette confessed. "I was sixteen at the time, and I chose to run from the horrible gossip and spiteful words being spewed at me."

"What happened?" she found herself asking.

Lord Morgan's smug voice came from the doorway. "She married a most dashingly handsome man, and Society fell at her feet."

"That's true, too," Josette said, turning her loving gaze towards her husband, "about the handsome man part, but not about Society falling at my feet. Morgan did manage a few well-placed articles in the Society page of the newspaper, and it turned the tide of public opinion towards me."

Coming to stand next to her, Morgan smiled. "Or it could have been that you were endorsed by the prince regent, the Duke of Remington, the Marquess of Bath, the Marquess of Lansdowne, the Earl of Camden, Lord Charles Beckett, Lord Jonathon Beckett..."

"We get the point, dearest," Josette joked.

Morgan turned his gaze towards her. "You need not fear, Emma. Some of the brightest minds are working on turning your Season around." He smirked. "And by brightest, I mean me."

Josette let out a slight huff. "You will have to excuse my husband. He is extraordinarily cocky about his abilities on... well, just about everything."

Leaning closer, Morgan whispered something in his wife's ear, causing a discernable blush on her cheeks.

"Newlyweds," Eliza jested before turning her gaze back to Emma. "The front page of the newspaper has the most fascinating article about the Highland Clearance by a Mr. *David* Blackmore. Have you read it?"

Emma reached for her teacup and took a long sip. After she placed the cup back to its saucer, she replied, "I have not."

"Interesting," Eliza muttered. "I enjoyed the perspective of the writer. The person interviewed many of these displaced Highlanders and eloquently explained the injustice of it all."

"Oh," Emma remarked innocently as she picked up her fork and resumed eating.

Eliza let out an exasperated sigh. "Let's speed this conversation along, Emma. Shall we? After all, Rachel already gushed about you having an article published in the newspaper."

"She did?" Emma asked.

Eliza's face softened. "We're all so immensely proud of you."

"I hardly know you, but I am proud of you as well," Morgan joked.

Josette nudged him in the side. "Hush, my love."

Placing her fork down, Emma straightened in her seat. "Luke wasn't exactly pleased that I submitted an article to the newspaper. He even offered me additional pin money to stop writing."

"Of course, he reacted that way. I wouldn't have expected him to act any differently," Eliza said with a wave of her hand. "But I have it on good authority that Luke is also proud of you."

"You think so?" she asked hopefully.

Eliza nodded. "I know so."

A little girl's laugh came from the doorway and was followed by Benedict's voice. "I am now prepared to tutor Emma in hand-to-hand combat training."

Emma looked over and saw Benedict holding his smiling twenty-month-old daughter, Lady Caroline, in his arms.

Morgan chuckled. "By accepting Benedict as your training tutor, you're setting yourself up for failure, Emma. I'm willing to impart my wisdom to you, as well."

"I beg your pardon?" Benedict asserted, walking closer to the table. "I could best you in a round of fisticuffs any day."

Eliza grinned and shook her head. "Gentlemen, this is getting us nowhere," she proclaimed as Caroline lunged out of Benedict's arms and into hers. "Perhaps it would be best if *both* of you demonstrate how to protect oneself."

Benedict removed his jacket and draped it onto the back of the chair. "It's best to provide you with some basic training in the unlikely event that someone attempts to abscond with you," he explained.

Rising from her chair, Emma responded, "Last week, Eliza gave me an overcoat pistol to keep in my reticule, and after much practice, I'm a decent shot."

"That's good," Benedict said, "but that isn't enough. You might not be able to reach for your pistol if the assailant is dragging you away." He waved his hand towards the lawn. "Come. Let us show you."

Once they stepped onto the lawn, Benedict turned back around, grabbed her arm, and yanked it behind her back.

"How do you get out of this hold?" he asked.

Rather than explain, Emma decided to show him. She lifted the heel of her kid boot and stomped it down hard on top of his Hessian boot. Immediately, he released her and let out a loud, pain-filled grunt.

"I am so sorry," Emma said as she watched him limp around on the lawn.

To add to her embarrassment, Eliza, Josette, and Morgan were all laughing at Benedict's discomfort.

"Well done, Emma," Morgan praised. "The element of surprise is your greatest ally." He waved her closer. "Come stand here."

Emma came to stand in front of him as she explained, "When I was younger, my brother showed me some moves to protect myself."

"Now you tell me," Benedict mumbled as he limped back over to the table.

Giving her an expectant look, Morgan explained, "I'm going to grab you. I want you to stop me, by any means necessary. Understood?"

She pressed her lips together. "I'm not sure this is such a good idea. I might hurt you."

"Hurt me?" Morgan huffed. "Fat chance of that."

Without saying another word, Morgan lunged at her, and Emma grabbed his shoulders and kneed him in the stomach.

Morgan groaned as he staggered back and looked up at her in amazement. "I may have underestimated you, Emma." He lifted his brow. "Again?"

"If you insist," she replied, waiting for him to make the first move.

His movements were precise and quick as he approached her. She went to jab him in his throat when he grabbed her arm, yanking it behind her back, and brought his arms tightly around her stomach. Reacting quickly, she dropped down low, ignoring the pain when her face connected with his clenched hands, and wriggled out of his hold. She turned quickly and punched his stomach.

Grunting, Morgan placed his hands on his knees and took a deep breath. "You have an impressive amount of agility, Emma. You said your brother taught you those defensive moves?"

She nodded as she brought her hand up to touch the throbbing pain in her right cheek. "He did. David was fiercely protective of me and wanted me to know how to defend myself, if the need ever arose."

Morgan eyed her cheek remorsefully. "I am sorry I hurt you. That was not my intention," he said as he straightened.

"I know that," she rushed to reassure him. "And I am sorry if I hurt you."

"You didn't hurt me," Morgan proclaimed forcefully, almost too forcefully.

Eliza spoke up from the table. "You are a woman with many hidden talents, Emma."

Turning back towards Eliza, she replied, "I daresay that I have never been in a situation where I needed to defend myself, especially now that I live with Luke and Rachel. After all, Luke ensures that I always have a companion and footmen to accompany me whenever I go into Town." She frowned. "Mrs. Ruth Morton is the most dutiful companion when Rachel is busy with Matthew."

Josette eyed her suspiciously. "You don't seem pleased by the arrangement."

"No, I am," she rushed to explain. "I am most grateful for everything that Luke and Rachel have given me. But sometimes, even though I am surrounded by people, I still feel alone. And I feel like

I'm hiding my true self from the world as I attempt to fit into Society." Her shoulders slumped slightly. "I know I'm probably not making any sense right now."

"You are making perfect sense," Josette reassured her.

Benedict scooped Caroline up in his arms as he asked, "Have you told Luke and Rachel how you feel?"

She started shaking her head profusely. "Heavens, no. I have been so blessed that I have no right to complain."

"Who is it that you want to be?" Eliza asked, tucking an auburn tendril behind her ear.

Emma bit her lower lip. "I want to be a writer like Rachel and write additional articles for the newspaper. I want to write about the Corn Laws and delve into how people are suffering from the exorbitant price of grain."

"And what is stopping you?" she pressed.

"I don't want to upset Luke."

Benedict chuckled. "If Luke asks you to leave, we will gladly take you in."

Her eyes grew wide. "Oh no, I hadn't considered that he might ask me to leave. Do you think that's a possibility?"

"Not at all," Benedict corrected. "He would never be callous enough to even consider that."

Rising from her chair, Josette started walking over to her husband. "I think it's fantastic that you had an article published in the newspaper. Would you consider being a guest teacher at The Beckett School for Girls?" She wrapped her arm around Morgan's waist. "Perhaps one day, it will even be commonplace for women to write for the newspapers."

"Wouldn't that be lovely?" Emma responded. "And, yes, I would love to be a guest teacher."

Morgan let out a scoff. "Women writers. What a terrible thought," he mocked, earning a jab in the ribs from Josette.

"What do you say?" Eliza asked her. "Are you going to keep writing articles for the newspaper?"

Turning her gaze towards the grand townhouse, Emma took a moment to mull over her answer. What harm could possibly befall her just for writing a few articles? She would have to do some research periodically, but she had already proven to everyone that she could protect herself.

With a bright smile on her face, she brought her gaze back to the group and proclaimed, "I think that's a splendid idea."

"Then you will need this," Eliza said, reaching into the folds of her gown and removing a small dagger. She placed it, unsheathed, on the table. "Tomorrow, we'll start training you to defend yourself with a dagger."

Emma put her hands up in front of her. "I assure you that I don't need a dagger, especially since I already have an overcoat pistol."

"You do," Josette stated firmly. "Furthermore, you will need multiple weapons when you visit The Beckett School for Girls."

Seeing that she was fighting a losing battle, Emma lowered her hands. "I must admit I am curious where you each went to boarding school. My school didn't teach any weapons training but emphasized needlework instead."

Eliza just laughed. "Why don't you change back into your gown, and I will see that your carriage is brought around front?"

"Good idea," she replied. "Luke would be furious if he saw me in these clothes."

"What does he think you are doing here?" Josette asked.

Emma grinned. "I told him that I come to see Caroline."

"Does Rachel believe that?" Benedict asked with a skeptical brow.

She shook her head. "Not at all. Rachel would have most likely joined me, if she wasn't so exhausted from Matthew not sleeping at night."

Glancing up at the position of the sun, Emma said, "I'd better hurry. I need to prepare for Mrs. Gupper's garden picnic."

Chapter Four

Simeon groaned in annoyance as he walked up the steps of Caddington Manor. Why had he agreed to this act of sheer folly?

I have no time in my life for an entitled debutante, he thought, as he brought his hand up to bang on the main door. No doubt Miss Pearson was still asleep at this early hour, since most ladies of the ton didn't wake up until much later in the day.

The door was opened, and a well-groomed blond-haired butler smiled cordially at him.

"May I help you, sir?"

"I am here to see Lord Downshire," Simeon said, extending his card to the butler. "He's expecting me."

The man looked down at the card before taking a moment to peruse Simeon's plain, blue jacket with matching waistcoat, ivory shirt, and grey trousers. He opened the door wide and stood to the side.

"Please come in, Mr. Martin. I will see if Lord Downshire is available for callers."

Whenever Simeon was on an assignment, he dressed in unobtrusive attire and rarely passed out calling cards that stated his title. The less people knew about him, the better. Besides, the people he usually dealt with cared little about his title and more about the money he supplied them for information.

Removing his top hat, he took a step into the entry hall, and his steps faltered at the sheer magnificence of it all. Massive pillars supported round-topped arches, with classical statues looking down from above, painted murals ran the length of the domed ceiling, and golden sconces hung on the wall.

The clicking of the butler's shoes on the tile alerted him to his approach. "Lord Downshire will see you, Mr. Martin."

"Thank you," he said, feeling a bit embarrassed that he was caught gawking.

Simeon followed the butler through a narrow hall lined with tapestries and portraits. The butler stopped outside of an open door and gestured that he should go first. Simeon walked into the room and saw Lord Downshire sitting at a large mahogany desk.

"Come in, Mr. Martin," Lord Downshire said, pointing to a chair in front of the desk. "Thank you for coming so soon."

Simeon walked over to the proffered chair and sat down. "Lord Lansdowne and Lord Jonathon indicated that time was of the essence."

Picking up the calling card on his desk, Lord Downshire gave him a long, curious look. "Why are you not making use of your title, Lord Wentworth?"

"I prefer not to use my title when I am working as a Bow Street Runner."

Lord Downshire dropped the card onto his desk. "Interesting," he muttered. To Simeon, he said, "My brother informed me that you are trustworthy and loyal."

He remained silent and lifted his brow. What did one say to that?

Sitting back in his chair, Lord Downshire wiped his hand over his chin in agitation. "I need someone that can keep my ward safe this Season, or at least until the threat passes."

"I'm afraid that I am unavailable for the entire Season," Simeon declared, rising abruptly from his seat. "I have other responsibilities."

Lord Downshire frowned. "I will pay you double your usual fee."

Tugging down on his waistcoat, Simeon asserted, "Money is not the issue."

"Is it the familial connection?"

It was Simeon's turn to frown. "No," he stated curtly.

"I apologize. I don't mean to imply that you harbor any residual feelings for Mrs. Martha Maddix," Lord Downshire stated.

Simeon eyed him with frustration. "I am well aware that Mrs. Maddix is married to your wife's cousin, but that's not why I am turning down this assignment."

Lord Downshire leaned forward and placed his forearms on the desk. "My ward, Miss Emma Pearson, is being targeted by a spurned suitor from her past, Mr. Peter Lockhart," he shared, grabbing a piece of paper from his desk and extending it towards him. "He has made false claims, sued me for breach of contract, and has made himself an utter nuisance."

Accepting the paper, Simeon looked down and saw the list of all the civil proceedings over the past two years. "It's expensive to file all these court cases. Is Mr. Lockhart wealthy?"

"No, but he is a solicitor."

"Ah," Simeon said, nodding. "That would make sense. But for what purpose?"

Lord Downshire rose from his chair and walked over to the drink tray. "Miss Pearson's brother was the agent assigned to guard my wife in Scotland. When Rachel was attacked, David gave his life to save her." He stopped speaking and poured two snifters of brandy. "When we went to pay our respects to his family, we found that Emma's father had also died, and she was left alone. She had little food on the shelves and an overbearing suitor pressuring her to marry."

Lord Downshire picked up the snifters and walked one over to him. "By taking Emma in as my ward, I feel that we are honoring David's ultimate sacrifice."

Simeon took a sip of his drink. "That is honorable of you," he remarked as he lowered his glass.

Waving a hand dismissively in front of him, Lord Downshire said, "Emma has become part of our family. I daresay we got the better end of the deal." He took a sip of his drink. "I can't forbid Emma to leave the estate, and I need someone I can trust to watch over her when she's in town."

"How exactly is Miss Pearson being targeted?" Simeon asked, silently cursing himself for even posing the question. He didn't want this job, so why was he asking pertinent questions?

Placing his empty glass down on his desk, Lord Downshire explained, "Someone placed a burr under her saddle and spiked her drink with laudanum at her ball."

"Why do you suspect Mr. Lockhart is behind this?"

Lord Downshire shrugged. "Who else could it be?" He shifted his gaze towards the opened window. "Outside of the Season, we live in Scotland. An outsider would be identified nearly immediately. Emma is a lively young woman and couldn't possibly have any enemies."

Swirling the liquid around in his snifter, Simeon asked, "What about you? Do you have any enemies in town?"

"None that I am aware of," Lord Downshire answered. "I rather detest being in Town. The only reason we're here is for Emma to have a Season."

Simeon brought the glass up to his lips and sipped his drink. He investigated crimes, went undercover, and arrested criminals. He did not have time to sit idly by and watch a pampered young woman mingle in Society. "I'm sorry…"

His words stilled when he heard a knock at the door, and he turned towards the noise. A young woman was standing in the doorway, dressed in a simple, white gown. She was tall, with dark brown hair and pale skin, but it was the way her smile reached her eyes that caused him to take notice of her. They reflected genuine happiness, something he had not known for some time.

"I apologize for the intrusion, but Munro just informed me that you wanted to see me," she said in a kind voice.

"Emma, please come in," Lord Downshire invited, waving her into the room. "I would like to introduce you to someone."

Simeon placed his snifter on the desk as he watched Miss Pearson approach them.

Coming to stand next to his ward, Lord Downshire said, "I would like to introduce you to…"

"Mr. Simeon Martin," he interjected loudly, ignoring Lord Downshire's annoyed expression. He had no desire to inform this young woman that he held a title. It was his experience that women only were interested in conversing with him when they found out he was a viscount.

Miss Pearson curtsied. "It's a pleasure to meet you, Mr. Martin."

"Likewise, Miss Pearson," he replied, bowing.

Lord Downshire gestured towards him. "Mr. Martin is a Bow Street Runner and…"

She let out a gasp. "You are a Bow Street Runner?" she asked with enthusiasm.

Simeon had not expected that reaction from a Society miss. "I am."

A bright smile came to her lips. "I would love to speak to you about your thoughts on the Corn Laws and…"

"Emma," Luke interrupted in a warning tone, "what have we discussed before?"

Clasping her hands in front of her, she replied, "Women do not talk to gentlemen about politics, religion, philosophy, history, or anything inherently interesting."

Simeon grinned at her exasperated tone.

"I hope I did not offend your delicate male constitution by speaking my mind, Mr. Martin," Emma said, her eyes twinkling with merriment.

"I assure you that you did not," he responded, finding himself entranced by her playful nature.

Lord Downshire pressed his lips together before saying, "I have hired Mr. Martin to…"

"Unfortunately, I am…" he started.

His words stopped when Luke stepped forward, and his eyes narrowed disapprovingly at his ward. "How did you get a bruise on your cheek?"

She brought her hand up to touch the bruise. "Oh, Lord Morgan was teaching me some defensive moves, and my face connected with his hands."

Lord Downshire's brow lifted. "Morgan hit you?"

She shook her head. "No. You misunderstood me. His arms were around me, and I dropped down low to escape his hold. But, in doing so, my face collided with his clenched fists."

"Where was Eliza when this was happening?" Lord Downshire asked with a clenched jaw.

"At the table with Josette and Benedict."

Taking his hand, he placed it to the bridge of his nose. "And Benedict just allowed Morgan to attack you?"

A mischievous smile came to her lips. "Benedict was still recovering. You see, I stomped on his boot and made him cry."

Simeon chuckled. "You made Lord Lansdowne cry?"

"Not on purpose, mind you," Emma said. "He asked me to escape a hold. The quickest way was to stomp down on his boot with the heel of mine."

Lord Downshire stared at his ward for a long moment. "I am not completely unaware of what my sister is teaching you, but you must avoid acquiring visible bruises."

"I understand," she acknowledged.

"Good," Lord Downshire declared. "Now, back to what I was saying. Mr. Martin will be assigned to guard you for the foreseeable future."

Simeon was opening his mouth to once again decline the job when Emma spoke first. "I don't need a guard."

"Pardon?" Lord Downshire asked in a forceful tone.

Her naivety was evident when she explained, "Eliza gave me an overcoat pistol and," she paused, pulling out a small dagger from the pocket of her gown, "this."

"Eliza," Lord Downshire mumbled under his breath.

Simeon stepped forward and held out his hand for the dagger. "Do you know how to use a dagger?"

Emma shook her head as she extended him the weapon with her gloved hand.

"Daggers can be a useful weapon or, if they are used improperly, can remove fingers," he said, fingering the weapon in his hand.

"We start training on the dagger tomorrow," she announced proudly.

"Do you now?" he asked, extending the dagger back to her.

Returning the dagger into the folds of her gown, Emma shared, "Josette asked me to be a guest teacher at The Beckett School for Girls and informed me that I would need multiple weapons on my person."

"No, no, no…" Lord Downshire started muttering as he stormed towards the door. "Munro! I need to speak to Lady Downshire… *now!*"

Emma put her hand next to her mouth and leaned closer. "Whenever Luke is displeased with me, he calls for Rachel so she can talk me out of my foolish behavior."

"Is Lord Downshire frequently displeased with you?"

She smiled. "All the time." Emma glanced over her shoulder at Luke, who was still standing by the door, looking agitated as he waited for his wife's arrival. "Do you know of any groups that are protesting the Corn Laws?"

"Pardon?" he asked, hoping he misheard her. After all, why would a lady of the ton care about the Corn Laws?

"I know there are groups that are actively protesting the Corn Laws," she whispered. "I just need to get in contact with one of their members so I can interview them for an article I am working on."

Simeon stifled a sigh. Miss Emma Pearson was a bluestocking, and he suspected, slightly mad.

He took a step back, creating more distance between them. "That's impossible. Even if I knew someone in one of these groups, no one would speak to a lady about the price of grain. Besides, we both know that women cannot write articles for the morning newspapers."

"That's not true," she asserted. "I have…"

He spoke over her, and his tone brooked no argument. "No, Miss Pearson. My answer is no."

Annoyance flashed over her features, and he expected a sharp-witted rebuke. However, to his surprise, a tense smile grew on her lips.

"I understand, Mr. Martin," she said, her words anything but cordial.

Simeon furrowed his brows. "You do?"

"I do." She curtsied. "It was a pleasure to speak to you."

Without saying another word, she turned and approached Lord Downshire. "With your permission, I would like to dress for Mrs. Gupper's garden party."

He nodded. "You may, but please join me in the study before you depart. I would like to revisit this conversation about working as a teacher at The Beckett School for Girls."

Emma smiled at her guardian before she departed from the room.

Lord Downshire tilted his head up and looked up at the ceiling. "Emma is quite opinionated and free spirited, but I assure you that she does behave in public."

"Does she?" Simeon found himself asking.

Bringing his gaze back down, Lord Downshire replied, "She was educated at a boarding school, but her education was lacking in many regards. She was not prepared for Society, so we hired tutors to fill in the gaps. Poor Emma grew up with less restrictions, and she thrived in Scotland. However, London poses its own set of problems, even before Mr. Lockhart started sabotaging her."

"Your ward claims she writes articles for the newspaper," he shared, picking up his snifter from the table and taking a sip.

Lord Downshire cleared his throat. "Please keep that to yourself, Lord Wentworth."

"It's true?"

"Yes," he reluctantly admitted.

Simeon found his curiosity piqued by this peculiar young woman. She was an anomaly amongst the women of the ton. But more importantly, he felt she conceded too easily. It struck him as ingenuine, and that perplexed him.

Miss Emma Pearson was up to something, and it irked him that he didn't know what it was. Perhaps guarding her for a day wouldn't be the worst waste of his time.

He tossed back the remainder of his drink and placed it onto the table. "I will guard Miss Pearson," he paused, "at least until another guard can be procured."

"Thank you, Wentworth. I will owe you a favor," Lord Downshire sighed in relief.

"Keep it," he declared, walking towards the door. "I'll be waiting outside to escort Miss Pearson to the garden party."

Emma was sitting perfectly still at her dressing table chair while her lady's maid used a hot curling tong to create small ringlets to frame her face. Her thoughts were on the infuriating Bow Street Runner she had just met. He had a strong jaw, piercing blue eyes, and thick, black eyebrows. His short, brown hair was brushed forward, and he had long sideburns. He may be handsome, but he was a dolt. She had been so excited to learn that Mr. Martin worked as a Bow Street Runner, but he had dashed her hopes of interviewing him. All she wanted to know was his thoughts on the Corn Laws and...

Her lady's maid's voice broke her out of her thoughts. "You seem distracted, miss," Peggy observed as she reached for another lock of hair.

Keeping her gaze focused on the mirror, Emma replied, "I am. The newspaper requested that I submit additional articles for their consideration, and I want to write an article about how the Corn Laws are affecting the people in the rookeries."

"Like you did for the Highland Clearance?"

"Yes, but this time I would like to attend a meeting of a group that is actively opposing the Corn Laws and interview multiple people," she confessed.

"That doesn't seem safe," Peggy mused, walking over and placing the hot tongs next to the hearth.

Emma shifted in her chair to face her lady's maid. "People are on the brink of starvation because of the high bread prices, and they have no money to spare to buy anything else."

"My cousin's family is starving because he can't find a job," Peggy revealed, blinking back her tears. "I send him all the spare coins that I can, but it isn't enough. He works side jobs whenever he has the chance, but there are no long-term prospects."

"Why didn't you say anything?" Rising from her seat, Emma went over to her reticule and removed the two one-pound notes. She extended them towards Peggy. "I hope this helps."

Peggy put her hands in front of her. "I cannot accept that. It's far too generous."

"Please, I insist," Emma replied, holding the money out. "No one should go without food, especially children."

Tentatively, Peggy reached for the money. "Thank you, miss. This will mean the world to my cousin," she said, slipping the notes into the pocket of her apron.

Turning towards the bed, her lady's maid picked up a white gown with a fine, sheer, yellow silk overlay. A blue trim ran along the hemline and along the sleeves. She held it up for her inspection. "I thought this gown would look beautiful for the garden party."

"Excellent choice, Peggy."

After she was dressed, Emma sat back on the bed as she put on her white satin slippers with their blue decorative ribbons.

Clutching a blue-striped parasol in her hand, Peggy appeared anxious as she diverted her gaze to the floor.

"What is it?"

Peggy brought her gaze back up to meet Emma's. "I do know someone who can help you. My brother, Jerome, belongs to the Anti-Corn Law rebels."

"Can you arrange a meeting with him?" Emma asked eagerly.

"I'm afraid he won't come to Caddington Manor, miss. It's much too grand for his taste, nor does he have the funds to come to this part of town."

"Then, where can I find him?"

Peggy shook her head. "It's not safe for you to go into the rookeries. If you write down some questions, I can ask him on my next day off and remember his responses."

Reaching for her white gloves, Emma pressed, "Where do you meet him?"

"At his job," Peggy replied. "He works at a public house called The Tubby Wench. It's on Bosky Street near the east side. It's also where the Anti-Corn Law rebels meet each week."

"That isn't quite in the rookeries, is it?" Emma asked.

"Right. If you continue down Bosky Street, it turns into a dead end at St. Giles." Peggy shuddered. "I have never ventured that far, mind you. I've only heard stories of how horrific the rookeries are."

"Mrs. Gupper's estate is not far from Bosky Street," Emma remarked out loud. "I could go to The Tubby Wench public house..."

Peggy spoke over her. "That's a horrible idea! You must get that thought out of your head."

Before she could respond, a knock came at the door before it was pushed open. Rachel walked into the room, holding Matthew in her arms.

"Emma," Lady Downshire proclaimed in a firm voice, "I've come to talk you out of being a teacher at The Beckett School for

Girls. That is completely…" she closed the door, "wonderful news."

Emma breathed a sigh of relief. "For a moment, I thought you were angry with me."

"I'm not," Rachel confessed, "but Luke is not entirely pleased." She walked over to the bed and laid Matthew down. "Don't worry. Luke will come around."

Sitting down next to Matthew, Emma replied, "I've been having such an enjoyable time at Eliza's house. She taught me how to climb down a wall, shoot a pistol, and she's going to start tutoring me on daggers tomorrow."

"I wish I could be there with you. But this little guy," Rachel said, turning her attention towards Matthew, "keeps me up at night."

Emma smiled. "You could employ a nursemaid for nighttime."

"I could, but I won't," Rachel stated.

Peggy extended her the parasol. "Do you care for your parasol?"

"Not today, but thank you."

For a long moment, Peggy watched her before asking, "I apologize for my bold speech, but you aren't planning to leave Mrs. Gupper's garden party for any reason, are you?"

Emma knew what she was not saying, so she answered, "We'll discuss it more later this evening."

"As you wish," Peggy sighed, turning to exit the room.

Before the door latched close, Rachel turned to her with an expectant look. "May I ask what that was about?"

Emma smiled down at baby Matthew as she explained, "I would like to write an article about the Anti-Corn Law rebels, and Peggy's brother belongs to the group. I was hoping she would arrange a time for us to meet."

"You're writing about the Corn Laws?"

"I am," she answered. "Furthermore, I assume my article would have a better chance of being accepted if I have a meeting with a member of this group."

Rachel nodded approvingly. "I agree, but you must be safe. Traveling to interview the displaced Highlanders was a vastly different experience than meeting with members of the lower class in London."

"I will. Are you coming to Mrs. Gupper's garden party?" she

asked in a hopeful tone.

Rachel yawned. "I plan to rest while you are gone, but I have arranged for Mrs. Morton to accompany you."

Leaning down, Emma kissed Matthew's cheek and earned a smile from him. "Mrs. Morton is attentive and genuine, but she is no fun at these social gatherings. She sits in a corner and practices her needlework."

"How awful for you," Rachel teased. "But be kind to Mrs. Morton. She is a dear family friend."

"I'm well aware of that," Emma said, rising from the bed. "Hopefully, if all goes well, I won't fall into a puddle or get inebriated at the garden party."

Laughing, Rachel picked up Matthew. "You will shine like the woman we know you to be."

Emma smoothed out her gown and walked towards the door. She picked up the reticule and ensured her overcoat pistol was inside. If the garden party was boring, as she anticipated, no one would notice if she disappeared over the back wall for an hour or so and took a short walk to The Tubby Wench.

After all, it was only a short jaunt to the public house. She'd be back before anyone knew she was gone.

Chapter Five

Simeon was questioning his life choices… again. He owned a highly profitable merchant company and had amassed a sizeable fortune. Still, he maintained his position as a Bow Street Runner because he needed a distraction from Martha's memory. Solving crimes and socializing with miscreants gave him the reprieve from his thoughts that he craved.

And yet, here he was, standing in front of Caddington Manor, waiting for a peculiar debutante to make an appearance so he could escort her to a garden party. He hated garden parties. Well, to be fair, he hated any type of social gathering.

The Marquess of Downshire's crested coach came to a stop on the paved courtyard as the door to Caddington Manor opened. An older, nicely dressed woman with white hair exited first, walking down the few stairs before spinning back around.

"Are you coming, dear?" she asked in a kind voice.

Simeon turned his gaze towards the door to see Miss Pearson step out of the manor with a bright smile on her face. He took a moment to admire her fair, oval face, and comely figure, but a vision of Martha flitted through his mind, causing his mood to turn sour.

Miss Pearson's smile dimmed when she saw him. "Mr. Martin," she said, her voice strained, "what a pleasure to see you again."

He wanted to laugh at her blatant lie, but instead replied, "I have agreed to stay on as your guard until another can be secured."

"Well, I hope you enjoy garden parties," she teased, walking gracefully down the steps.

"I do not."

She stopped in front of him, and he detected the aroma of

rosewater. "Then we have something in common, Mr. Martin."

He lifted his brow. "Every lady enjoys garden parties."

"I am not a lady," she replied as she brushed past him.

"You look like a lady to me."

"Looks can be deceiving," she said over her shoulder as she accepted the footman's offered hand.

Glancing up at the main door, he saw Lady Downshire smiling, holding a baby in her arms as she waved down at him. He tipped his hat to acknowledge her, and her smile grew. The Beckett family was quite odd. Some were agents of the Crown, some were obnoxiously cheerful, and they all held secrets. Secrets that weren't his business to know.

Simeon walked up to the carriage and stepped inside. "Ladies," he said as he sat down on the opposite bench.

The older woman smiled back at him. "Aren't you a handsome young chap?"

He shifted in his seat uncomfortably as he saw Miss Pearson bring her gloved hand up to her lips to cover a growing smile.

"I am Mrs. Morton," the woman said, introducing herself.

He didn't smile at the nice woman, but he didn't frown either. "I'm Simeon Martin, ma'am."

His lackluster introduction didn't seem to bother the woman, and she pressed on. "I understand that you will be guarding Miss Pearson from that sneaky Mr. Lockhart."

"We don't know if Mr. Lockhart is behind this," Simeon responded, amused despite himself.

"Back in my day, this whole situation would be rectified with a steely round of fisticuffs," Mrs. Morton declared, punching the air in front of her.

Miss Pearson giggled at the antics of her chaperone.

Removing his top hat, Simeon placed it next to him on the bench. "I understand that Mr. Lockhart was a suitor of yours."

The smile dimmed from Miss Pearson's lips. "That's not accurate. We grew up together, but Peter was a year older than my brother, David. From a young age, he had it in his mind that we would marry, but I continually rejected his courtship."

"May I ask why?" he asked.

Simeon noticed that she'd begun wringing her hands together in her lap.

"Peter was a bit possessive, and he was known to have a nasty temper. He never struck me, but it was rumored that he struck the maids at his home if they displeased him," she explained.

"If you hadn't become the ward of Lord Downshire, would you have married Mr. Lockhart?" he asked directly.

"No," she answered without hesitation. "My father owned a store in town, and I planned to work there to support myself."

Fearing he misheard her, he repeated, "You planned to work?"

"I am fully capable of working, Mr. Martin, and I do not appreciate the censure in your tone," Miss Pearson huffed.

"My apologies, I just assumed that a lady of your station…"

"My station?" Miss Pearson pressed her lips together, drawing his attention to their crimson color. "Before I became Lord Downshire's ward, I was just a constable's daughter. My boarding school taught me the usual subjects, but my father paid extra for me to be taught plain and fancy needlework, music, drawing, dancing, and French. Furthermore, I learned the skills that would allow me to find employment, if I ever needed to."

"Which boarding school did you attend?"

"Westmoreland House Boarding School in Witney," she informed him.

He stared back at her in disbelief. "You went to Westmoreland House Boarding School?"

Miss Pearson gave him a baffled look. "I did."

"My younger sister is there now, at the cost of thirty-five guineas a year."

Her brow lifted. "I daresay that my father did not pay that inflated amount."

"Do you know how much your father did pay?"

Miss Pearson shook her head. "I do not. But I know he did not have the funds to pay a fee of thirty-five guineas."

Simeon adjusted his jacket. "Was your father's shop profitable?"

"I assume so."

"But you don't know for sure?" he pressed.

For a quick moment, Simeon saw irritation flash in her green eyes, and he knew he'd pushed her too far with his line of questioning.

"Lord Downshire has been gracious enough to handle my father's business deals. I encourage you to direct your questions to him," she replied, turning her gaze out the window.

The carriage came to a stop in front of a stately townhouse. The door was opened, and Mr. Martin exited the carriage first so he could assist the ladies. However, the moment Miss Pearson placed her gloved hand into his, he felt a jolt of something indescribable. He waited until her foot was on the ground before he drew back his hand, not understanding what had caused that reaction.

Miss Pearson gave him a tentative smile. "We will be inside for at least a few hours. I'm not entirely sure what a Bow Street Runner does, but you are welcome to rest your eyes while you're waiting."

Placing his hat on his head, he replied, "A Bow Street Runner does not take naps while on assignment."

"Pity," Miss Pearson teased as she followed Mrs. Morton up to the iron gate. A footman opened the gate, and they stepped inside.

Once he saw Miss Pearson walk inside the townhouse, Simeon started walking around the property, looking for anyone that might be surveying the surrounding area.

The townhouse sat on the corner within a few blocks of a rough section of town. It always amazed him how closely the wealthy and the poor lived, but they had little or no interaction. A stone wall ran along the back of the property, and it appeared to be fairly easy to climb, assuming the need arose.

Simeon had just turned the corner when he heard a noise coming from the back of the property. He took a step back, shielding himself, as he waited to see if the noise repeated itself. He was surprised when he saw Miss Pearson appear on the top of the wall and was even more surprised when he saw her climb down with slow but sure movements. What in the dickens was she doing?

Miss Pearson glanced both ways before she started walking down the pavement away from Mrs. Gupper's townhouse. Staying far enough away to avoid detection, he followed her as she turned onto Bosky Street where the streets narrowed, the buildings were darkened, and the odor of excrement was pungent.

To add to his confusion, she stopped a scruffy older man on the street, and she appeared to ask him a question. The man pointed further down the street. She smiled and continued on her way, appearing blissfully unaware of the commotion she was causing among the men milling about. They were eyeing her as if she was a piece of candy. Did this woman not have a lick of sense?

Miss Pearson gripped her reticule tightly in her hand as she approached The Tubby Wench public house. To his horror, she gripped the handle and opened the door.

Forget keeping himself concealed, he thought, as he charged towards the door, I need to save this madcap woman!

The moment Emma opened the door to the clamorous pub, she knew that she hadn't fully thought this through. Raggedly dressed men filled the small, dimly-lit hall, and a few scantily clad women were pushing through the crowd to serve drinks. Between the smell of ale and the odor emanating from the dirty-faced men, a foul, putrid stench engulfed the hall.

A few men glanced her way, with a lecherous gleam in their eyes, causing her to shudder in fear. Emma realized that the one bullet in her overcoat pistol would not be sufficient to protect her against these men and their vile intentions. Now was not the time to question herself, she thought. She would accomplish what she came here for and then figure out the rest later… assuming she made it that far.

Banishing that wayward thought, she approached the crude bar and waited for a round-faced barkeep to acknowledge her. She waited and waited as he filled tankard after tankard of ale, barely sparing her a glance. Finally, she found her voice and spoke up.

"Excuse me, sir."

He huffed. "You're wasting your breath, lady. I'm not serving you a drink."

Looking down at the grime-coated tankards, Emma was thankful for that. "I just want to ask you a question."

The man stilled with a tankard in his hand. "Why?"

"I was hoping you might know a man named Jerome."

Lowering the tankard to the table, he repeated his question. "Why?"

Emma took a step closer to the bar and lowered her voice. "I want to ask him a few questions about the Anti-Corn Law rebels."

Giving her an exasperated look, the barkeep tossed a rag over his shoulder as he yelled, "Jerome!"

A thin man, no older than she, dressed in a faded shirt, trousers held up by twine, and boots that had more holes than tread, ran up to him.

"Yes, sir," he asked breathlessly.

The barkeep jabbed his thumb towards her. "This lady wants to speak to you."

Jerome turned his attention towards her. "How may I help you, ma'am?"

"I'm a friend of your sister's."

His eyes grew wide and fearful. "Oh no. Has something happened to Peggy?"

Emma shook her head. "No, not at all." She took a step closer, attempting to keep their conversation private. "Peggy is my lady's maid, and she told me where I could find you. I was hoping to ask you a few questions."

"Ye're Miss Emma Pearson," Jerome responded knowingly, his eyes darting around the room. "Ye shouldn't be here. This place is dangerous for any woman, but especially for a respectable lady such as yerself."

"I wanted to speak to you about the Anti-Corn Law reb…"

"Say no more," he declared forcefully. "Are ye mad?"

She frowned at his aggressive tone. "I am not. I want to interview…"

Her words were stilled when he grabbed her arm and led her towards an unoccupied corner of the room. He remained close and kept his voice low. "It's not safe to speak here. Bow Street Runners could be in this very room." He glanced nervously over his shoulder. "I can't risk talking for too long. This job is the only thing keeping me and my family from starving."

Emma pulled out three shillings and extended it towards him. "I would like to pay you for your time." She could see the regret in his eyes as he accepted the coins in his red, blistered hands.

"It ain't right that ye are paying to speak to me, but I thank ye for your generosity, Miss Pearson."

"You're doing me the favor," she assured him.

He deposited the coins into his pocket. "What do ye want to know?"

"I'm writing an article about the Corn Laws, and I wanted to meet with a few members of," she hesitated, "the rebels."

Jerome sighed as he looked up at the rafters. After a moment, he brought his gaze back down. "I'm sure the members would be willing to speak to you, assuming you'd be willing to make a small donation to the cause."

Emma felt her excitement growing, but she worked to keep her face expressionless. "That would be my pleasure."

"We're meeting tomorrow night at nine," he revealed. "We meet in the upstairs hall."

"I'll be here," she assured him.

Jerome perused her gown and remarked, "It might be best if you borrowed a gown from my sister. It may help you blend in better."

"I think I shall."

Shifting his gaze over her shoulder, he said, "Make sure you bring your guard with you, as well. This is a bad part of town during the day, but it becomes downright devilish at night."

She gave him a puzzled look. "I didn't bring a guard with me."

"Really? Then who's he?" he asked, pointing over her shoulder.

Emma followed the direction of his finger, and her heart stopped when she saw who he was pointing to. Mr. Simeon Martin. And judging by the scowl on his face, it was clear that he was not pleased to see her, either.

Mr. Martin walked slowly over to her, his step emanating power and confidence, and he didn't stop until he was in front of her.

"Miss Pearson," he growled, "what in blazes do you think you're doing?"

Bringing her hand up to her chest, she feigned outrage. "Language, Mr. Martin. My delicate constitution cannot handle your vulgar choice of words."

Mr. Martin clenched his jaw so tight that a muscle pulsated under his right ear. Perhaps it was not the right time to tease the man, she thought, as she took a step back.

His hand reached out and grabbed her arm. He turned his gaze towards Jerome. "Is there a back door to this public house?"

Jerome nodded. "There is. Follow me," he said, leading them through the crowd.

Mr. Martin kept a firm hold on her as they followed behind Jerome. She gave him a side glance. "I can walk perfectly well on my own."

"I have no doubt about your walking ability. It's your sanity that I call into question," he huffed.

They reached a closed door in the rear of the room. Jerome pulled out a key from his pocket and unlocked it.

"Go, before anyone sees you," he encouraged.

Mr. Martin led her into the dimly lit alley, and her kid slippers slipped on the grime-coated ground. She brought her hand up to cover her nose.

"What is that horrid smell?" she asked.

"Urine and excrement," he answered without sparing her a glance.

They had just stepped out of the alleyway when three men pushed off from the wall of the public house and approached them. They were all of similar height and were covered in a thick layer of filth, but that's where the resemblance stopped. The first man had a dark face and restless eyes, whereas the second man had a shapeless face with large, pale eyes, and the last man had a long, pointy nose.

Mr. Martin released her arm and corralled her back behind him. "Step aside," he ordered.

The dark-faced man chuckled. "I don't think so, mate."

"I am not your *mate*," Mr. Martin replied, his hands forming into tight balls.

Large, pale eyes landed on her, and she could see lust in them. "We just want the girl," he said with a leer.

"The girl is with me," Mr. Martin asserted. "Let us pass."

The man with the pointy nose started cracking his knuckles in an exaggerated fashion. "You may leave, but not with the girl."

Emma fumbled with her reticule and pulled out her overcoat

66

pistol. She tucked it against her side. She would never be a willing participant to what these men wanted. She would die first. Besides, she wasn't the helpless woman they thought her to be.

The first man swung at Mr. Martin, and he ducked easily. While he was low, he punched the assailant in the stomach, causing him to double over. Another man lunged at Mr. Martin as the third grabbed her arm and yanked her towards him.

Taking her pistol, Emma slammed it into his face, causing his large, pointy nose to gush blood. She reared back again and hit him in the side of the head. This time, he crumbled to the ground.

Mr. Martin was still fighting with the assailant, both throwing punches at each other. She removed the dagger from the pocket of her gown and plunged it into the man's leg. He roared in pain and reached for the wound as she yanked it out.

Without saying a word, Mr. Martin grabbed her hand, and they started racing down the street. He didn't stop until they arrived at the stone wall outside of Mrs. Gupper's townhouse.

His breathing was labored. His eyes were closed. But Emma knew that she had fueled Mr. Martin's anger, and she couldn't rule out that he might take that out on her. She slipped her hand out of his hold, took a step back, and held firmly to her pistol.

Mr. Martin opened his eyes, his unrelenting gaze latching onto hers. "You foolish, witless girl..." he started.

"Stop!" she ordered. "You have no right to speak to me like this."

His mouth dropped. "No right? You almost got us killed back there!"

"I did no such thing," she retorted. "In fact, I would like to point out that I took out two of the attackers, and you only took out one. I believe a thank you would be in order."

"Thank you?" he growled. "You want me to thank you?"

She shrugged. "It would be the polite thing to do."

Advancing towards her, his eyes sparked with fury. "What *exactly* was so important that you risked going into a public house in that part of town?"

She tilted her chin to look up at him. "It matters not."

"You are unbelievable!" He pointed towards the ground. "You

will tell me this instant what you were doing at that public house."

"I will not," she answered, returning his ire.

Mr. Martin spun back around and took a few steps away. She heard him muttering curse words under his breath, and she pressed her lips together to refrain from smiling.

He turned back around and surprised her by asking, "Will you *please* tell me why you went to The Tubby Wench?"

Despite his boorish tone, Emma now knew that she had no reason to fear Mr. Martin. She even felt safe around him. Which was odd, especially since he insulted her constantly. She placed her pistol back into the reticule around her wrist.

"As I mentioned previously, I intend to write an article for the newspaper about the Corn Laws…"

"Which is rubbish."

Emma raised an eyebrow. "Thank you for that," she remarked dryly. "By going there today, I have arranged for a meeting with the members of an Anti-Corn Law movement."

Mr. Martin stared at her in silence for a long moment. Finally, he inquired, "When?"

"I don't think so, Mr. Martin. If you recall, you weren't willing to help me when I asked earlier today."

"That's different," he stated, stepping closer to her. "These rebels are dangerous."

"Do you believe starving, desperate men to be dangerous of their own volition?"

"Clearly."

She frowned. "Men, women, and children are starving because of the high price of bread. The poor are suffering so the landowners can line their pockets. Whom, may I ask, is the guiltier of the two?"

"Are you saying the ends justify the means?"

Tucking a lock of hair behind her ear, she clarified, "I'm saying, that there are two sides to every story, and it's important to know both sides before casting judgement."

He stiffened a little, his face settling into hard lines. "Your logic isn't entirely faulty."

"Was that a compliment, Mr. Martin?" she mocked.

A brief smile came to his lips, but it happened so quickly that she feared she'd imagined it.

"I propose a bargain," he stated.

Crossing her arms over her chest, she replied, "I'm listening."

He took a step closer to her, bringing him within arm's length. "We go to this meeting… *together*," he hesitated, "and I will allow you to interview me."

Emma studied his blue eyes as she attempted to gauge his sincerity. Could she trust him? Or would he betray her at his first opportunity? He appeared genuine, which irked her for some unknown reason.

"I will agree," she paused, holding her hand up, "but I request five separate interviews."

"Two," he countered.

"Three."

"Deal."

She held out her gloved hand, ignoring the blood splatter on the white fabric. "It appears that we have struck a bargain, Mr. Martin."

He accepted her hand. "It does, indeed, Miss Pearson."

Mrs. Morton's voice came from the other side of the stone wall. "Emma… it's time for you to come back to the garden party."

"Thank you, Mrs. Morton," she acknowledged, dropping his hand.

Mr. Martin eyed her with suspicion. "Mrs. Morton knew that you were leaving?"

Emma laughed. "I expect better from you, Mr. Bow Street Runner."

She walked over to the stone wall and quickly climbed up it. Once she dropped on the other side, Mrs. Morton whispered, "Did you have a good adventure?"

"I did," she confirmed. "I truly did."

Chapter Six

Emma watched in frustration as her dagger sailed past the target… again. She let out a loud, unladylike grunt. What was she doing wrong? How did Eliza make it look so easy?

Adrien's jovial voice came from behind her. "Perhaps she doesn't see the large, chalked circle on the tree."

"I fear that she might be partially blind," Benedict replied in a concerned voice.

Standing next to her, Eliza glanced over her shoulder and gave the men an exasperated look. "Your commentary is not appreciated."

"Well, I never!" Adrien declared in a haughty tone.

Turning around to face the men, Emma asked, "What am I doing wrong? My throwing stance and grip are perfect."

"You're too tense," Benedict observed.

Adrien chimed in. "You're throwing the dagger with too much force. Just a moderate throw will be sufficient if you have the correct stance and grip."

She glanced over her shoulder to look at the target. "I have been trying to hit the target all morning with a single rotation dagger throw."

"Would you like to try again?" Eliza asked as she handed her another dagger. "Don't fret. It will just take time. A single rotation throw is much more difficult than the half rotation throw."

Relaxing her stance, Emma gripped the dagger at its hilt and eyed the target. She threw it with moderate force and was rewarded when it hit the tree, albeit not on target. In response, she jumped up and down, clapping her hands. "I hit the tree!"

"Well done, Emma," Eliza praised. "Now, go collect the daggers and join us for breakfast."

Emma practically skipped the ten feet towards the cluster of trees. She had been practicing all morning and discovered that throwing daggers did not come easily to her. It required a lot of concentration, but she had to keep her body relaxed. Frankly, it didn't make a lot of sense. But that didn't matter, because she'd finally hit the tree on a single rotation toss.

Reaching down, she picked up the three daggers and then proudly retrieved the dagger sticking out of the tree. She hurried back towards the veranda and placed the daggers on the table.

"May I come back tomorrow for more practice?" she asked as she stepped over to the buffet table.

Eliza sat down on a chair. "You are always welcome, you know that."

Her back was to the group as she placed food onto her plate. "I am grateful for this training, especially after I was forced to hit a man in the face with my pistol," she shared, placing a piece of toast on her plate.

Her words were met with a deafening silence. She turned towards the group, and they were all staring at her.

Benedict was the first to speak, and his words were slow and deliberate. "Why did you have to hit a man in the face with a pistol?"

Emma scrunched her nose. Perhaps telling them that detail had been unwise. Everyone's eyes tracked her as she walked over to the table. "I went to a public house in hopes of securing an interview with a member of an Anti-Corn Law rebel group." She smiled victoriously. "And I was successful."

Eliza's lips parted. "What were you thinking? It's never safe for a woman to be anywhere near a public house, especially a refined lady."

Sitting down in the chair, she began to defend herself. "I just went into The Tubby Wench..."

"The Tubby Wench?" Adrien groaned, speaking over her. "That is a hotbed of criminal activity."

With a clench jaw, Benedict asked, "Where was Wentworth?"

"Who?" she asked.

His frown deepened. "Lord Wentworth. The Bow Street Runner

assigned to protect you."

"I thought his name was Simeon Martin?"

Benedict nodded. "It is. But he is also the Viscount of Wentworth." He eyed her curiously. "Did he not inform you of that?"

"No, he did not," she murmured, feeling a bit uneasy discovering that piece of information had not been revealed to her. If he was lying about his title, what else was Mr. Martin lying about?

Adrien placed the plate down on the table and sat down. "Regardless, where was Martin when this all happened?"

"Right next to me," she answered.

Eliza's brow lifted. "He went with you into the public house?"

She shook her head. "No, not exactly. I climbed over Mrs. Gupper's stone wall, walked the few blocks to the public house, went in, and met my contact. I had failed to notice that Mr. Martin had followed me. When I realized he was there, he offered to escort me home."

Eliza's gaze grew stern. "That was a foolhardy thing to do, Emma. You could have been killed... or worse."

Lowering her gaze towards her lap, she nodded her understanding. It hadn't been entirely wise on her part, and it could have ended much differently if Mr. Martin hadn't intervened when he had.

Adrien chuckled, breaking up the tension. "Who would have thought that our sweet Emma had it in her to walk brazenly near the rookeries."

"I, for one, did not," Benedict said, turning his head towards the lawn. "If we hurry and eat breakfast, we could practice some more defensive moves before you leave."

Emma brought up her gaze and smiled, grateful for the change in topic. However, that did not last long. For the rest of breakfast, she filled them in on what she had learned and the details of her harrowing escape.

It was much later when her coach pulled up in front of Caddington Manor. She exited the carriage, but her steps faltered when she saw Mr. Martin was standing next to one of the columns. By the frown on his face, it was clear that he wasn't pleased to see her.

"Where have you been?" he demanded.

"I was having breakfast with Lord and Lady Lansdowne," she responded, smoothing out her gown.

His eyes focused on her ungloved hands. "Why do you have dried blood on your fingers?"

Hiding her hands behind her back, she replied, "I was doing some target practice."

"Do you often go over to the Lansdowne's townhouse for breakfast?"

"I do," she revealed. "I've gone every morning since we arrived in Town."

He lifted his brow. "And Lord Downshire approves of this?"

Emma smirked. "Define 'approve'?"

"What time do you leave in the morning?"

Turning her gaze in the direction of the sun, she said, "Typically, I try to arrive at dawn. Lady Caroline is an early riser and runs that household ragged with her energy in the morning."

"Ah, that would explain it," he replied, drawing back her gaze. "I didn't think any respectable lady would be out of bed before nine in the morning."

She placed a hand on her hip. "I believe I already explained that I am not a lady. I am just a country miss that used to wake up before dawn to do my chores."

"Be that as it may, my job is to guard you, and I am unable to accomplish that task if you wander off whenever you see fit."

"I see," she replied, stepping closer to him. "You want me to keep you abreast of my comings and goings."

"Yes, so I may accompany you."

Her eyes narrowed slightly. "Do you want honesty between us, as well?"

"I do."

"Well, is there anything that you would like to tell me, Mr. *Martin*?" she asked, drawing out his last name.

"Not that I can think of."

Emma stepped closer, challenging him. "Nothing?"

"Nothing." His face was expressionless, giving nothing away.

"I see," she sighed as her eyes trailed over his blue jacket and white waistcoat. She immediately noticed that he was dressed in finer articles of clothing this morning. Interesting, she thought.

Stepping back, she said cheerfully, "I am going to freshen up, and then I'm heading into town to visit Miss Cosette's Dress Shop. You are welcome to join me, *Mr. Martin.*"

He bowed. "I'll be waiting."

Emma watched him for a moment. Why would a viscount work as a Bow Street Runner? She couldn't wait to interview him. This man had secrets, and she couldn't wait to discover all of them.

Simeon watched as Miss Pearson entered Caddington Manor. Her behavior was odd, but that was to be expected. She was a most unusual young lady. Yet, he had an uneasy feeling that she knew more than she was letting on.

The entrance door opened, and Lord Downshire's frame filled the doorway. He looked down at Simeon with an exasperated look. "May I ask why you are loitering outside my townhouse?"

"I am here to guard your ward," he announced, leaning his shoulder against a column.

Lord Downshire glanced over his shoulder. "I hate to be the bearer of bad tidings, but Emma is safely inside Caddington Manor."

"I'm aware of that."

"I can tell that you are extraordinarily busy guarding my ward, but may I have a moment of your time?" Downshire asked, stepping back. "My brother dropped off the agency's report on Mr. Lockhart this morning."

"This morning?" he repeated in disbelief as he jogged up the few steps. Did all of the Beckett family rise at this extremely early hour, he wondered.

Downshire chuckled. "My sister-in-law, Hannah, just had twin girls. No one sleeps in their house." He closed the door behind him. "It would be best if we had this conversation in my study."

"As you wish," Simeon said, following closely behind Downshire.

Once they stepped into the study, Downshire closed the door and walked over to his desk. He reached for a file and sat down on his chair.

"We have a problem," he stated, removing a paper from the file. "Mr. Peter Lockhart is nowhere to be found."

Simeon straightened in his chair, fully alert. "He's gone? I thought he worked as a solicitor in the village of Totternhoe."

"He does… or, he did, until recently," Downshire explained. "Three weeks ago, Lockhart locked up his home and office and rode out of town."

"Where did he go?"

Downshire shrugged. "Agents interviewed Lockhart's neighbors, but they could give no additional insight." He gave him a pointed look. "Did you have a chance to read those letters?"

"I did," he said, removing the stack of notes from his jacket pocket and placing them on the desk. "There was nothing in there to indicate he would go off half-cocked."

"Exactly," Downshire agreed. "Lockhart wouldn't put his entire life on hold unless he had a plan. And I'm afraid that plan revolves around Emma."

"But why? Why would he give up all that he has for a woman that does not favor him?"

Downshire removed another paper from the file. "The agents broke into his office and confiscated several ledgers. After reviewing them, they discovered multiple suspicious deposits every month from different clients. However, someone with the initials of A.B. has deposited £75 every month into Lockhart's account for the past five years."

"Dare I ask if they discovered the identity of A.B.?"

Downshire shook his head as he extended him the paper. "No. The agents are attempting to identify all the clients that made monthly deposits."

Reading the rather long list, Simeon asked, "All this money is being deposited into Lockhart's account? Is any money going out?"

"It doesn't appear so, but the most recent ledger disappeared along with Lockhart." Downshire picked up another paper. "There's more. A large stack of contracts was in the hearth when the agents searched the room. Most of them were burned beyond recognition, but one managed to survive." He extended the paper across the desk. "This is a re-creation of the contract."

Simeon accepted that paper and began reading the copy. He found himself growing incredibly infuriated at the renter's contract. It stated the rental price at one rate, but Lockhart charged the tenant an inflated monthly fee. Furthermore, if the tenant defaulted on the payment, he would be required to pay a fee directly to Lockhart.

"This contract is rubbish. Lockhart was bamboozling the people in his own village," he declared, tossing the paper onto the desk.

"It appears that way," Downshire remarked. "He was the only solicitor in the town, and he exploited the citizens' inability to read."

"What a horrid man," Simeon mumbled. "But none of this explains why he's sabotaging Miss Pearson's Season, assuming that it's even him. There's been no proof to corroborate that."

Downshire sighed. "Who else could it be?"

Simeon sat back in his chair and asked, "Did Miss Pearson receive an inheritance after her father passed away?"

"She did," Downshire confirmed. "Constable Pearson owned his cottage, the surrounding land, and a general store in town."

"Was the store profitable?"

Downshire gave him a baffled look. "I suppose so. There were no liens on it when I sold it for Emma, and I negotiated a generous sum for her."

"Have you sold the cottage or land off?"

Downshire shook his head. "No. That will be Emma's decision, but there are tenants in the cottage. Currently, she is earning a small income every month." He pressed his lips in a frown. "Mr. Lockhart had taken it upon himself to secure buyers for Emma's land, and he was furious when I informed him that the land was not for sale. *Irate* would be a better word."

"Did Constable Pearson have a savings?"

"A modest one," Downshire shared, his expression growing curious. "Why are you asking all these questions?"

Simeon glanced over at the door. "Did you know that Miss Pearson went to Westmoreland House Boarding School in Witney?"

"I did know that, because I am her guardian," Downshire said in a mocking tone.

Simeon frowned at the marquess' tone. "Did you know that school costs thirty-five guineas a year?"

"I did not," he replied, letting out a low whistle.

Rubbing his chin thoughtfully, Simeon asked, "So the question remains, how did the daughter of a constable afford to go to an elite boarding school?"

"I cannot answer that, but perhaps Emma can," Downshire suggested.

"No, she doesn't know either." He dropped his hand. "What of Miss Pearson's relations?"

Downshire leaned back in his seat. "She has none."

"None? I find that hard to believe."

Rising from his chair, Downshire walked over to the window and looked out. "Emma's paternal grandparents are buried near her father's grave, and she learned from a young age that her mother's parents died from diphtheria."

"Poor Miss Pearson," he found himself saying.

A knock came at the door. "Come in," Downshire ordered.

The door opened, revealing Emma, and she let out a sigh of relief when her eyes landed on Simeon. "Oh, good. I found my protector. I was worried that you were abducted and were being held for ransom by a group of ruthless ruffians."

He rose from his seat, slightly baffled. "And why would you think that?"

"Simple," she remarked, smiling, "you weren't outside."

A chuckle came from behind him. "Please give Miss Cosette our regards when you see her," Downshire requested.

Turning her smile towards her guardian, Miss Pearson replied, "I will. I am excited to visit her shop and collect my new gowns." She shifted her gaze back to him. "Afterwards, I was hoping we could go to the square near Gunther's and have some lemon ice."

"I will agree to that only on one condition," Simeon said, giving her a stern look.

She arched an eyebrow. "Which is?"

"You will behave, and there will be no more attempting to hoodwink me."

Lowering her brow, Miss Pearson's eyes had a mischievous twinkle in them. "You offend me, sir. I would never, *ever*, attempt to deceive a Bow Street Runner."

Ignoring Downshire's chuckle, Simeon cast her an irritated look.

Why did I come back today, he asked himself. However, he already knew that answer. Without Miss Pearson, he wouldn't know when and where that meeting was with the Anti-Corn Law rebels.

Drat! When he signed up to be a Bow Street Runner, he never thought it would take him to the dangerous fields of a dress shop.

Chapter Seven

Simeon leaned up against the wall of Miss Cosette's Dress Shop and started counting all the ways his life had gone terribly wrong. Here he was, standing outside a modiste shop waiting for the most infuriatingly stubborn young woman that he had ever met.

He was a blasted Bow Street Runner. Not a for-hire guard. He had brought down criminal networks, gone undercover in the rookeries, and even worked alongside agents of the Crown to help put an end to The Cursed Lot gang in Gravesend. Yet again, he cursed himself for agreeing to guard Miss Pearson. It didn't matter that her eyes sparkled when she talked about something that excited her. She may be a beautiful young woman, but she was foolhardy, brazen, and she was going to get herself killed.

The door to the modiste shop opened, and he straightened from the wall. Miss Pearson stepped out with a beautiful woman with black hair, creamy white skin, and red, pouty lips.

Miss Pearson put her hand out towards the woman and provided the introductions. "Mr. Simeon Martin, may I introduce you to Miss Cosette. She owns this dress shop."

Simeon bowed, admiring her long-sleeved, ornate blue gown. "It's a pleasure to meet you, Miss Cosette."

"The pleasure is all mine, Mr. Martin," she replied with a French accent.

"You're French," he remarked.

Miss Cosette let out a light, airy laugh. "I am so much more than French." She arched a brow at him. "I wanted to speak to you about the protection you are offering my dear Emma."

"Pardon?"

She eyed him thoughtfully. "How many pistols are on your person?"

Simeon frowned, confused by the turn of the conversation.

"Three, I'm assuming, if you aren't lax on your safety," Miss Cosette stated, her eyes dropping to his Hessian boots before turning towards Emma. "But I am worried that Mr. Martin is a person of low intellect. He can't seem to follow this conversation adequately."

Miss Pearson giggled, causing him to break out of his stupor of thought.

"I assure you that is not the case, Miss Cosette," he huffed.

Taking a step closer to him, Miss Cosette's next words were laced with an even thicker French accent. "If any harm comes to Emma, I will hold you accountable." Her eyes narrowed slightly. "And, trust me when I say this, you don't want that to happen."

Simeon lifted his brow in surprise, finding himself unnerved by this beautiful woman's threat. "I understand, but no harm shall come to Emma on my watch," he asserted.

Pressing her lips together, Miss Cosette watched him with an intense gaze that baffled him. Then, she bobbed her head and announced, "I think you shall do, Mr. Martin. You shall do." And with that, she turned and went back into the dress shop.

Simeon furrowed his brow at that peculiar interaction. Another example of a beautiful, but odd woman.

Coming to stand next to him, Miss Pearson informed him, "Miss Cosette just opened her shop a month ago, and she's already the most popular modiste in town. The only reason she agreed to make me gowns is because of our familial connection. I've been told that she has turned women away because she has too many orders."

"What did you tell her about me?" he asked curiously.

She shrugged one shoulder. "Nothing. Other than the fact that you were assigned to guard me."

"Was she in earnest?"

A smile came to Miss Pearson's lips. "Indeed, she was. Miss Cosette is a very capable woman, and she is fiercely loyal to her family and friends."

Simeon glanced over at the door. "She's quite frightening."

"She is, isn't she?" Miss Pearson looped her arm through his.

"Are you ready to go get some lemon ice? I am famished."

Being uncomfortable by her nearness, Simeon knew he couldn't step away or he would be considered rude. Instead, he led her towards the curricle.

"Lemon ice will not provide you sustenance," he pointed out as he assisted her into the curricle.

She scooted over to the far side and waited for him to climb in before responding, "It is dreadfully warm, and I could use a delicious treat."

"It is warm," he agreed. "Why do you suppose Miss Cosette was wearing a long-sleeved gown on such a beautiful day as this one?"

"I'm not rightly sure," Miss Pearson replied. "I have only ever known Miss Cosette to wear long-sleeved gowns."

He reached for the reins and merged the carriage into the traffic. "You have never asked her?"

A look of sorrow came to Miss Pearson's face. "My family has an enormous number of secrets, which I am not privy to. As much as I want to discover the truth, I know that it's not my place. I hope one day I will be taken into their confidences."

Simeon could hear the sadness in her voice, but he didn't dare continue his line of questioning. He could tell that her admission had cost her dearly. Unsure of what to say, he focused on driving the team until they arrived at the square outside of Gunther's Tea Shop. He parked the curricle underneath the shade of the maple trees.

A large line of carriages filled the square, and waiters dodged between the carriages to take and deliver the customers' orders.

"It's quite busy today," Miss Pearson mused as they waited for a waiter to approach their carriage.

"What shall it be today?" the waiter asked politely.

Simeon looked over at Miss Pearson expectedly.

She smiled. "I would like the lemon ice, please."

"Good choice, miss," the waiter said. "And for you, sir?"

"I suppose lemon ice for me, as well."

The waiter nodded his acknowledgement and headed back towards Gunther's. Simeon stepped out of the curricle and came around to Miss Pearson's side. He leaned up against the square's railings as he saw the other gentleman escorts do.

Miss Pearson's eyes scanned over the other curricles and remarked, "Gunther's Tea Shop is the only establishment where a lady can be seen eating alone with a gentleman without harming her reputation."

Simeon hadn't even had a chance to respond when she surprised him by saying, "It's time for our first interview."

He gave her a look of exasperation. "Do be serious."

"I am," she said with a determined tilt of her chin. "If you recall, you promised me three interviews in exchange for attending the meeting with me tonight."

He huffed. "Fine. What would you like to know?"

"Why did you become a Bow Street Runner?"

Simeon froze. He had not anticipated that question, nor did he want to answer it truthfully. He opened his mouth to lie, but he saw the innocent, curious expression on her face. He couldn't lie to her, but he refused to tell her the full truth.

"I... uh... became a Bow Street Runner to help people," he replied lamely.

"That's admirable." Her eyes seemed imploring when she asked, "What has been your toughest case?"

"Blazes!" he muttered under his breath. He shifted his gaze over her shoulder as he took a moment to mull over her question. His toughest case had been to find Martha. "I was searching for someone," he hesitated, before adding, "someone that I truly cared about."

Miss Pearson watched him with compassion in her eyes. "Did you find that person?"

"I did," he admitted, lowering his gaze towards the ground.

Reaching out, Miss Pearson touched the sleeve of his jacket. "Were you too late?"

"I was," he sighed. "By the time I found her, her heart belonged to another."

Miss Pearson removed her hand, and he could hear the sympathy in her voice. "How long were you searching for her?"

"Five years."

"Five years?"

He nodded. "A long, painful five years."

"I'm sorry, Mr. Martin."

Turning his gaze towards Gunther's Tea Shop, Simeon didn't want to continue this line of questioning. He didn't want to reveal anything more about himself. His assignment was to protect Miss Pearson, not befriend her.

Miss Pearson spoke up, breaking him out of his grumbling reverie. "I'm attending another ball in a few days, and I'm hoping to dance with a marquess or an earl."

Simeon stiffened at her pretentious attitude. "But not a viscount?"

"No, viscounts are typically stuffy, boring men," she said with a flick of her wrist.

He turned back to face her. "Viscounts?"

"It's true," she admitted without a hint of remorse. "I have not met one viscount that was young and vigorous. Have you?"

"I... uh..." His voice stopped. How did he respond to that? Should he reveal that he was a viscount and contradict her statement, or just pretend her comment didn't affect him?

Simeon was still debating how to answer when the waiter walked up with two bowls of lemon ice. He extended both bowls towards him and stepped back.

Before he could retrieve coins to pay for the lemon ice, Miss Pearson extended her hand and dropped a few coins into the waiter's awaiting hand.

His jaw dropped as he saw the waiter turn on his heel and headed towards another carriage. "What in blazes do you think you are doing?" he exclaimed in annoyance. What was it about this woman that just kept infuriating him, over and over?

"I believe it was quite obvious what I was doing, Mr. Martin," she said, reaching for a bowl of lemon ice. "I was paying the waiter."

He stood there, dumbfounded. A woman didn't pay for items in a man's presence. It just wasn't done. "It was my right, as a gentleman, to pay for your ice."

Taking a bite of her ice, she savored it for a moment before responding, "I didn't mean to offend you, but you work as a Bow Street Runner. I can't imagine your income would allow you to pay for such extravagances as ice from Gunther's."

Tarnation! That was correct, and incredibly thoughtful. Curse her kindness! His salary for being a Bow Street Runner was a paltry sum, and he would barely be able to afford food and lodgings on what he made. However, he couldn't very well tell her that he had acquired a fortune in trade. That would lead to more questions.

"Be that as it may…" he started.

Miss Pearson placed the bowl down on the carriage bench next to her. "Don't be angry with me. I was the one who suggested Gunther's, and I have more than adequate funds to pay for it."

"I assure you that I have more than enough funds at my disposal to pay for Gunther's ice." There. That was simple, and it was the truth.

Her eyes grew wide. "I truly meant no ill will. How was I to know that a Bow Street Runner had sufficient funds to pay for such a scrumptious treat. It's not like you're a viscount…" Her voice trailed off as she looked at him knowingly.

His eyes snapped back up to hers. "When did you find out?"

She smirked as she picked up her bowl of lemon ice. "This morning," she confessed. "Lord Lansdowne told me."

"Ah, I should have known from the comments you were making," he said, taking a bite of his treat. "I suppose you're mad that I lied to you."

Miss Pearson shook her head. "Not at all. I was surprised, but not upset, especially since I understand your secrecy. No one would care about me if they knew I was a lowly country miss, but I have titled suitors because Lord Downshire is my guardian."

"Indeed," he acknowledged. "Women have no interest in me until they find out that I am the Viscount of Wentworth. Then, they start fluttering their eyelashes at me."

She nodded thoughtfully. "I tire of gentlemen attempting to woo me because they strive to gain favor in my guardian's eyes. I want a gentleman to fall in love with me because I'm a constable's daughter, and not in spite of it."

Simeon lowered his bowl of lemon ice. "I hardly believe that's the only reason you have suitors, Miss Pearson."

He didn't dare tell her that she was beautiful, for he had no doubt that Miss Pearson would chastise him for being disingenuous.

"It may not be," she murmured, "but I don't know who is genuine and who is not."

"I agree with your sentiments."

She gave him a weak smile. "I know you do, Mr. Martin."

An unspoken bond passed between them, and Simeon found himself returning her smile. However, the smile was wiped off his face when he heard a man's voice shout from across the square.

"Miss Pearson!"

Simeon turned and saw an impeccably dressed middle-aged man. He was tall, broad-shouldered, and had dark brown hair. However, it was his piercing gaze that caused him to be concerned, because that gaze was focused solely on Miss Pearson.

He heard her whisper, "That is Peter Lockhart."

Emma placed her half-eaten bowl of lemon ice onto the bench of the carriage and forced a smile onto her face as she watched Peter cross the square. She noticed that Mr. Martin had stepped closer to her, trying to shield her from Peter's view.

Peter had an unassuming smile on his face as he approached her. "Emma…" His words trailed off when Mr. Martin took a commanding step forward and placed his hand onto his chest, stopping him.

Mr. Martin leaned closer to Peter and growled, "Stay away from Miss Pearson."

Turning his head to look at her, Peter asked, "Who is this man?"

"That is Mr. Martin," she replied. "Lord Downshire hired him to guard me."

Peter's face grew slightly pale at her admission. "Is someone attempting to hurt you?"

"You should know," Mr. Martin interjected.

His mouth gaped. "How dare you make such an outlandish accusation? I grew up with Emma, and I am still her solicitor." He turned his gaze back towards her. "Tell him, Emma."

Emma's eyes darted between the two men, and she noticed that their interaction was starting to draw unwanted attention. Knowing she must act quickly, she said, "Mr. Martin, please release Mr. Lockhart. I would like a moment alone to speak to him privately."

"No," Mr. Martin replied, but lowered his hand. "Absolutely not."

"Then at least step to the side so I may converse with him." She hesitated before adding, "Please."

With his gaze firmly set on Peter, Mr. Martin stepped to the side, leaned against the side of the carriage and crossed his arms. To some, it might appear that he was relaxing, but Emma could tell he was alert and poised for a fight.

Peter stepped up to the carriage and smiled at her. "Are you well, Emma?"

"Yes, I am. Thank you." She turned her attention towards the pavement.

He placed his hands on the sides of the carriage, eliciting a low growl from Mr. Martin. "You look beautiful."

Ignoring his compliment, she asked, "Why are you here?"

"I work in town now."

Her eyes scanned the bustling crowd of the square and the stream of carriages driving through the center. How had he seen her? Rather than question him about that, she asked, "When did you seek out new employment?"

He shrugged. "It was a recent change, but I needed a break from the drudgery of living in a small village."

"Won't your family miss you?"

"I suppose, but I hope to return soon," his gaze grew intense, "assuming I find what I'm looking for." He was silent for a moment before saying, "My mother misses you."

A smile came to her lips. "Please tell Mrs. Lockhart that I said hello."

"You could tell her yourself," he urged. "Come back to Totternhoe with me… just for a visit."

"No, I am here for the Season."

Peter watched her for a long moment before changing the subject. "Do you remember fishing in the stream on your property?"

Her smile grew. "I do. I also remember when you pushed me in

86

and laughed."

"I recall it quite differently." He chuckled. "You were trying to catch a fish with your hands."

She brought her gloved hand up to cover her laugh. "David was furious and challenged you to a duel."

"A duel with tree branches," he joked. "We had such fun together."

A silence descended over them before he said, "As your solicitor, you should know that I have received multiple offers for your cottage and surrounding land. Are you interested in selling?"

"No, I am not," she stated in a firm tone. "I will never sell my family's home."

"That's ludicrous, Emma," he responded in a disapproving tone. "I've received good offers that I want you to consider…"

She spoke over him. "I'm not interested, Mr. Lockhart. Furthermore, I have granted leave for Lord Downshire to handle all of my financial matters."

"I perceive that you do not lack for income at this time," he remarked, frowning.

Deciding to take hold of this conversation, Emma shifted her gaze from his as she said, "Well, I hope you have safe travels."

Peter had always been intense, but she had never found herself uncomfortable. At least, until now. Reaching out, he placed his hand over hers. "Are you happy?"

"Peter," she admonished in a low tone, pulling back her hand and scooting over on the bench to create more distance between them, "you are being too familiar."

"Are you in earnest?" he huffed.

Smoothing out her gown, she replied, "Very much so."

"Why haven't you returned any of my letters?" he asked, the hurt visible in his tone.

"I was only recently made aware of them, but that would not have changed anything," she responded, picking up her bowl of lemon ice. "It's inappropriate for a woman to write letters to a man that is not her family or her betrothed."

She wanted to laugh at her own words, because Rachel would be so proud that she was standing on ceremony with Peter.

"But, Emma... we were betrothed," he stated cautiously.

She shook her head. "No, we were not, Peter. You kept insisting that we were, but I have only ever considered you a friend."

"How can you say that?" he asked, his voice rising.

Mr. Martin took a step closer to them and shot Peter a warning look.

Emma glanced down at her melted ice and sighed. So much for a delicious treat. She brought her gaze back up to Peter. "I appreciate everything you've done for me and my family but..."

"No buts, Emma," he said, speaking over her. "I promised your father that I would care for you on his deathbed. He gave us permission to wed."

"Regardless, I have no desire to marry you, Peter."

Unexpectedly, Peter's expression turned thunderous. "You pompous chit," he growled. "You are trying to rise above your station."

Her gaze snapped back to his. "How dare you speak to me like that!"

He scoffed. "You're just a country bumpkin. You don't belong in this world," he proclaimed, tossing his hands up in the air. "You belong with me."

"I do not," she asserted. "And I do belong in this world, because Lord Downshire is my guardian..."

Peter cut her off. "I have read about you in the morning papers, you know," he began in a mocking chide. "You fell off a horse in Hyde Park, rolled in a mud puddle, and then you became inebriated at your own ball." He shook his head. "I daresay that Lord Downshire is not the spectacular guardian that you are making him out to be."

Mr. Martin stepped closer and warned, "Keep a civil tongue towards Miss Pearson, or this conversation is over."

Taking a step back, Peter declared, "You don't belong with these people. You would be nothing without me, and now you want to erase me from your life. I don't think so, Emma." His words were cruel and stiff. "We are connected, you and I."

"It is time for you to leave... *now*," Mr. Martin asserted, stepping in front of her. "If I ever see you speaking to Miss Pearson again, I will have you arrested."

Peter gave him an irate look. "You can't make that threat. You're just a lowly guard."

Removing a pistol from the back of his trousers, Mr. Martin brought it down to his right side. "I do have that authority. I am a Bow Street Runner, and I can make your life very uncomfortable, Mr. Lockhart." His gaze turned hard, unyielding. "Stay away from Miss Pearson."

A flicker of fear came to Peter's eyes before he blinked it away. "As you wish," he replied, performing an overexaggerated bow. He turned his gaze back towards Emma and winked.

Emma watched as he spun around and stormed away.

"Are you all right?" Mr. Martin asked, his eyes not wavering from Peter's retreating figure.

She shuddered. "Thank you for stepping in when you did. I had no idea he would create a scene in the middle of the square."

Her eyes scanned the square, and she saw women and men watching her, all with looks of censure on their faces. She let out a loud sigh. "This Season keeps getting worse and worse."

"Would you like to leave? Or we could go on a walk through the maple trees?" Mr. Martin surprised her by asking.

"A walk sounds delightful," she replied, placing her hand on the side of the carriage and allowing Mr. Martin to assist her down. Once her feet were on the ground, Mr. Martin stepped to the side, and she noticed that he begrudgingly offered his arm.

She couldn't help but notice that he did not enjoy being near her. Or was it any woman? She would have to ask him that during their next interview.

"Do not give any heed to what Mr. Lockhart said," he remarked, leading her onto the pavement. "His words were inaccurate and in no way reflect the woman that I have had the privilege of getting to know."

She gave him a grateful smile. "Thank you."

"Do you think your father granted him permission to marry you?" he asked, giving her a side glance.

"Heavens, no," she stated with conviction. "My father did not want me to marry at sixteen, nor would he have ever selected Peter as a suitable candidate."

She could feel the taut muscles under Mr. Martin's jacket, making her feel safe.

"May I ask why?" Mr. Martin pressed. "After all, he employed Lockhart as his solicitor."

Up ahead was a break in the iron fence that led towards an established footpath through the maple trees. She kept her eyes on the trees while she explained, "My father always said that Peter was good at business but lousy at life. Furthermore, he was the only solicitor in our village, and his family's land neighbored ours."

The sound of horse hooves pounding on the cobblestone caused her to turn her eyes towards the direction of the street. A black coach, with two horses and a lone driver, was charging right for them.

Women and men started screaming as they darted out of the pathway of the carriage. Immediately, Mr. Martin grabbed her arm and pulled her behind the safety of the iron fence in such a hurried fashion that they both toppled to the ground with Mr. Martin landing on top of her.

The carriage roared past them and down the street before turning the corner.

"Thank you for saving me," Emma murmured, their faces now only inches apart. She couldn't help but admire his handsome face, and she had an immense desire to reach up and touch the dark stubble along his jawline. Thankfully, she was still in control of her senses.

"You are welcome, Miss Pearson," he breathed as his eyes landed on her lips.

A growing number of people were congregating near the fence, and they started whispering loudly back and forth. A few of the women even had fans in front of their faces. It was evident that they were talking about her... again.

Mr. Martin rose and extended his hand to assist her in rising.

Emma straightened and started dusting off the dirt and leaves from her once-pristine gown. Perhaps Peter was right. It appeared that the universe was telling her that she did not belong in this world.

With her head held high, she allowed Mr. Martin to escort her back to his carriage. She felt confident that this was the worst Season ever!

Chapter Eight

Sitting on a brown leather settee in Lord Downshire's study, Simeon held a snifter in his hand, but it had long been forgotten. He was watching Lord Downshire pacing back and forth, and the anger radiating off him was almost palpable.

Miss Pearson was sitting next to Lady Downshire on a settee, and her eyes were downcast. Whenever she glanced in his direction, he couldn't help but notice the sadness that lingered in her eyes. Her normal air of cheerfulness was replaced with gloom. He had to admit that it tore at his heartstrings.

Why does it matter what her reputation is, he wondered. Miss Pearson is a beautiful young woman, well connected, with a large dowry. He had no doubt a gentleman of the ton would recognize her for the rare beauty that she was, and she would have a blissful life. He frowned at that thought. It was a life he would never know.

The door to the study opened, and to his surprise, Eliza, the Marchioness of Lansdowne, rushed into the room, followed by Lord Lansdowne and Lord Jonathon.

"Good gracious, Luke, what was so urgent that you called for an immediate family meeting?" Eliza asked.

Simeon quickly rose and bowed. "Lady Lansdowne," he greeted her politely.

A gracious smile came to Eliza's lips as she acknowledged him. "Lord Wentworth. What a pleasure to see you again."

"No, it is not," Downshire huffed as he stopped pacing. "Wentworth is fired."

Not offended in the least, he placed his snifter onto a table and remarked, "I shall take my leave, then."

Downshire glared at him. "You will not," he ordered. "You were the one who got Emma into this blasted mess."

"Language, dear brother," Eliza chided, tipping her head towards Emma. "Your ward is present."

"My apologies, Emma," Downshire said, his eyes darting to her, "but she has landed herself into a most bothersome situation."

"Another one?" Benedict joked.

Lord Jonathon walked over to the drink cart and poured himself a drink. "And what situation would that be exactly?"

Downshire lifted his brow at him. "Why don't you explain, Wentworth?"

Simeon glanced over at Emma, and he saw that she had a pained expression on her face. Poor girl, he thought. He turned towards the group and started to explain.

"After we went to Miss Cosette's dress shop…"

Eliza cut him off. "How is dear Cosette doing?"

"Very well," Emma said, speaking up for the first time. "She sent her regards and informed me that she will be joining us for breakfast tomorrow morning."

"That's wonderful news," Eliza replied.

"Eliza…" Downshire grunted.

Pressing her lips together, Eliza turned her expectant gaze back towards Simeon.

"As I was saying," he began, "we ran into Mr. Lockhart…"

Benedict spoke over him. "Did you arrest him?"

"I had no grounds. He didn't do anything criminal in the square near Gunther's," Simeon explained.

"Pity," Jonathon mumbled, sipping his drink.

Downshire tossed up his hands in the air. "Will everyone stop asking questions?" he exclaimed. "Wentworth hasn't even gotten to the worst part, yet."

All eyes turned towards him, and he continued. "After Lockhart departed, a closed carriage came barreling towards us, and I pulled Miss Pearson to safety." He hesitated before admitting, "Unfortunately, I landed on top of her, and there were many witnesses."

The room grew silent, but he could tell by the expressions that something had passed between the members of the Beckett family.

Rachel spoke first. "It matters not. We are here for Emma's Season, and we are not going to retreat. We will face this latest hinderance head on."

"It isn't that simple, my love," Downshire sighed. "Emma's reputation is in tatters, and it may never recover from this."

Walking over to the settee, Eliza sat down next to Emma. "We will sort out this mess. This isn't the first time that a member of the Beckett family has done something scandalous."

"No, but it is the first time that the ton has witnessed it," Jonathon said, lowering himself down into an armchair.

Benedict walked over to the drink cart. While he was pouring himself a drink, he asked, "What is our battle plan?"

"Emma should marry, and quickly," Jonathon remarked.

"No! Absolutely not," Downshire exclaimed. "I will not force Emma into a marriage of convenience."

Jonathon spoke up from his seat. "There are a few outstanding gentlemen that I could recommend…"

"No!" Downshire repeated.

Miss Pearson turned her gaze towards her guardian. "Perhaps it would be best if we left for Scotland. This Season has been a disaster for me, anyway."

"Honestly, Emma, if you run away from this, I doubt your reputation would ever recover," Eliza pressed gently.

"So, I should stay and fight?" Miss Pearson asked in disbelief.

Knowing this was his fault, Simeon found himself doing something he didn't think he was capable of. He approached Miss Pearson and reached for her hand in her lap. He dropped down to one knee and held firm to her hand, despite her trying to pull her hand away.

"Miss Pearson," he paused, correcting himself, "Emma. I don't want to get married any more than you do, but it is inevitable. I can't promise love, but I can promise you the protection of my name." Ignoring the furrowing of her brow, he continued. "We get along nicely, and you would have a title. Since this is a marriage of convenience, I wouldn't expect an heir, or any intimacy of that nature."

Simeon stopped speaking and wasn't prepared for the deafening silence in the room. Furthermore, everyone was frowning deeply at him. He turned his gaze back towards Emma, and she was staring at him with her mouth gaping.

Finally, her mouth closed, and she yanked back her hand. "Was that a proposal?"

"It was," he confirmed.

"My answer is no," she replied immediately.

He gave her a baffled look. "No?" he repeated, surprised by her rejection.

Before she could respond, Jonathon muttered under his breath, "That was awful."

Benedict chuckled. "I stand corrected. Jonathon did not deliver the worst proposal ever."

"Get up," Downshire ordered. "You're making a fool of yourself. My ward will never marry you, Wentworth."

As he rose, he found his anger pricked by Downshire's rejection. "May I ask why?" he growled.

"Emma will not marry a lowly viscount," Downshire said. "Or a Bow Street Runner, for that matter."

"I beg your pardon!" he shouted.

"Stop!" Miss Pearson exclaimed, rising from her seat. "I have my own voice." She turned towards him. "Mr. Martin, your gesture is appreciated, but I do aspire for a love match. Besides, you don't want to marry me, any more than I want to marry you. We are two vastly different people."

"Is it because I am a lowly viscount?" he muttered.

Miss Pearson gave him a look of censure as she approached him. "You forget yourself, milord. I am just a constable's daughter, and I do not aspire for a title. I will marry for love, no matter how lowborn or highborn he may be."

"But an earl or higher is better," Downshire mumbled.

Rachel sighed in exasperation. "Good heavens, my love. Leave it be."

Downshire frowned, but his eyes softened when his eyes landed on his wife. "As you wish." He leaned back against his desk. "We will all need to ponder on how to repair Emma's reputation, but first, let's discuss the other pressing matters."

"Finally," Lord Jonathon said, placing his snifter on the side table and leaning forward. "I don't believe in coincidences, which makes me suspect that high speed carriage was no mere accident."

"I concur," Eliza replied. "Furthermore, Mr. Lockhart was quite brazen to approach Emma in public."

"Perhaps it's time to bring in agents to guard Emma," Benedict suggested.

"Absolutely not!" Simeon proclaimed, tugging down on the lapels of his brown jacket. "I am more than capable of guarding Miss Pearson."

"It would appear not." Jonathon smirked.

His eyes narrowed slightly. "She didn't get hit by the carriage, did she?"

"That's a low standard for protection detail," Benedict remarked.

Downshire drummed his fingers on his desk. "We need to keep Lockhart away from Emma at all costs," he stated. "Wentworth, can you fill in everyone on Emma's conversation with Lockhart?"

"I can," Simeon said. "Lockhart supposedly found employment in town…" He went on for a few moments, reciting the whole conversation. He finished with, "Lockhart is extremely possessive of Emma, and I doubt he is going to let her go without a fight."

Miss Pearson walked over to a tray on the back table and poured herself a cup of tea. She took a sip, then said, "Why would Peter want me to sell my ancestral home, and the lands my family has held for almost a century? He knows how important those are to me."

Downshire reached for a file on his desk and opened it up. He pulled out a piece of paper. "Lockhart did send over an offer for the land, but my solicitor informed me that the amount was grossly less than it is worth. He wants to burn your cottage to the ground and plans to build small cottages to rent out."

"Why not rent out the cottage that's already there?" Eliza asked.

Downshire nodded. "Currently, it is being rented out, and Emma is making a small income every month."

"I propose we go and see if there is anything in the cottage that makes it worth burning to Lockhart," Benedict suggested.

"I'll join you," Jonathon offered eagerly.

Benedict smiled. "Won't Hannah be disappointed that you would be gone for two days?"

"Possibly, but twins are a loud lot," Jonathon remarked. "I fear that I need a break, or I may go mad."

Simeon placed his hands on the back of the camelback settee and leaned in. "I'll go to the Bow Street Magistrate and ask for another agent to trail Lockhart. We need to learn where he's working, where he's living, and all of his habits."

"Lovely. Another Bow Street Runner on the case," Jonathon mumbled under his breath.

"Until then," Downshire placed the file back onto the desk and turned his heated gaze towards Emma, "you are not allowed to leave Caddington Manor... for any reason." He lifted his brow. "Do I make myself clear?"

Emma tipped her head. "As you wish."

Simeon frowned. Now that Miss Pearson wouldn't be attending the Anti-Corn Law rebels meeting, would she confide the location and time of the meeting to him?

Straightening from the desk, Downshire announced, "I have a meeting with my father about our investments. Perhaps he can provide some insights on what we can do to salvage Emma's reputation."

"If he doesn't, then I am sure my mother will," Eliza remarked, rising from her seat.

As everyone started to leave the study, Simeon waited until Emma walked out, then quickly followed behind. He tapped her on the shoulder and indicated she should follow him around the corner.

Once she turned the corner, Simeon asked, "Since you won't be attending the meeting, will you tell me the location?"

"I am attending the meeting," she answered, glancing over her shoulder.

He eyed her with frustration. "Downshire just issued an order for you to stay inside the estate. You would defy his order?"

Stepping closer to him, she lowered her voice. "I already borrowed a dress from my lady's maid, and I plan to skip dinner by feigning exhaustion."

"But Downshire..."

She waved her hand dismissively. "He won't even know. We will attend the meeting and be home before anyone is the wiser."

Simeon didn't know if he should throttle Miss Pearson or admire her spunk. Either way, he would be helping her defy an order from her guardian. He was confident that Downshire would send him to Newgate if something happened to his pretty little charge.

"I could go and tell Downshire what you're planning," he threatened.

"You could," she paused, smiling, "but you won't."

He stepped closer to her. "Why do you say that?"

A mischievous glint came to her eyes. "If you tattle on me, then you won't know the location of the Anti-Corn Law rebels."

"You doubt my ability to find it out on my own?" he questioned.

Emma shrugged smugly at him. "I'll remain here all afternoon while you attempt to learn the location of the meeting." She paused, before adding, "But if you don't discover the location or time of the meeting, then meet me at the back of the gardens at eight tonight."

He pushed his brows together. "You would go to the meeting without me?"

"I have no doubt that you will be meeting me in the garden tonight," she replied, giving him a complacent smile. "Until tonight, Lord Wentworth."

As she turned to leave, he grabbed her arm. "I do not like being called by my title."

"Then what would you prefer me to call you?"

"Simeon," he blurted out before he realized what he was about.

Her brow lifted slightly, but she responded, "Then you must call me Emma."

A smile came to his lips. "I would like that very much, Emma."

"As would I, Simeon."

Simeon released her arm and watched as she hurried away. He took out his pocket watch and looked at the time. He only had four hours to discover what he had been trying to uncover for weeks.

He'd better get to work.

Dressed in a drab, borrowed gown, Emma hurried across the expansive garden of Caddington Manor. It had just started to grow dark as she stepped into the cover of the trees along the back wall.

She sighed in disappointment when she saw that Simeon wasn't there. She'd been hoping that he wouldn't have been able to discover the information on his own. Glancing at the rising moon, she decided that she would only wait for a few moments before heading to the meeting herself.

Tucked into the pocket of her gown was a pound note and some coins. That was the last of the pin money she'd been saving. Luke had been most generous with her allowance, but she would often give it away to people who needed it more than she.

The sound of crunching leaves caused her head to snap towards the direction of the noise. She slid her hand into the pocket of her gown and gripped her overcoat pistol. If the noise wasn't caused by Simeon, then she was in a lot of trouble.

A shadow emerged from the trees, its footsteps crackling the fallen twigs.

Her breath caught as the shadow took another step closer, directly into a gap between the trees, revealing a man.

"Emma," the man whispered as he came closer.

She breathed a relieved sigh when she heard Simeon's voice. "You must have missed me," she joked, removing her hand from her pocket.

"I did no such thing," he declared in a haughty fashion. "I was unable to ascertain the location of the meeting."

Emma shrugged one shoulder. "Or perhaps you missed my witty conversational skills?"

"You surely jest," he grumbled.

She grinned. "And you, milord, are way too reserved."

"I am not reserved," he growled.

Walking over to the black iron fence, Emma quickly jumped over and watched for Simeon to follow suit. They hurried towards the pavement and the bustling street. Raising her hand, she tried to hail a hackney, but none would give her any heed.

Simeon came to stand next to her. "No respectable hackney will carry a single woman," he informed her. "Allow me." He lifted his hand, and a black hackney came to a stop in front of him.

"Where to, sir?" the fair-skinned driver said.

"To The Tubby Wench," he replied.

"No, sir, I don't get that close to the rookeries," the driver declared. "I can drop you off at Busby Street."

"That will do," Simeon answered, turning to assist her into the hackney. Before he climbed in next to her, his eyes scanned the street until he gave a curt nod.

Once he sat next to her, Emma murmured, "Why is another Bow Street Runner following us?"

He looked at her in surprise. "How did you know that?"

"I'm basically a spy," she joked. "I can scale walls, I'm good at defending myself, and I am quite intuitive."

"What do you know about spies?" he asked cautiously.

She put her hand next to her mouth as she shared, "I am wise enough to know that Jonathon, Benedict, and Adrien are agents of the Crown."

"Do you now?"

"I do." She lowered her hand. "Anyway, do you think it is wise to include another Bow Street Runner?"

He nodded. "Pembrooke is one of the best. I sent him a missive, asking him to trail us to the meeting. I haven't yet spoken to him about Peter Lockhart, but I intend to shortly." He gave her a pointed look. "You can trust Pembrooke."

"I suppose I'll give Pembrooke a chance."

Turning her head towards the street, Emma watched as the vendors closed their stands, and hungry children eyed the remaining food with longing.

"That's awful," she murmured to herself.

"What's awful?"

Shifting on the bench towards him, she answered, "All the children that are starving and no one is helping them."

"It's the parents' job to feed their children."

Emma furrowed her brows. "And if the parents don't have money to pay for the high price of bread?"

"I can't answer that," he replied with a slight wince.

Her eyes shifted back towards the street, and she watched

women carrying baskets as they scurried along. She bit her lower lip to keep from crying. If Luke and Rachel hadn't rescued her when they did, this could have been her life. Who knows where she would have ended up?

Simeon's voice broke through her musings. "What's the matter?"

"Nothing," she replied. "Just anxious, I suppose."

Thankfully, Simeon left it at that, since the hackney jerked to a stop. They quickly walked the distance towards The Tubby Wench pub. Once they stepped inside, Emma waded through the large group of patrons as she headed towards the stairs. A lone door was at the top of the stairs, and she knocked loudly.

The door opened, and a short man with long hair stared back at her. "How can I help you?"

"I'm a friend of Jerome's," she revealed, raising her voice so she could be heard over the crowd downstairs.

He nodded, opened the door wide and waved them through.

Inside the small, crowded hall, a rectangular table sat in the middle, and a large group of people congregated on both sides. The table held multiple sheets of paper. Men and women approached and signed their names.

Stepping closer, Emma asked a petite, blonde-haired young woman who was standing near her, "What is everyone signing?"

"We're signing a petition for Parliament to overturn the Corn Laws," she explained. "The more signatures we have, the more likely we can affect change."

"Indeed," Emma responded.

The woman looked at her, glancing down at her brown gown. "You're new here. My name's Janet."

"I'm Emma." She tilted her head towards her guard. "That's Simeon. He does speak, but he's more of an observer."

In response, Simeon grunted with his familiar air of annoyance, confirming her statement.

"Do you know how to read and write, Emma?" Janet asked, reaching for a quill from the table.

"I do," she acknowledged as she accepted the quill.

"Take a moment to read our petition and sign under the other signatures," Janet explained.

Stepping up to the table, Emma and Simeon both read the petition. It was straight-forward. The petition was urging Parliament to redact the Corn Laws, citing how people were starving due to the rising food prices and chronic unemployment. Furthermore, it pressed the point of writers, such as William Cobbett, who were denouncing the inequality of the electoral system, as evidenced by rotten boroughs.

"What are rotten boroughs?" she whispered to Simeon.

Simeon leaned close to her, and she smelt his scent of musk and a hint of orange. He spoke next to her ear. "A rotten borough is an area that has found a way to unjustly gain unrepresentative influence in the House of Commons. It has a very small electorate, but it has the same influence of a large town."

The warmth of his breath on her ear was immensely distracting, but she was able to concentrate enough to acknowledge his words. Not daring to move her face, she murmured, "How awful."

Thankfully, Simeon stepped back, and she leaned over to sign her name. She completely agreed with this petition. She extended the quill to Simeon and noticed that he placed the quill down on the table without signing his name.

"May I have your attention," a man's voice shouted from the front of the room.

Turning her gaze, she saw Jerome standing next to a taller man, who was lean and dark, with sideburns growing down to almost his jawline. "Mr. Hatcher, our esteemed orator, wants to say a few words," Jerome stated.

The man stepped forward. "Thank you for coming tonight and signing the petition. I hope that everyone plans to attend the *peaceful* demonstration in Templeton Square tomorrow. I've met with other districts, and they will be marching through the streets of London, as well. We hope our demonstration will garner more support for the cause, and we can gain more signatures for our petition."

A collective cheer went up around the room. Mr. Hatcher put his hands out to silence them. "Do not bring weapons of any kind. We do not want to give the magistrates or constables any just cause to resort to violence." His intense gaze traveled over the crowd. "Our families are starving because of the wealthy landowners passing these

Corn Laws. The laws were passed even with riots outside of the House of Lords. Violence is never the answer, but we need to do something. We must act."

As Mr. Hatcher started pacing in the front of the room, he urged, "If you have any coins to spare to help the cause, please consider donating them. Anything that we don't use will go to buy bread for our next meeting. With any hope, that bread will feed the families that are struggling to put food on the table."

Emma glanced over to a table near the front and saw a large pile of loaves of bread. She noticed that a few people approached it, and each ripped off a section of bread. The way they savored the bread in their mouths caused her heart to mourn. How she took for granted the bread on her tray every morning.

Jerome made his way over to her with Mr. Hatcher by his side. Stopping in front of them, he made the introductions. "Miss Emma, may I introduce you to Mr. Graham Hatcher."

She tipped her head graciously. "Mr. Hatcher. You are truly a gifted orator."

Mr. Hatcher smiled kindly at her. "Thank you, my dear. I heard that you wished to speak to me about the cause."

"It's true," she said, reaching into her pocket and retrieving the pound note.

Accepting the note, Mr. Hatcher bowed. "Thank you, Miss Emma. Your generosity will help feed a large group of people."

"I read the petition and heard you speak about the peaceful demonstration in Templeton Square, but is there anything else I should know about the Anti-Corn Law rebels?"

"May I ask why?" Mr. Hatcher asked, giving Simeon a baffled look.

Simeon stepped forward and answered for her. "I plan to write an article for the morning newspaper about the Anti-Corn Law rebels, but sometimes my cousin," he paused, glancing disapprovingly at her, "is overzealous. I assure you that it will be most favorable."

"Splendid news," Mr. Hatcher replied. "I must admit that at first I thought Miss Emma was writing the article." He let out a dry chuckle. "Which, of course, is ludicrous."

"A woman writing newspaper articles. Can you even imagine?"

Simeon let out a loud laugh.

Emma pursed her lips as she watched the two men converse about the Anti-Corn Law rebels, and Mr. Hatcher barely acknowledged her while explaining their mission.

Once Mr. Hatcher stepped away, Emma crossed her arms over her chest and muttered, "That was rather insulting."

Simeon nudged her shoulder and kept his voice low. "Dear cousin," he teased, "you can't go around telling people you are a writer for the newspaper. If you say that, it confirms that you are of higher social standing than them because you can afford the luxury of a morning paper, not to mention the leisure and education to write. Or they'll consider you mad because women aren't hired by the newspaper agencies. Either way, neither are good for our assignment."

Reluctantly, Emma knew that he had a point. She lowered her arms and asked, "Cousins?"

"We arrived together so, it's logical that we would be related."

"Good point," she said as someone brushed past her. "Should we tarry any longer?"

Simeon's alert eyes scanned over the room. "I think we got all that we came for."

"I can't wait to attend the demonstration tomorrow," she said, heading towards the door.

Increasing his stride, Simeon arrived at the door first and opened it up for her. In a hushed voice, he asked, "How do you propose leaving Caddington Manor during the middle of the day without detection?"

A wry look of mischief crossed her face. "I am practically a spy, remember?"

Letting out a frustrated sigh, Simeon drawled, "No, you are not. I'm concerned that you truly believe you are."

Laughing, she replied, "Call on me tomorrow at ten, and we will go on a carriage ride."

"A carriage ride?" he asked, giving her a puzzled look. "That is your genius plan?"

Accepting Simeon's proffered arm as they headed down the pavement, Emma remarked, "I haven't worked out all the details yet, but I'll find a way to go to that demonstration."

"Perhaps it's best if you sit this one out," he asserted. "After all, a rally is no place for a lady."

Emma admired the gas lights along the pavement before saying, "Mr. Hatcher says it is a peaceful demonstration, and I have no doubt that other women will be attending. Women desire change too, not just men."

"Fine, but after tomorrow, no more sneaking out or attending demonstrations," Simeon grunted. "Just write your blasted article and be done with it."

She smiled at his brash tone. "Thank you, Simeon."

"For what?" he asked, stopping on the pavement.

"For being my guard," she hesitated, "and my friend."

"I hate to disappoint you, but we are not friends." Simeon resumed leading her along the pavement. "My job is to guard you, not befriend you."

What a stubborn, vexing man, she thought. Keeping pace with his increasing stride, she attempted again. "Fine. Thank you for accompanying me to the meeting this evening."

"You are welcome," he said, barely sparing her a glance.

Taking a moment to admire his handsome face, she boldly asked, "Why am I not your friend?"

"What?"

"I said 'why am I not your friend'?" She stopped on the pavement and removed her arm from his. "I consider you a friend."

With a clenched jaw, Simeon turned to face her. "Friends are liabilities."

"I disagree. Friends can be your greatest assets."

"They are," he hesitated, shifting his gaze over her shoulder, "until they die."

She stepped closer to him. "Who did you lose, Simeon?"

An enraged look came over his features. "No! You have no right to ask me those questions!" he exclaimed, earning a few scowls from people passing by. "My life is my own. I have a right to maintain secrets!"

Taking a step back, Emma stared at him with wide eyes. "I am sorry... I... uh..."

"You are an infuriating chit," he declared. "I would never have a friend like you."

Tears pooled in her eyes, and her lower lip started to tremble as she murmured, "I'm sorry you feel that way."

"No more words," Simeon stated in a firm tone as he held up his hand to secure a hackney.

Once she was in the hackney, Emma kept her back rigid and pretended that his sharp words hadn't cut her deeply. He was right, of course. She had no right to ask him personal questions, but she truly had considered him a friend.

Chapter Nine

Reaching his hand out the window of the hackney, Simeon opened the door and waited until it came to a complete stop before he stepped down onto the pavement. He extended the driver a few coins and hurried up the steps of his brick townhome in Mayfair.

He opened the door and slammed it shut. "Confounded, insufferable woman," he muttered under his breath as he walked across the entrance hall towards his study in the rear of his home. Why was Emma plaguing his thoughts?

After he had secured a hackney, they traveled in silence to Caddington Manor, which is what he had wanted... silence. But then the stubborn girl refused his assistance as she exited the hackney and wouldn't even glance in his direction when she climbed over the fence. He knew he'd hurt her with his sharp words earlier, but why did she insist on being his friend? She had no right! Why could she not leave it be?

His tall, stoic butler stepped out from the library. "Mr. Pembrooke is in your study, milord," Mr. Baxter informed him.

Acknowledging his butler's words with a grunt, Simeon didn't slow his stride until he arrived at his study and had closed the door behind him. His fellow Bow Street Runner, Officer Edwin Pembrooke, sat on an armchair with a snifter in his hand.

Pembrooke took a long sip of his drink. "It took you long enough to drop off the girl."

Ignoring his friend, Simeon walked across the room to the drink cart and poured himself a brandy.

"I must admit that she is a pretty little thing."

Simeon took a long sip, not feeling a need to contradict

Pembrooke's words.

"Good heavens, Officer Martin," Pembrooke admonished, "sometimes I feel like I would have a more informative conversation with a settee than you."

Turning to face him, Simeon leaned back against the wall. "Sorry. I have some things on my mind."

"It wouldn't be a beautiful, brown-haired, young woman, by any chance would it?"

He frowned. "No… yes, actually. But only because she is maddening."

"Aren't most women?"

Not amused by his friend's teasing, Simeon pressed, "Miss Pearson is the most vexing woman I know. She climbs walls, defends herself from ruffians, and chats incessantly."

Pembrooke chuckled. "I agree that she is unconventional, but I must admit I am confused about why you find her so vexing."

Bringing the snifter up to his lips, he asked, "Why are you here anyway?"

"Justice Ford wants an update on the Anti-Corn Law rebels," Pembrooke explained. "He wants to know if he needs to issue any warrants ahead of the demonstration tomorrow."

Simeon swirled the drink in his hand. "No. I was at the meeting, and Mr. Hatcher intends for the demonstration to be peaceful."

"You believe that?" Pembrooke asked, lowering his drink to his lap.

"I do. These demonstrators are angry about the Corn Laws, but I don't believe they'll resort to violence."

Pembrooke studied him for a moment. "Sheriff Blundell is pressuring Justice Ford to issue a warrant for the orator. He wants this uprising squashed."

"It's hardly an uprising," he declared, placing his empty snifter down on the drink cart.

"There is talk that upwards of four thousand people will march to Templeton Square."

Crossing his arms over his chest, Simeon sighed. "I understand, but I do not perceive this group to be a threat to the Crown… yet."

"I believe you," Pembrooke said, sitting back in his seat. "Now about your other assignment."

"Go to the devil," he growled.

"I would prefer not to." Pembrooke smirked. "I understand you were spotted laying on top of Miss Pearson near Gunther's yesterday."

He let out an exasperated huff. "A carriage was barreling towards us, and I shoved her out of the way. Unfortunately, I tripped on her skirts, and I landed on top of her."

"I've noticed that you haven't posted the banns yet."

"Not that it's any of your business, but Miss Pearson rejected my proposal," he grumbled.

Pembrooke let out a loud, drawn out laugh. "I knew I liked this girl. She's choosing a life of spinsterhood over marrying you."

"She's doing no such thing," he contended. "Miss Pearson is well connected, and I have no doubt that the Beckett family can save her reputation."

"That will be no small feat. She has had a rather unfortunate series of accidents befall her," Pembrooke said, suddenly serious.

Simeon pushed off from the wall. "They were no accidents. Mr. Peter Lockhart is behind this."

"Who?"

He came to sit down across from Pembrooke. "Lockhart is mad, and he truly believes that Miss Pearson belongs to him. I have a few friends looking into this..."

"What friends?" Pembrooke asked. "Because I happen to know for a fact that you don't have any friends."

"We are quasi-friends."

Pembrooke gave him a curious look. "Are these other friends Bow Street Runners?"

"No. Will you drop it?" he asked firmly.

Pembrooke put his hands up in front of him.

"We need to get into our criminal system and find out all that we can about this Lockhart."

"What do you hope to find?"

Simeon shrugged. "I don't know."

"I will look into it."

"Thank you."

Bringing his hand up to his chin, Pembrooke rubbed it thoughtfully. "You seem out of sorts, Martin." He paused, before adding, "At least, more than usual."

"I am fine, Pembrooke," he remarked dryly.

"Ford wants us to officially work the Anti-Corn Law rebels assignment together," Pembrooke informed him, his words starting off slow.

He clenched his jaw. "I work alone. I do not have a partner anymore."

Sighing, Pembrooke lowered his hand. "Jared died over a year ago at the hands of The Cursed Lot gang. No one blames you for his death."

"I blame myself!" he shouted. "He was my partner, and my friend."

"He chose to work undercover as a customs official in Gravesend. He knew the risk! Blazes! We all know the risks associated with this job," Pembrooke asserted.

Simeon refused to yield. His last partner had been found dead, floating face up in the River Thames. He wouldn't do that to anyone again. "I work alone, and that's final."

"You caught the men responsible for Jared's death," Pembrooke pressed. "They hung for their crimes."

He scoffed. "Does their death suddenly bring Jared back?"

Pembrooke gave him a look filled with pity. "I will relay the message to Ford, but he won't be pleased."

"Regardless, I sent you a missive about the meeting planned tonight," he attempted.

"You wanted me there in case things went awry, not to be your partner."

"It's true," he commented. "I can ensure my own protection, but I wanted an additional set of eyes to help keep Miss Pearson safe."

Pembrooke grinned. "You two appear close."

"We are not. I am assigned to guard her, nothing more."

His smile grew. "I saw you smiling when you were talking to her."

"I don't smile."

"True, your normal resting face is between a grimace and a

scowl, but when you are with Miss Pearson, you occasionally smile."

"Please leave," Simeon said, rising from his seat. "I have had my fill of you for the moment."

Pembrooke rose and jested, "These moments are special to me, as well."

"You will look into Lockhart?"

"I will, and I will continue to trail you until you acknowledge that I am your partner."

"It won't happen."

Tugging down on his paisley waistcoat, Pembrooke didn't seem perturbed by his rejection. "I will wear you down, just like a good pair of Hessian boots. We will be partners soon enough."

Simeon watched as Pembrooke walked out of his study. He was the closest thing he had to a friend. They had worked a few cases together when he was a new recruit, but then he had been partnered with Jared.

His partner's death had been his fault. He knew it. It didn't matter what everyone else thought. Jared had been working undercover as a customs official and had left him a note saying that he was on to something big. However, he had been tracking a shipment of contraband and was staking out The Cloven Hoof public house. The next morning, Jared was found dead.

Simeon winced as he poured himself a drink. He had failed his friend. He should have been there to help him. He blinked back his tears of remorse. He was bloody awful at keeping people safe. He deserved to be alone. He wanted to be alone!

Emma's crestfallen expression came to his mind as he slammed his glass onto the cart, spilling his drink on his hand. His sharp words had hurt her, and he'd seen the pain in her eyes. He could have apologized, but he was angry. She had no right to ask those questions. But, on the other hand, he had no right to yell at her like that, either. He was raised better than to yell at a woman in such an appalling fashion.

Simeon knew he needed to apologize, despite every fiber of his being telling him not to. He would do it tomorrow, and he hoped the apology would be better than his marriage proposal had been.

Emma sat at her dressing room table as Peggy styled her hair into a chignon. Simeon's words echoed through her mind. "*I would never have a friend like you.*" What a terrible thing to say to someone. She had a lively personality, and she had no problem making friends... until now. Which was fine with her. If Simeon didn't want to be her friend, then she didn't need him as her friend either. Her lips twitched in amusement. She sounded as if she was back at the early days of her boarding school.

"Are you all right, miss?" her lady's maid asked, breaking through her thoughts.

Emma smiled at Peggy's reflection in the mirror. "Just woolgathering, I suppose."

"You aint' dreaming about that handsome Bow Street Runner, are you?" she teased, placing the final pin in her hair.

"Heavens, no," she declared as she turned in her seat. "Mr. Martin is rude and big-headed."

"I see," Peggy replied, but clearly she did not, judging by the smile on her face.

Abruptly rising from the chair, Emma wanted to be finished with this futile conversation. She smoothed out her primrose gown with its rounded neckline.

"I'd better hurry if I want to arrive on time to break my fast," she said.

"Yes, miss," her lady's maid replied with mirth in her voice.

As she headed down the hall towards the family's dining room on the first level, Emma recognized that she would not be able to attend the rally today in Templeton Square without Simeon's help. She didn't dare go by herself, and Luke would never grant her permission, even if she took along one hundred footmen. She sighed. Perhaps she should just write an article about the meeting that she attended and hope that it would be good enough to be accepted by The Morning Post.

Stepping into the dining room, Emma greeted Luke and Rachel with a smile. "Good morning."

Luke was sitting at the head of the table, and he lowered the paper when she walked in. "Good morning, Emma. Did you sleep well?"

"I did, thank you."

Sitting on Luke's right, Rachel smiled up at her. "How was visiting Eliza this morning?"

Luke groaned. "Did I not confine you to the estate?

"My apologies. Since Eliza's townhouse is only a few blocks away, I assumed it was safe to visit," she replied honestly. "As a precaution, I took four footmen along with me."

"I suppose you can continue your morning visits to Eliza's," Luke said. "But next time, take six footmen along with you."

"Understood." Accepting a plate from a footman, Emma started filling it with food. "Cosette was there this morning. She sends her regards."

"I will have to join you tomorrow," Rachel said.

"You should," she replied. "Cosette showed me how to sweep an attacker's foot, causing them to fall, and how to escape a choke hold."

Luke let out a groan. "What happened to needlework and reading Latin?" he asked, placing the folded paper on the table. "It's much more feminine and civilized."

Coming to sit down next to Rachel, Emma waited as a footman pulled out her chair for her. "Do not fret. I do those, as well," she assured him.

The butler walked into the room with a tray filled with missives and extended them towards Rachel. "These came in the mail this morning, milady."

Accepting the pile, Rachel placed them on the table next to her and reached for her letter opener. She opened the first missive and pursed her lips before she placed it down next to her.

"What is it?" Emma asked, glancing curiously at the discarded missive.

Rachel gave her a forced smile. "Nothing to concern yourself about," she replied in a strained voice.

"You are a horrible liar," Emma said. "May I see the note?"

Picking it up, Rachel shared, "Your invitation to Lord Baskett's ball this evening has been rescinded."

"What?" Emma asked, her mouth parting in shock. "Were you uninvited as well?"

Rachel shook her head. "No."

"Oh," she managed to say before she diverted her eyes to her lap and started blinking back her tears. Her actions had not only embarrassed the Beckett family, but now members of the ton were distancing themselves from her.

"Rachel," Luke growled, reaching over and grabbing the note, "send a note that none of the Beckett family will be attending this evening." He crumpled it up and tossed it over his shoulder. "Furthermore, let it be known that if anyone shuns Emma, then they will receive the cut direct from us."

Emma's eyes snapped back to her guardian. "No, I won't let you do that. This is my fault, and mine alone."

Luke placed his forearm on the table and leaned in. "I am the Marquess of Lansdowne, and one day, I will be the Duke of Remington. No one will dare defy me, Emma. We will find a way to restore your reputation, I promise."

"You can't give the whole ton the cut direct," she insisted.

Rachel reached out and placed a hand over hers. "You'll find that there are many families that are loyal to the Beckett family. Don't worry, Emma."

"How can I not?" she questioned.

"Lockhart wants you to fail," Luke pressed. "He wants you to be an outcast of Society, to prove that he was right. But he's wrong, and he always will be. You belong in this world, Emma."

"Do I?" she asked, her voice rising. "I'm just your ward. I was not raised in this world."

Rachel patted her hand. "You are part of our family; whether you were born into it or not, it doesn't matter."

A knock came at the door and the butler announced, "Lord Wentworth is here to call on Miss Pearson." He turned his gaze towards her. "Are you available to receive him?"

Rachel and Luke's eyes both landed on her, and Luke spoke first. "Wentworth is calling on you now?" His words were slow and deliberate.

Ignoring their curious expressions, she directed her comments to Munro. "Please inform Lord Wentworth that I am not receiving any callers at the moment."

He nodded and excused himself from the room.

Rachel's brow lifted. "You are refusing to see him?"

"I am," she answered, picking up her fork. "He said some rather cruel things last time I saw him."

"Yesterday? Did you speak to him after that awful proposal?" Rachel pressed.

Just before she took a bite of food, she muttered, "I did. Just for a moment in the hall." She didn't dare confess that she had seen Simeon the night before when she had snuck out of Caddington Manor and attended a meeting.

"Would you like me to secure you another guard, then?" Luke asked.

She shook her head. "Lord Wentworth may be cruel and unfeeling, but he is a proficient guard. I feel safe with him. However, I don't want to spend any additional time with him."

A knock came at the door before Munro walked back into the room. "Lord Wentworth refuses to leave. He says he needs to speak to Miss Pearson about an urgent matter."

She was about to turn him away again when Luke spoke up. "This is ridiculous. Send him in," he ordered with a wave of his hand.

"Yes, milord," the butler said, departing from the room.

Luke furrowed his brow as he asked, "Is Wentworth attempting to court you?"

She shook her head adamantly, causing the curls framing her face to swish back and forth. "Heavens, no. He is my guard. There's nothing more between us."

"Good," Luke admonished. "I would prefer you to marry someone greater than a viscount."

Emma frowned. "You know I don't care about titles."

"As long as you don't marry Wentworth, I will be hap…" His words trailed off as Simeon walked into the room holding a bouquet of flowers.

She turned to face Simeon, and immediately noticed the quality of his fine garments. He was wearing a blue jacket, grey trousers, and a white waistcoat. His brown hair was brushed forward, and it almost appeared as if he had a smile on his face... almost. If she had to guess, she would assume he dressed up specifically to call on her.

Simeon stopped short of the door and bowed. "Miss Pearson, thank you for agreeing to see me."

"I didn't," she informed him. "Luke did."

"I see," Simeon said before he acknowledged Luke and Rachel with a tip of his head. He brought his gaze back to hers. "May I have a moment of your time?"

Emma pressed her lips together. Part of her wanted to know why he was here, but she wasn't in the mood to chat with him. Not yet, anyway.

"I am busy at the moment, Lord Wentworth," she started, ignoring Rachel's knowing gaze, "perhaps another time."

Simeon moved quickly to stand next to her and extended her the flowers. "Just hear me out, please."

Emma kept her face expressionless as she tilted her head to look at him but didn't move to accept the flowers.

"I said some rather hurtful things to you, and I wanted to offer my deepest apologies," he said. "I had no right to speak to you that way."

Hearing his apology caused some of her anger to dissipate. "You were right, though. We aren't friends."

Grabbing the chair next to her, Simeon pulled it out and sat down. "I assure you that you don't want to be friends with me. I have had a string of bad luck when it comes to friends."

She smiled. "It couldn't have been worse than my series of unfortunate incidents."

"My last friend, who was also, coincidentally, my partner, was murdered while on assignment with me," he shared solemnly.

"Oh, I am so sorry," she murmured.

Emma heard Luke whisper to Rachel, "Wentworth won that argument."

With a grateful look, Simeon once again extended her the flowers. "I was hoping we could go on that carriage ride we previously talked about."

"Absolutely not!" Luke declared. "Emma is not allowed to leave this house for any reason."

Rachel turned towards her husband. "Darling, I think it would be permissible for them to travel to Hyde Park, which is only a short distance away by carriage."

"Fine. But only to Hyde Park and back," Luke declared.

Simeon leaned closer to her. "If you say yes, I would be willing to be interviewed again."

"How could I refuse, then?" she said, accepting the flowers.

"Good. Then I shall pick you up within the hour."

They sat there, looking at each other, saying nothing. But Emma felt something shift between them.

"Pardon me, but I am late for a meeting." Luke rose and kissed Rachel on the cheek. "You will stay and chaperone."

"It would be my pleasure," Rachel answered with a smile.

The moment that Luke walked out of the door, Rachel turned back towards them with a questioning brow. "What's going on between you two?"

"Nothing," Emma replied innocently.

Rachel let out a huff. "Do not patronize me, Emma. I know you snuck out of your room last night. Did you meet up with Wentworth?"

With a side glance at Simeon, Emma lowered her voice and shared, "We did meet up, but only so he could guard me while I went to a meeting for the Anti-Corn Law rebels."

"For what purpose?" Rachel asked.

She clasped her hands in her lap. "For research on my next article for The Morning Post."

"And the carriage ride today?" Rachel prodded.

Simeon cleared his throat. "I promised to escort Miss Pearson to a peaceful demonstration in Templeton Square."

Rachel was silent for a long moment, and Emma could see the indecision cross her features. "I would be a hypocrite if I attempted to stop you, but you must use caution. There are dangerous men afoot." She glanced over her shoulder. "I can't keep this secret for long from Luke. Go to the rally, return home unharmed, and write your article. Then, no more of this sneaking out. Do we understand each other?"

Emma let out a sigh of relief. "Thank you, Rachel."

Turning her piercing gaze towards Simeon, Rachel said, "You will keep my Emma safe. Understood?"

"Yes, Lady Downshire," Simeon replied in a firm tone.

Rachel's eyes roamed her gown. "You can't wear that to Templeton Square. You'll stand out."

"I'm borrowing Peggy's drab gown again," she informed her.

Giving her an exasperated look, Rachel stated, "No more climbing down walls. Change your clothes and walk out the main door. I will ensure that Luke is occupied."

"Thank you," Emma said.

"Your brother would not have been amused by your antics. That's for sure," Rachel remarked with a shake of her head.

"Oh no, he would have locked me up in my room if he even got wind of me sneaking out of my bedchamber," she responded.

Rachel gave her a look of wry disapproval. "That thought may have crossed my mind, as well."

"I'll be safe," she rushed to assure her. "What harm could possibly come to me at a peaceful demonstration?"

Simeon let out a chuckle. "Where there's a will, there's a way."

Emma scowled at him. She wasn't worried. The Anti-Corn Law rebels weren't ruffians. They were planning a peaceful demonstration. Besides, she had full confidence that no harm would befall her with Simeon by her side.

Chapter Ten

Simeon was finding Emma to be a vastly entertaining partner. Her eyes would light up with excitement every time they turned the street corner. She found the storefronts fascinating, the street urchins entertaining, and she even stopped to buy wafers from a street vendor. How was it possible that she found such mundane things amusing? Whereas he found the storefronts to be tedious, the street urchins to be horridly filthy, and the street vendors to be pesky.

They had started their march with their chapter of the Anti-Corn Law rebels from The Tubby Wench, and they were about to reach Templeton Square. Along the route, hundreds of people joined their protest, eager to show their support.

With her arm tucked safely into the crook of his arm, Emma was chatting with Miss Janet as they walked side by side. He didn't even attempt to follow the conversation, because he was fairly confident that they were speaking about womanly topics. Whatever those may be. Besides, Simeon was too busy scanning Templeton Square and the growing crowd.

The square was filled to capacity, and everyone was facing a large, wooden stage that had been constructed in the middle. Men and women stood side by side, and some were even carrying signs about repealing the Corn Laws.

As their chapter of the Anti-Corn Law rebels started making their way closer to the stage, Simeon stopped on the outskirts. "We stay here."

Emma looked at him with curiosity. "Why are we so far away?"

"It's safer this way. We'll be less likely to be trampled," he informed her. "Don't fret. I have no doubt that we'll be able to hear the orator from here."

Rather than argue with him, Emma just nodded and turned her gaze back towards the stage.

Not quite ready to look away, Simeon's eyes roamed the curls that framed her face perfectly to the radiant glow on her face. He noticed how long her black lashes were, and her lips were parted in exuberance as she fixed her eyes on the square. Tarnation! He shifted his gaze away from Emma. What was he thinking, ogling her? She was his responsibility, nothing more.

A smile was still on her lips as she turned to face him. "When do you think Mr. Hatcher will arrive?"

He shrugged one shoulder. "I suppose anytime."

Her eyes landed on his lips, and he felt rooted to his spot. Could she feel his growing urge to kiss her, to feel her lips on his own?

"I can't hear you!" she shouted as the crowd grew more boisterous.

Did he say something? Oh, yes. He leaned closer to her and raised his voice. "I suppose Hatcher could come at any time."

A slight blush came to her cheeks. It was barely noticeable, but he caught it nonetheless.

"Is this peaceful demonstration everything that you thought it would be?" he teased, enjoying their nearness.

Her eyes left his and scanned over the people, and she nodded. "Yes. If Luke and Rachel hadn't rescued me from my situation, I could have easily been in many of these people's situations."

"Is that so?"

She nodded. "I was fortunate enough to inherit my father's shop in the village, our cottage, and property surrounding our home. However, working for an income is not beneath me."

Simeon gave her a quizzical look. "You would have had to work?"

"Frankly, I don't know," she replied. "Lockhart insisted we wed so he could take care of me. He said that my income was too meager for me to support myself."

He pressed his lips together to prevent a vulgar word from slipping out in the presence of Emma. He had no doubt that Lockhart was trying to force her to marry him. But why? Was it just because she was beautiful, or did she have something that he wanted?

"And what of now?" he asked.

"Pardon?"

Simeon leaned closer to her ear. "Have you not asked Downshire to explain your inheritance to you?"

She shook her head. "I have not. His solicitors are handling my financial matters, and I trust Luke completely."

"As well as you should, but you should have some concept of your inheritance."

Tilting her head towards him, their eyes locked. "From the moment Luke and Rachel brought me back to their home, I've never wanted for anything. Love, money, attention…" Her voice drifted off. "It's been like a dream for someone like me."

"Someone like you?"

Emma gave him a tentative smile. "I'm a nobody, a country bumpkin. Yet, because of my brother's sacrifice, I've been given everything." She shifted her gaze away from him. "I've done nothing to deserve it."

With compassion swelling in his breast, he reached out and placed his finger under her chin, turning her to face him. "I want you to listen to me very carefully, Emma," he started. "You are not a nobody. You are a beautiful young woman," he paused, "and are admirably unique."

A sad smile came to her lips. "You may not have noticed, but everyone in the Beckett family is extraordinary, and I don't fit in with them."

"That's rubbish," he declared, pleased when a soft laugh escaped Emma's mouth. "You already have one article published in The Morning Post. Has anyone else in the Beckett family accomplished that feat?"

"No, but Rachel wrote a book, and Eliza is…"

He released her chin but remained close. "Don't compare yourself to anyone else. Go at your own pace and believe in yourself. Because I do," he hesitated, "and I don't normally believe in people anymore."

Emma's face softened. "Thank you, Simeon. That means a lot."

He gave her a curt nod and straightened to his full height. Why did he feel the need to praise the girl? He already knew the answer. He spoke from his heart. Something that he used to do a lot more when he was younger... with Martha.

Simeon knew he had become jaded over these past few years, but more so when Martha married another. Could he even remember who he used to be?

A loud, collective cheer came from around the men and women assembled together in Templeton Square. Glancing towards the stage, he saw Mr. Hatcher stepping up to the podium. He put his hand up, and everyone went quiet.

"My brothers and sisters, I have been told that our numbers are nearly four thousand today. The members of Parliament will have to stand up and take notice of our growing movement!" Hatcher exclaimed. "The Napoleonic wars are over! The blockade that Britain had put into place to stop goods from coming into the continent is gone! However, the greedy British farmer and landowner doesn't want to drop the price of corn and other grains. They only care about profit, and they don't care about our starving children at home."

A roar of grumbling came from the assembly, and Hatcher put his hand up to quiet them. "The Corn Laws state that no foreign corn will be allowed into Britain until domestic corn reaches a price of eighty shillings per quarter. *Eighty shillings!* That is nigh impossible."

Hatcher stepped away from the podium and started pacing across the stage. "Landowners are getting rich on the high bread price. Except for the rich, everyone is suffering from these high prices. Some are on the brink of starvation, and for what? So, the landowners can have more coins?"

Simeon noticed that a large group of about fifteen brawny men were starting to approach the assembly, with wooden batons in their hands, and they all seemed to be focused on Hatcher.

Hatcher didn't seem to notice as he continued his speech. "Workers are being fired because their employers can't afford to pay them. They must choose between feeding their own children or having additional workers, and now these men can't find new jobs. There are none! The Corn Laws have caused panic amongst the people."

Simeon watched as this group of men started knocking people

out of their way with batons as they approached the stage. What were they thinking? He turned towards a man near him, who was holding a baton in his hand. "What is the meaning of this?"

The stone-faced man sneered at him. "Mind your own business."

"Or what?" he challenged.

The man spat near his feet. "Or I will force you."

Stepping closer to the man, Simeon towered over him, and declared, "On what authority are these men here disturbing a peaceful protest?"

"We have a warrant for Mr. Hatcher's arrest," the man remarked dismissively as he eyed his clothing, obviously viewing him as unimportant.

Simeon clenched his jaw. "Then wait until after the demonstration. This is a peaceful protest."

"There's no such thing," the man said, tapping the baton in his hand. "Why should you care?"

He met the man's gaze and held it. "I'm a Bow Street Runner."

"It appears to me that you are sympathizing with these rebels," the man stated.

"Don't you?" he asked.

The man huffed. "I am Constable McKay, and I don't report to your magistrate."

A loud commotion came from near the podium as a fight was breaking out. The constables were hitting men and women with their batons, but this time, the people were fighting back. A bloody-armed Janet emerged from the crowd near them.

"Get out of here," she urged. "These constables are beating us for no reason. We weren't resisting!"

Simeon grabbed Emma's arm and yanked her towards him. "She's right. We need to leave *now*."

"Not without Janet!" she declared, holding her hand out for Janet to grab.

Without waiting for another moment, he started heading towards an alley when another man stepped in front of them. "Where do you think you are going?" he asked gruffly.

"I demand that you let us pass," Simeon declared.

His eyes perused the length of Emma's body lewdly. "I don't

think so. It looks to me like you rebels could benefit from some time in prison."

Simeon squared himself up to his full height. "I am a Bow Street Runner, and I am on assignment."

"Well, I'm Constable Stone, and we have strict orders to bring each of these worthless rebels into prison," he stated dismissively.

"Our prisons can't handle this influx of people, and you know it," Simeon argued. "Whose authority are you working under?"

"Justice Keats, the district magistrate." Constable Stone's eyes focused on Janet's wounds. "You can go, Runner, but I'm taking these ladies to the Bridewell prison in Westminster for a spell," he asserted, reaching out to grab Emma's arm firmly.

"I don't think so," Simeon growled, knocking his hand to the side.

Reaching for the dagger in the waistband of his trousers, Constable Stone wasn't even bright enough to consider Emma a threat. She came around Simeon and jabbed the constable in the throat, causing him to fall onto his knees.

"Let's go," she admonished.

The sound of a pistol cocking behind them made them all stop in their tracks. Simeon put his hands up and turned in the direction of the sound. A man dressed in a brown suit was holding a pistol, and it was aimed at Emma.

The man's glare intensified as he watched her. "You're under arrest for striking an officer of the law."

Keeping his hands up, Simeon said, "I am a Bow Street Runner, and this young lady is my partner."

The man gave him a look of disbelief. "Bow Street Runners do not hire women. We both know that women do not have the mental fortitude to handle such work."

"Regardless, you don't want to arrest this girl," he attempted again.

"And why is that?" the man scoffed.

Slowly, he lowered his hands and took a step closer to the man. "That is Miss Emma Pearson, and she is the ward of the Marquess of Downshire."

His pistol wavered slightly at Simeon's words, but then the man ran his eyes down the length of Emma's gown. "She doesn't look like a lady to me."

Simeon heard a loud slap behind him, followed by Emma crying out. He turned and saw that Emma had a hand over her reddened cheek, and Constable Stone was gripping her other arm tightly.

"This one goes to Westminster Bridewell, and it doesn't matter if she's the queen of England," Constable Stone said.

"Then I'm going with her." Simeon approached Constable Stone and knocked his hand off Emma's arm. He kept his voice low and controlled. "You are going to pay for your ill-treatment of Miss Pearson, constable. I guarantee it."

A hint of fear came into his eyes, and Constable Stone was wise enough to step away from Emma.

"Get into the wagon," the constable said, pointing towards a wagon not far away.

"Are you all right?" he asked, leading her towards the wagon.

Emma looked up at him with red-rimmed eyes. "I have never been slapped before."

A surge of protection coursed through his body, and he found raw anger building up inside of him at the sight of her tears. He knew he could take out the five constables milling around the wagon, who were arresting people at their discretion. However, his main concern needed to be Emma's safety.

Simeon had no doubt that Pembrooke had witnessed the attack and knew he would contact Justice Ford, the magistrate of Bow Street, to sort this mess out.

As he assisted Emma and Janet into the carriage, he heard a shot fired in the direction of the stage. He turned his head and saw people running in the opposite direction, attempting to flee the violence. Men and women were laying on the ground, bloodied and bruised as the constables continued to attack the unarmed people. This was a travesty, and he couldn't wait to speak to Justice Keats about his supposed warrant and questionable tactics.

Emma and Janet were huddled up in the corner, and Simeon sat down next to Emma. He placed his arm on her shoulder, and she leaned into him.

"Do you think I am truly going to prison?" she murmured.

Surprising even himself, he kissed the top of her head. "Not on my life."

The wagon was filled with mostly women, and a few bruised and bloodied men. Everyone was silent as they rode the short distance towards Westminster Bridewell, one of the worst prisons in London.

The wagon jerked to a stop in front of a decaying stone structure with iron bars over the windows. The glass in many of the windows was broken out. Simeon jumped out of the wagon and came around to start assisting everyone out of the wagon. When it was Emma's turn, he heard horses' hooves pounding on the cobblestone, getting increasingly louder.

He turned his head and saw the black-crested coach of the Marquess of Downshire barreling towards the prison. Before it came to a complete stop, the door opened and a stone-faced Lord Downshire stepped out. His eyes sought out Emma, and he visibly relaxed when he saw her.

Without hesitation, Lord Downshire headed straight towards Emma and pulled her into a tight embrace. He murmured something into her hair before he released her and stepped back. Immediately, his eyes narrowed, and his hand came up to touch her reddened cheek.

His eyes snapped up, and he addressed Constable Stone, who was standing guard near the wagon. "Who in blazes struck my ward?"

Constable Stone visibly froze with trepidation before saying, "I did. She was resisting arrest…"

Downshire spoke over him. "You had the audacity to arrest my charge. For what?"

"For… uh… striking an officer of the law."

Taking a commanding step closer, Downshire proclaimed, "I could see why. I, too, would like to strike you for your complete and utter incompetence."

A pudgy, short man with a receding hairline walked out of the prison's main door and approached Downshire cautiously. "May I ask what the problem is, milord?"

"This imbecile," Downshire pointed at Constable Stone, "falsely arrested and assaulted my ward, Miss Emma Pearson, and I demand her release at once," he declared forcefully. "If not, I vow that I will get the Prince Regent himself to demand her release."

"I assure you that will not be necessary," the man rushed to say. "I am Mr. Beacon, the director of Westminster Bridewell. I would like to formally apologize for Constable Stone's mistake." The man bowed. "Your ward is free to go with my apologies."

"Not good enough," Downshire proclaimed, again pointing towards Constable Stone. "This man had the nerve to lay his hand on my ward."

Mr. Beacon turned towards Constable Stone. "I will recommend to Justice Keats that you should be fired immediately."

Downshire walked over to the group of people near the wagon. "May I suggest that all these people be released, as well, because of this man's incompetence."

"Excellent idea, milord," Mr. Beacon remarked. He turned his attention towards the group. "You are all free to go, with my apologies."

Downshire turned his heated gaze towards Simeon. "Wentworth," he growled, "get in the coach."

Simeon escorted Emma to the coach. Once she was situated, he sat across from her. He noticed she was wringing her hands in front of her.

"It'll be all right," he assured her.

Her brows dipped inward. "I've never seen Luke so angry."

The coach door was wrenched opened, and Downshire came to sit down next to him with a clenched jaw.

Emma spoke up, hesitantly. "I am so…"

"Not now, Emma," Downshire said, interrupting her. "I am so incredibly disappointed in you."

A soft sob came out of her lips as she turned to stare out the window.

Downshire turned towards him and asserted, "I'm still debating about killing you, Wentworth."

"Fair enough," Simeon replied. "I deserve that."

A grunt was the last noise they heard out of Downshire until they arrived back at Caddington Manor.

For what seemed like hours, Emma kept her gaze on her lap as Luke paced back and forth in his study, ranting and raving about all the awful things that could have happened to her today. He was furious, and he had every right to be. She had deceived him.

Rachel was sitting next to her, and she could see the disappointment on her features, as well. She had made a terrible mistake going to Templeton Square, and she was grateful that Luke had interceded when he had. After all, she had no desire to go to prison. Even the courtyard in front of the prison smelt horrid.

Luke stopped pacing and leaned back against the desk. His piercing gaze landed on her. "Explain to me what you were thinking, Emma."

Slowly, she raised her eyes until she met her guardian's. "I wanted to do research for my article for The Morning Post."

"That is asinine!" he declared. "You could have been seriously hurt today, or worse, killed."

Her eyes sought out Simeon, who was sitting across from her in an armchair. Just meeting his gaze provided her with much reassurance.

"I understand," she murmured.

"Have you done any research other than just today?" Luke questioned with a frown.

Emma winced. "I attended a meeting for the Anti-Corn Law rebels at a public house."

Luke's expression went hard. "You attended a meeting at a public house," he repeated slowly. His hardened gaze turned towards Simeon. "Dare I presume that you took her to this meeting?"

"I did," Simeon answered. "I ensured she was kept safe."

"Blazes," Luke muttered under his breath, crossing his arms over his chest. "What do you think your brother or father would say about your actions today?"

"They would be furious," she answered honestly.

"You put yourself at risk, you put Wentworth at risk," Luke started. "For what? To make two pounds for an article." He huffed.

"I will give you £1,000 if you stop this ridiculous notion of writing articles."

Feeling bold, she replied, "It's not about the money."

"Then what is it about?" Rachel asked softly from the chair next to hers.

Squaring her shoulders, she met Luke's firm gaze. "Surely, you must agree that I don't fit in with this family."

"Emma…" Rachel gasped.

Emma turned towards Rachel. "My brother died to give me this life, but I have done nothing to earn it. I am ordinary in every sense of the word."

"That is not true…" Rachel attempted.

"It is," she contended. "If you and Luke hadn't rescued me that day, I could have been one of those people in Templeton Square. I might have been struggling to pay for the increasing cost of bread."

Luke uncrossed his arms. "Emma, this is nonsense…"

"It is not," she replied, speaking over him. "Rachel has written a book, Hannah runs a horse farm, Kate manages a refuge for women, and Eliza…" She hesitated before saying, "I'm not quite sure what she does, but I have an idea, and it's extraordinary."

Luke straightened. "You need not compare yourself to others. Every person has unique talents that benefits others. More importantly, being yourself *is* being unique because there is only one of you."

"But I pale in comparison to them," she murmured.

"Comparison takes the joy out of life," Rachel said. "By constantly comparing yourself to others, you tear yourself down."

Tears came to Emma's eyes. "Have you ever felt like you were supposed to do more with your life?"

"I know that feeling well," Rachel assured her.

Swiping a tear that ran down her cheek, Emma explained, "I'm grateful for everything you've done for me, I truly am, but I feel as if I am not doing enough to help others." She pressed her lips together for a moment. "I have no doubt that people in my village are suffering because of the Corn Laws. Am I to sit by and do nothing?"

Rachel shook her head. "No, of course not. You must do what your conscience dictates."

Emma turned towards Simeon. "What I don't understand is why those constables were using force during a peaceful demonstration."

"I agree," Simeon replied, "and I intend to call on Justice Keats after this meeting to discuss just that."

Luke let out a loud sigh. "Regardless, you can't keep sneaking out and attending these meetings. Lockhart is a madman, and he intends to make you his."

A knock came from the opened window. "I believe that's my cue," a man said from outside the window. He climbed through the window. "I've been waiting to announce myself."

"What is the meaning of this?" Luke demanded.

Rising, Simeon cleared his throat. "Lord and Lady Downshire, allow me to introduce you to Officer Edwin Pembrooke."

"We've already met. Pembrooke was the bloke who notified me that Emma was being carted off to prison," Luke informed him.

"Indeed," Simeon replied. "However, I am as confused as you are about why he's in your study."

"Because I found some information about Lockhart that you both will find beneficial," Mr. Pembrooke said, removing a few folded pieces of paper from his blue jacket pocket.

Luke eyed him with annoyance. "May I ask why you were skulking outside my window, Officer Pembrooke?"

"I was not skulking, Lord Downshire," Mr. Pembrooke replied, amused. "When I arrived at the estate, I heard shouting, and I came around to ensure everyone was unharmed."

Pressing his fingers to the bridge of his nose, Luke remarked, "You're an imbecile."

Mr. Pembrooke grinned. "I've been called much worse." He turned his gaze towards Emma. "And you must be Miss Emma Pearson."

She tilted her head towards him. "I am. It's a pleasure to meet you, Mr. Pembrooke."

"I had the privilege of watching you jab that constable in the throat. I must admit, I was impressed," Mr. Pembrooke stated, respect in his tone. "Have you considered applying as a Bow Street Runner?"

"Under no circumstances will my ward ever be a Bow Street

Runner!" Luke exclaimed.

Mr. Pembrooke winked at her. "I understand."

"What do you want, Pembrooke?" Simeon growled.

Emma turned her gaze towards Simeon, surprised by the anger resonating in his voice. Weren't they friends?

Holding up the papers in his hand, Pembrooke shared, "Lockhart is not a good man."

"Thank you for that," Luke drawled. "Now get out of my home."

Pembrooke smirked. "There's more." He unfolded the papers. "Lockhart is not working in London at any law office, nor is he staying in any legitimate housing."

"Then where is he living?" Rachel asked.

"Most likely at a disreputable public house," Pembrooke answered. "A man fitting Lockhart's description has been hiring ruffians from the rookeries, and my sources revealed that the sum is quite generous."

Emma frowned. "Where is Peter getting all this money?" she asked.

"That's an excellent question, Miss Pearson," Pembrooke said, smiling, "and I'm afraid I don't have the answer. However, I do urge you to remain diligent about your safety."

Luke turned towards her. "You are not allowed to leave the estate for the foreseeable future, and that includes no visits to Eliza," he said in a tone that brooked no argument. "Do you understand, Emma?"

She nodded. "I do."

"Do you understand why?" Rachel pressed.

"I do, but I don't understand why Peter is doing this," she answered. "We never had an understanding between us."

"Men can lose rational thought when it comes to a beautiful young woman, such as yourself," Pembrooke remarked.

Simeon rose. "With your permission, I would like to investigate this matter further."

"Granted, but you are fired from guarding Emma," Luke stated.

Simeon tugged down on the lapels of his jacket. "I've decided to decline your firing."

Luke lifted his brow. "You can't decline being fired."

"I believe I just did," Simeon replied.

Walking over to the door, Luke opened it and shouted, "Get out of my home!"

Simeon chuckled as he approached Emma. "I'll be back later to call on you, Emma."

"I might be too busy for callers," she joked.

He grinned as he tipped his head towards her.

Emma watched as Mr. Pembrooke and Simeon exited the study.

"Those men are ignoramuses," Luke mumbled as he sat down in his desk chair.

Rachel gave her a curious look. "That interaction with Simeon was rather telling."

"In what way?" she asked.

Leaning closer, Rachel revealed, "He was smiling at you."

"And?"

"Haven't you noticed that he only smiles at you?"

She shook her head. "I hadn't noticed."

"Interesting," Rachel said, leaning back.

Emma placed her hands in her lap. "You're wrong. Simeon has already informed me that we aren't friends."

Smiling, Rachel remarked, "That's even more intriguing."

Luke's grumpy voice came from his desk. "Leave it, Rachel. No ward of mine is going to marry Wentworth."

Emma rose. "If there are no objections, I'm going upstairs to write my article." She looked down at Rachel. "Would you mind reviewing it once it's finished?"

"Yes," Rachel said, rising. "I'll be in the nursery with Matthew."

Before she took a step, Rachel threw her arms around her. "I'm so relieved that you're home safe. You scared me."

Emma returned her embrace. "I'm sorry, Rachel. I truly am."

"I understand your need for adventure, but perhaps you could do it from the safety of the estate for the time being."

"I can do that," she promised, stepping back.

"Good," Rachel said. "Now, off with you. But just so you know, we're proud of you, whether your article is accepted or not."

"Thank you," she murmured, exiting the room.

Chapter Eleven

Simeon exited the hackney in front of a three-level, white-washed building, which housed the public offices of Justice Thomas Keats, a magistrate for the 34th District.

Pembrooke came to stand next to him. "I question the validity of your plan."

"I think it's brilliant," Simeon replied, not bothering to spare him a glance. "Besides, I don't have time to wait for an appointment. If Justice Keats is in his office, he will see us."

Pembrooke gestured towards the front door. "After you."

They entered the building and were approached by a brawny man wearing no jacket, with a pistol tucked into the waistband of his trousers.

"You blokes lost?" the man grunted, placing his right hand on the pistol.

Reaching into the pocket of his waistcoat, Simeon pulled out his calling card. "Please inform Justice Keats that I would like a moment of his time," he said, extending the card.

The man accepted the card reluctantly and read it. Immediately, his head snapped back up. "Yes, milord. I will inform Justice Keats of your arrival."

Once the man had stepped away, Pembrooke chuckled. "I have never seen you play that hand before."

Simeon gave a one-shoulder shrug as he removed his top hat. "I've found that my title has opened up doors, whereas being a Bow Street Runner typically slams the door shut."

The man reappeared from a side door and said, "Justice Keats will see you now, Lord Wentworth."

"Thank you," he replied as he moved towards him.

They stepped into a small office with a lone window, with weathered, papered walls, and a simple rug. An older gentleman sat behind a desk and greeted them with a frown more than a smile. He had dark hair, woven with gray, and deep frown lines between his eyes.

The man rose from his chair. "What brings the Viscount of Wentworth to my office today?" he asked, pointing towards two chairs in front of his desk.

Unbuttoning his jacket, Simeon sat down. "I was at Templeton Square today, and I saw some atrocities on behalf of the warrant that *you* issued, Justice Keats."

Keats returned to his seat, appearing undisturbed. "May I ask why you were at Templeton Square?"

"It's no secret that I work as a Bow Street Runner," Simeon shared. "I was there on official business. However, Constable Stone struck my female companion and arrested her for resisting arrest."

With a frown, Keats commented, "That's most unfortunate. I've taken Mr. Beacon's recommendation and fired Constable Stone for his deplorable actions today. His conduct was not becoming an officer of the law or this office."

"And what of the others' actions?"

"Pardon?" Keats replied.

Simeon considered the justice of the peace for a moment. Either this man was a simpleton and he truly did not know what took place at Templeton Square, or he was involved in the corruption. He would need to proceed cautiously.

"Under the warrant *you* issued, the constables attacked unarmed men and women as they attempted to arrest the orator of the protest," he explained.

Justice Keats sat back in his chair. "I assure you that is not what happened. Those men and women were bearing arms, and my constables were merely protecting themselves."

"That's rubbish. I was there," Simeon contended. "Your constables started hitting people with batons as they made their way towards the stage. Only after people were bloodied and bruised did the fighting break out."

Threading his fingers over his waist, Justice Keats remarked, "It's against the law to hit an officer of the law. Those people's actions were criminal."

"Out of curiosity, how long did you suppose those people would suffer injustices before they fought back?" Simeon asked.

"Careful. It almost sounds if you are a sympathizer of the Anti-Corn Law rebels and their aggressive tactics," Justice Keats remarked dryly.

Attempting to keep his voice controlled, Simeon replied, "The only aggressive tactics I saw were your constables executing *your* warrant."

"Why exactly are you here, officer?" Justice Keats asked indifferently.

Simeon narrowed his eyes at the impertinent magistrate. "I prefer Lord Wentworth, if you don't mind," he stated in a steely tone. "I am here to discover who ordered you to issue a warrant for Mr. Hatcher's arrest."

"It was of my own volition," he responded. "We needed to squash the growing demonstration, which demanded I issue a warrant for the arrest of the orator."

"But it was a peaceful demonstration," Pembrooke objected. "There were no incidents until your constables arrived."

Justice Keats sighed impatiently. "Gentlemen, you're wasting my time…"

"Did Sheriff Blundell pressure you to write that warrant?" Simeon asked, speaking over him.

"He did not. We discussed the case, and both acknowledged that the Anti-Corn Law rebels were becoming too strong in numbers," Justice Keats explained. "If we'd continued to let the people gather, riots would have erupted all over London." He leaned forward and rested his forearms onto his desk. "I would think that Bow Street Runners would prefer *not* to have riots."

"Now that you have arrested Mr. Hatcher, what do you intend to do with him?" Pembrooke asked.

"Eventually, he will be granted a trial, but we shall wait until these rebels dissipate before we order one," the magistrate said in a bored tone.

"Do you intend to make an example out of him?" Pembrooke asked.

"I do."

Rising, Simeon inquired, "Pray tell, what if you're wrong, and by arresting Hatcher, you've stirred the flame of rebellion even more?"

"Then, we shall squash them, one by one," Justice Keats asserted, looking up at him. "I was under the impression that you're a Tory."

"I am," Simeon replied, placing his hat on top of his head.

"Tories are *for* the Corn Laws, not against them," Keats pointed out.

Simeon stepped forward and tapped the desk with his finger. "I'm on the side of right, whatever side that may be."

"That is a dangerous way to live," Keats said.

He let out a light huff. "No more than allowing innocent people to be attacked for attending a peaceful demonstration."

"I would proceed cautiously, Lord Wentworth," Justice Keats advised. "Powerful men want this rebellion to be squashed."

"Which men?"

Justice Keats scoffed. "You're a fool for getting involved."

They continued to stare at each other with contempt until Pembrooke tugged on the sleeve of Simeon's jacket. "Come, Wentworth. We have another meeting we must attend."

Reluctantly, he broke his gaze from Keats. "Of course." He tipped his hat towards the magistrate. "I personally will ensure that Hatcher is treated fairly in the court system."

Keats rose from his desk slowly. "Are you implying that he won't be?"

"I apologize," Simeon started dryly, "I wasn't implying anything. I am boldly stating that I question your integrity in this matter."

"How dare you come into my office and speak such blatant untruths," Keats declared. "Who do you think you are?"

Simeon straightened to his full height. "I am the Viscount of Wentworth, a peer of the realm, and a decorated Bow Street Runner. I have every right to speak to you in such a manner."

He spun around and left the room, ignoring the guard standing outside of the door.

Without saying a word to each other, Simeon and Pembrooke flagged down a hackney, and sat across from each other.

It wasn't until the hackney had eased its way into traffic when Pembrooke lifted his brow. "Do you want to explain what happened with Justice Keats?"

"That man is corrupt."

"I agree. But what can we do about it?"

"What magistrate issues a warrant for the arrest of a man during the middle of a peaceful demonstration?" Simeon removed his hat and placed it on the bench next to him. "It was almost as if he was sending a message."

"What message?"

"I don't know," he replied honestly, "but I intend to find out."

Pembrooke stretched his legs in the cramped hackney. "May I suggest we seek out Justice Ford later. Perhaps he might have insight on what Justice Keats is attempting."

Simeon nodded and closed his eyes. "Wake me when we arrive at my townhouse."

He almost smirked when he heard Pembrooke mumble, "Lords have it rough."

Simeon had just stepped out of his carriage at Caddington Manor when he heard pounding horses' hooves on the cobblestone. He turned to see Lord Jonathon and Lord Lansdowne reining in their horses.

"Afternoon, Wentworth," Benedict greeted, dismounting his horse.

He tipped his hat. "Afternoon, Beckett. Lansdowne."

"We just arrived back from visiting Totternhoe," Jonathon said as he handed off the reins to an awaiting footman. "Benedict and I found some alarming information about Lockhart."

"Which was?" he asked eagerly.

Lansdowne gave him an amused look. "Patience, Wentworth. Downshire will want to hear this as well."

A few moments later, Simeon followed the men into Downshire's study.

Downshire looked up from his desk and his eyes landed on him. "Wentworth," he growled. "Don't you have your own home to go to?"

"I do," he replied, smirking, "multiple homes, in fact."

With a shake of his head, Downshire remarked, "At least you didn't bring Emma flowers this time."

"This time?" Benedict asked, his brows lifted. "Are you courting Emma?"

"No, no, no... I am not," he insisted. "Those were apology flowers."

"Interesting," Jonathon muttered.

"There is nothing interesting about it," Simeon assured them as he walked over to a camelback sofa and sat down. "Emma and I are just friends."

"You're *friends* now?!" Downshire exclaimed, dropping the quill onto the desk.

Benedict glanced curiously between Downshire and Simeon. "It appears that a lot has transpired since Jonathon and I left for Totternhoe. Perhaps it would be best if we start with what we discovered about Lockhart."

"Proceed," Downshire said, sitting back in his chair.

Jonathon walked over to the drink cart and picked up the decanter. "We searched Emma's cottage from top to bottom, and other than the usual critters living in the thatched roof, we found nothing that would indicate why Lockhart would want the property so badly." He popped off the lid. "Then I asked myself, 'if I wanted to hide something valuable, where would I hide it?'"

Benedict laughed. "It's true, Jonathon did say that exact question... aloud."

"But it worked," Jonathon said, pointing the decanter lid at him. "Inside Constable Pearson's bedchamber, we started searching the stones around the hearth and discovered a loose one. We pulled it out and found... contracts."

"Contracts?" Simeon repeated. "What kind of contracts?"

"Four bill of sale contracts for cottages near Emma's land, and all of them listed Lockhart as the solicitor," Jonathon answered, pouring himself a drink.

"We also found this," Benedict said, removing a gold locket from his jacket pocket. He walked over and extended it towards Downshire. "We assumed it belonged to Emma's mother."

Downshire accepted the necklace. "This is an expensive piece of jewelry."

"Exactly," Benedict agreed. "It's not quite befitting a constable's wife."

"I will ensure that Emma is given the necklace." Placing the necklace into the top desk drawer, Downshire said, "Now, back to the matter at hand. What did you uncover about the contracts?"

Jonathon took a sip of his drink while Benedict answered for him. "We went into the village and started asking around. We learned that the men on the bill of sale contracts had all gone missing at different times over the past few years."

Simeon moved to the edge of his seat. "Are you implying that Lockhart had a hand in their disappearances?"

"It sounds like a grand coincidence, does it not?" Jonathon remarked.

Benedict leaned his shoulder against the wall. "We went to speak to the new constable, and we discovered that Lockhart was known to engage in unscrupulous business practices."

"That's not a surprise to us," Downshire said. "My investigation turned up the same thing."

"Yes, but Jonathon and I are of the same mindset that Constable Pearson's death was a little too convenient."

Simeon lifted his brows in surprise. "You think he was murdered?"

Jonathon shrugged. "We confirmed that he was investigating Lockhart for those men's disappearances, and then he suddenly takes ill shortly thereafter. It sounds mighty suspicious to me."

"We encouraged Constable Brown to open up an investigation into Constable Pearson's death; discreetly, of course," Benedict stated.

With a curious glance, Simeon asked, "How did you convince the constable to open up an investigation into a death that happened over two years ago?"

"We just asked… nicely," Jonathon replied, bringing the snifter up to his lips.

"Jonathon and I decided to visit these cottages, which coincidentally neighbored Emma's land, and discovered an extensive channel of chalk quarries instead," Benedict shared.

"Chalk quarries?" Simeon repeated.

Benedict nodded. "Apparently, Emma's land is rich in chalk, including a desirable hard chalk stone, known as Totternhoe stone."

"I've heard of that stone," Downshire remarked. "It's strong enough to be used as a building stone and has been used to construct buildings such as St. Albans Cathedral and Westminster Abbey."

"At least we discovered why Lockhart was so keen on Emma selling her land," Simeon pointed out.

"Besides Lockhart potentially murdering five people and learning that Emma's land is rich in resources, did you discover anything else in Totternhoe?" Downshire asked.

"Yes, we are closer to discovering the identity of the initials 'A.B.'. Again, we asked the man at the bank very nicely for that information," Benedict replied, smiling smugly. "A man named Daniel Booth has been depositing money into Lockhart's account for the past five years."

Downshire groaned. "Who in blazes is Daniel Booth?"

"We're looking into it," Benedict replied.

"I may not be an agent, but even I can recognize that Daniel Booth does not have the initials 'A.B.'," Simeon joked.

Jonathon placed his empty snifter down on the drink cart. "True, but Daniel Booth must be depositing the money into the account for someone with the initials 'A.B.'. We have asked Uncle Charles to look into it."

"Poor Emma," Simeon muttered. "Do we tell her that we suspect Lockhart murdered her father?"

"No!" all the men in the room shouted in unison.

"Are you mad?" Downshire asked, glaring at him. "No one will breathe a word about this to Emma until we have absolute proof that Lockhart was behind the death of her father. Agreed?"

"Agreed," they all said in unison.

Simeon adjusted his green jacket. "While you were gone," he said, "a colleague of mine discovered that Lockhart isn't working at any law office in town, and no one can find his place of lodging. Furthermore, a man fitting Lockhart's description has been hiring a band of ruffians from the rookeries."

"For what purpose?" Jonathon asked. "What does Lockhart intend to do?"

Simeon rose and walked over to a large window, overlooking the gardens. "Lockhart has come to town, not for employment, but to hire mercenaries."

"It doesn't make sense. What does he hope to gain?" Downshire asked.

Simeon felt his hands ball into clenched fists. "He wants Emma."

"If that's his end game, then we'll depart for Scotland tomorrow," Downshire asserted.

"No," Benedict stated. "With enough men, they could easily overpower your traveling party."

Downshire tossed his arms up in the air. "Then I'll hire a militia."

"And what of Rachel and baby Matthew? You would put them in danger?" Jonathon questioned.

"It's not safe to travel now," Benedict asserted.

Leaning back against the edge of his desk, Downshire asked, "Then what do we do?"

"There's a place we could take Emma where she would be protected," Benedict said.

Downshire eyed him with concern. "Where?"

"It's best that you don't know," Jonathon stated firmly. "It's not a place we discuss lightly."

Simeon didn't dare ask for more details. Instead, he suggested, "I could go along to guard Emma."

Benedict started laughing but turned it into a cough when his gaze landed on Simeon. "Trust me, Wentworth, Emma will be well-protected."

"So, it's settled," Downshire declared. "You will take Emma to an undisclosed location, and we will wait out Lockhart. Eventually, he will run out of money and hopefully scurry far away from town."

"First, let me speak to Eliza, but it shouldn't be a problem,"

Benedict said. "We all have a fierce desire to keep Emma safe."

After a long moment of somber silence, Benedict declared, "I shall take my leave."

"As shall I," Jonathon said as they both walked towards the door.

Simeon leaned back against the sill. He wasn't ready to leave until he had a chance to see Emma again, especially if he wasn't going to see her for a while.

"Care to join us, Wentworth?" Benedict asked, standing in the doorway.

"I was hoping to speak to Emma before I depart," he answered.

Downshire let out an exasperated sigh. "Fine. But no courting nonsense. Just speak to her and be done with it."

"As I have stated on numerous occasions, I have no intention of courting your ward."

With a knowing gaze, Benedict teased, "Didn't you offer for her already?"

"I did, but that was only because I fell on top of her near Gunther's. Neither one of us *actually* wanted to marry."

"Ah, well, thank you for clearing that up," Benedict said in an amused tone.

Downshire walked into the hall and shouted for the butler.

Simeon found himself grinning. At his townhouse, they had a bell system to alert his staff, but Downshire still preferred that old fashioned way of shouting for his butler. It was quite humorous to him.

Now that Emma was leaving to an undisclosed destination, Simeon felt his heart begin to mourn for the loss of her company.

Chapter Twelve

Emma was waiting impatiently for the ink to dry on the paper when Rachel walked into her bedchamber.

"It's been hours," Rachel started, "have you finished the article?"

"I have," she replied, lightly blowing on the page.

Rachel stopped next to her at the desk and started reading. Her face remained expressionless as she read each line. Finally, she read the last line aloud.

"The Corn Laws are both morally and economically damaging, and we must put aside our political differences to take a stand for what is right."

Rachel looked over at her and smiled. "Well said, Emma. I have no doubt this article will be picked up by The Morning Post."

"Do you truly believe so?"

Picking up the paper, but being careful of the ink, Rachel read,

"Constables exercised underhanded tactics as they executed the warrant. The demonstration started off peacefully, but the constables beat everyone in their paths with batons, turning the tide. The images of bloodied and unarmed women and men scattered across the stones of the square will forever be emblazoned on my mind."

Lowering the paper back to the desk, Rachel said, "Your perspective is unique. You attended not only the meeting, but the rally, as well. You saw firsthand the atrocities those constables committed."

"It's true," Emma agreed, leaning back in her seat. "Those men had no regard for anyone's welfare as they plowed through the people."

"Why don't I have a footman deliver this article directly to the newspaper?" Rachel suggested.

"Do you mean it?"

Rachel smiled. "I do. With any luck, it will be in the tomorrow's edition."

"Wouldn't that be grand?"

Leaning her hip against the side of the dressing table, Rachel asked, "After submitting this article, what do you intend to do next?"

Emma tucked a lock of hair behind her ear. "I plan to write a series of articles about the Bow Street Runners."

"Interesting. And who will be the inspiration behind those articles?" Rachel asked innocently.

"Wentworth, of course."

"Of course," Rachel repeated, amused. "I came up to inform you that Wentworth is downstairs. He wishes to speak to you for a moment."

Rising from her chair, Emma took a moment to smooth out her gown, ignoring Rachel's growing smirk.

"Would you like me to chaperone?" Rachel asked.

She shook her head. "We'll just take a turn in the gardens."

"But not in the east gardens," Rachel admonished. "Those gardens are backed up to the woodlands. It's not appropriate for you to travel that far together."

Emma feigned an exasperated sigh. "I suppose I can follow that one rule."

"One?" Rachel chuckled. "We've gone over hundreds of rules."

Emma left her bedchamber and hurried down the stairs. For some reason, she found she was excited to see Simeon. It must be because she planned to interview him today. That has to be it, she thought.

The door to the drawing room was opened, and she walked in. Simeon was standing next to the window, the sun illuminating his face.

He turned to face her. "Did you have a pleasant afternoon?"

"I did. How was yours?"

"It was... uneventful," Simeon said, clasping his arms behind his back.

She arched an eyebrow. "Why don't I believe you?"

A chuckle escaped his lips. "You would make a brilliant Bow Street Runner, if not for your gender."

"My gender?"

He took a step closer towards her. "Women are not apt to handle espionage and such."

"That's ridiculous. I believe I proved myself at Templeton Square."

"Ah," he smirked, "how could I forget? You jabbed the constable in the throat, and you allowed yourself to get arrested."

"At gunpoint, may I add."

He gave her a look of disapproval, but she saw the teasing glint in his eye. "A pistol would not have stopped me," he declared dramatically.

Deciding to play along, she asked, "Pray tell, how would you have stopped a bullet?"

He took another step closer to her, and now they were only an arm's length apart. "My dear girl, the constable wouldn't have had time to get a shot off before I knocked him unconscious."

"I fear you are prone to exaggeration, milord," she joked.

Simeon chuckled. "And I fear that you are an impertinent thing."

A smile graced her face. She enjoyed bantering with Simeon. It was quickly becoming her favorite pastime.

"Would you care to take a stroll in the gardens?" she asked.

Simeon eyed her suspiciously. "If you are suggesting a tryst, then I am most assuredly not..."

"Good gracious, no," she rushed to say. "I was just thinking..." Her voice trailed off as her face grew increasingly warm, and she brought up her hands to cover her cheeks.

To her surprise, Simeon let out a loud, unrestrained laugh before he took another step towards her. "You're fun to tease."

"You are a horrid, insipid man," she declared, lowering her hands from her cheeks. "It was cruel of you to tease me."

"No, you're just angry because I bested you at your own game."

She had to concede that he did have a point. Tilting her head to look up at him, she replied, "You laughed."

He gave her an odd look. "I've laughed before."

"Not like that," she remarked. "You almost sounded happy."

He extended his arm. "A stroll in the garden does sound delightful."

"Indeed," she replied. "It will give me time to interview you."

With a side glance, he asked, "What is it that you wish to know?"

She tapped a finger to her lips. "What is your favorite dessert?"

"Lavender cheesecake."

"Favorite drink?"

He gave her a playful grin. "I love chocolate."

"You drink chocolate?"

"I do, every morning," he replied, puffing out his chest. "Sometimes two cups."

She tsked. "What a rebel you are, milord."

They reached the rear door to the gardens, and Simeon opened it for her. "Do you love chocolate?" he asked, standing to the side.

"Every woman loves chocolate," she replied, smiling. "Do you like to read?"

He nodded. "I have an extensive library. However, I don't utilize it enough."

"Do you have a large family?"

A wistful expression came over his face as he responded, "No, but I have a younger sister."

"Are you close with your parents?" she asked as they strolled through the paved pathway.

He stopped and grew serious. "There was a time when I was, but that was so long ago."

"What happened?" she asked, turning to face him.

Simeon's eyes held pain and anguish. "There was a girl that I loved from the moment I laid eyes on her. I knew we were destined to marry." He huffed. "We even eloped."

"You did?" she asked in surprise.

He shifted his gaze to over her shoulder. "I took all my money and went to secure a special license, leaving her behind in a rented room at the inn. But when I returned, she was gone."

Hearing the agony in his voice caused her heart to tremble for him. Reaching out, she placed her hand on his sleeve. "Where did she go?"

"At the time, she vanished without a trace, and I continued to search for her for the next five years," he said, his voice hitching with emotion. "My parents told me that she must be dead and to forget the girl, but I knew she was alive. I felt it here." He placed his hand over his heart. "That's why I became a Bow Street Runner, so I could investigate her disappearance."

"When you found her, was this the girl who…" she hesitated, "whose heart already belonged to another?"

He nodded. "It was. I was devastated. I pleaded for her to love me, but it was too late."

"I'm so sorry, Simeon," she said, knowing her simple apology wasn't adequate.

A silence descended over them, but it wasn't uncomfortable. After a long moment, she broke the silence by asking, "After you found her, why did you continue working as a Bow Street Runner? Why not enjoy the life of leisure of a viscount?"

He chuckled. "You know nothing about being titled, do you?"

"I do not. In case you forgot, I don't have one," she joked.

His face grew solemn. "To answer your question, I was bestowed the title of Viscount of Wentworth a little over a year ago by Prince George."

"You were?"

His broad shoulders slumped slightly, and his eyes reflected the tiredness of his soul.

Feeling a need to comfort him, she reached for his hand and held it tenderly. "You may not consider me a friend, but I consider you one. And friends share each other's burdens."

"My burdens are too great, Emma," he whispered with pain in his voice. "I have carried them for far too long."

"Then let me help you."

His eyes grew misty. "My struggles and pain might bring you down."

She brought her other hand up to cup his cheek. "Don't worry about me. I'm stronger than I look."

Simeon's eyes implored hers, and she hoped that he would trust her with his secrets.

He closed his eyes and asked, "What has Martha told you about her past?"

"Are you referring to Rachel's cousin's wife, Martha?"

He nodded. "I am."

"She hasn't told me much about her past," she replied. "Over this past year in Scotland, we have grown close, but she hasn't spoken about life before she was married. She just discovered she was pregnant..." Her words stilled when realization washed over her.

"It was Martha," she breathed, "wasn't it?"

Hearing her name out loud caused his heart to lurch, and Simeon kept his eyes closed. "It was," he confirmed.

To his surprise, Emma wrapped her arms around him and embraced him. Her actions spoke louder than her words would ever have, and he found himself touched.

She stepped back but remained close. "I had no idea, Simeon. I can hear in your voice how much you loved her."

He gave her a weak smile. "Emmett won her heart, and I got a blasted title."

"How did you earn a title?"

Tilting his head towards a bench, he said, "I received it after an assignment that went horribly wrong."

"Will you tell me about it?"

His initial response was to refuse her, but he saw the hopeful expression on her face. It was time for him to share his story, to trust another.

He led her over to the bench and waited until she was seated before claiming the seat next to her. "My partner and I were assigned to root out the leader of The Cursed Lot gang in Gravesend, but my partner was deceived and was murdered."

"How awful," Emma gasped.

He gave her a weak smile. "That isn't even the worst part."

Clasping her hands in her lap, she replied, "Please continue, then."

"After my partner's death, I was assigned to work with Dr. Maddix, but I found him to be intolerable."

"Emmett?" she asked. "He is quite possibly one of the nicest people I know."

He sighed. "Eventually, he grew on me as well, especially since he wasn't completely incompetent at his job."

"As a doctor? Or was he an agent of the Crown as well?"

He ran his hand through his hair. "What has your family told you about agents?"

"I know that Adrien, Benedict, Jonathon, and Lord Charles Beckett are agents," she said, lowering her voice. "I haven't figured out what Eliza, Cosette, and Josette are exactly, but it's fairly obvious they're more than they let on."

Deciding to change the subject, because frankly he didn't know either, he continued with the story. "Emmett became my partner, and together we brought down The Cursed Lot and their entire smuggling operation." After a moment, he reluctantly added, "Adrien, Benedict, and Jonathon may have played a role in the case, but their contribution was limited."

Simeon decided not to reveal that Eliza and Josette also contributed to bringing down the leader of The Cursed Lot and saving Martha from the clutches of her evil father.

He angled himself towards her. "Martha was working as a nurse in the hospital at Gravesend with Emmett," he hesitated, his voice becoming strained, "and that's when I saw her again. For the first time in five years."

"What did Martha say?"

He huffed. "She pointed a gun at me and threatened to kill me."

"Why?"

Frowning, he said, "I can't share that without betraying Martha's trust. Her past is her story to share, not mine."

Emma nodded thoughtfully. "I understand."

"I tried to convince her to love me, but it was too late. She'd already fallen in love with Emmett."

"I am sor…" She hesitated, then softly said, "I'm at a loss for words. I fear my words are inadequate."

He placed his hand over hers. "It's all right. You don't have to say anything." He gave her a tentative smile. "This is the first time I've shared this story with anyone. I never thought I'd be able to without my emotions taking over."

"I'm so glad you did," she murmured, her eyes full of compassion.

He turned his gaze away from hers. "Two weeks after we caught the leader of The Cursed Lot, I got a missive from the palace. It informed me that Prince George wanted to meet with me."

"What an honor."

"It was," he agreed, "but I didn't care about the title. The only thing I wanted was Martha's love, and I had lost it." He sighed deeply. "After that, I spiraled out of control. I stopped reading the letters from my parents, I avoided my friends, and I allowed others to run my company. I felt empty inside."

"Do you still feel that way?"

Furrowing his brows, he thought for a moment, then answered, "Not anymore."

"That's good," she said, smiling.

He brought his gaze back to hers. "We aren't so different, you and I. After all, I don't belong in this world, either."

"But you're titled and..."

He interrupted her. "Just because someone has a title, doesn't mean they belong in this world. I own a trading company and work as a Bow Street Runner. I daresay my actions are more scandalous than falling off a horse into a mud puddle."

"Did you forget that you landed on top of me near Gunther's?" she asked with an uplifted brow.

He cleared his suddenly hoarse throat. "How can I forget that?"

"Does your family know that you found Martha?"

He shook his head. "No. I have yet to tell them."

"And the title?"

"I assume they've discovered I was given a title."

"We could write them together, if you wish," she suggested.

Bringing his elbows to his knees, he leaned over and said, "I shall do it on my own. Besides, I'm not sure I'm ready yet."

"I'd give anything for my family to still be alive," Emma

remarked wistfully.

"Now it's my turn to be sorry."

Turning her gaze back towards Caddington Manor, she grew silent for a moment. "I am truly happy living with Luke and Rachel, but sometimes my grief overtakes me. I miss my brother and my father dearly."

"Not your mother?"

"Her, too, but she died a little over seven years ago," she admitted. "Her death isn't as recent."

Simeon leaned back and put his arm on the bench. "Tell me about your brother."

A genuine smile came to her lips. "David was vexing, infuriating, overprotective, and the best brother anyone could ask for. Don't get me wrong, he teased me unmercifully when I was younger, but I always knew that he loved me."

"And your father?"

Her face softened at the mention of her father. "He was a good man. He tried to care for me the best he could, but it took an enormous amount of time to be a constable and keep a shop going. He decided to send me off to boarding school for my education."

Simeon was still attempting to understand how a constable could afford the price of the boarding school. "Did your father come from privilege?"

She shook her head. "Heavens, no. He worked hard from a young age until he earned enough money to buy a dilapidated building on the outskirts of Totternhoe, eventually turning it into a general store."

"Did your mother come from privilege?"

"I don't know much about my mother's side, other than her parents died from diphtheria," she admitted. "My parents always had funds to cover expenses, but I do recall my mother would often take in sewing jobs when I was younger."

"Did you have no other relations to care for you?"

She bit her lower lip, drawing his attention to their fullness. "I was very much alone in this world before Luke and Rachel rescued me," she said. "And what of your extended family?"

"What of it?" he said defensively.

Emma let out a huff of amusement. "You entertain me, Simeon."

"I do?"

Leaning back against the bench, her shoulder was mere inches from his arm. "You have a kind heart, yet you hide it behind a mask of anger and hostility."

"I fear you're mistaken. I'm not hiding behind anything."

Emma studied him for a long moment, and he felt like squirming under her scrutiny. Finally, she spoke. "Your heart was horribly broken, and I believe *you* feel that it's become impenetrable and irredeemable." She brought her hand up and cupped his cheek, her eyes imploring. "To love is to be vulnerable. You'll never find love again if you keep your heart locked away."

"What you speak of is impossible," he murmured. "How does one move on from someone they loved so fiercely?"

Her eyes crinkled as she smiled. "You can't forget your past, or you forget the good times, as well. You must find the courage to let go of what you cannot change. It's the only way to move forward."

"I'm not ready to open my heart again, nor do I have a desire to ever marry," he admitted painfully.

Emma lowered her hand and leaned back. "Love isn't practical, and it's not meant to be easy. One day, your heart will be ready to love again, and it may come at the most inopportune moment. But you must be prepared."

"You should write for the society page." He chuckled. "How are you so wise in love?"

A playful glint came to her eyes. "I'm not, but I've read many books on the subject."

"Books?"

"Yes, and I believe in the immeasurable power of true love."

He huffed. "You mean fairy tales."

"No, I believe two people can fall so desperately in love with each other that they can create their own happily ever after."

Shifting away from her, he teased, "To think, I once considered you sane."

"Being sane is overrated, milord."

Laughing, he turned his head back towards the estate and saw the sun was starting to dip below the horizon. "I've enjoyed our time together, but I'm afraid I have some business I must attend to."

He rose and extended his hand towards her. "I shall call on you tomorrow to ensure you don't plan to sneak out of Caddington Manor."

"Perhaps I'll sneak out before you even arrive," she answered, accepting his assistance.

He gave her a lopsided grin. "You are a minx."

As he walked her back to the estate, Simeon realized that he'd been deceiving himself. Emma was most assuredly his friend, but she could be nothing more to him. His heart was impenetrable, and he could never risk the heartache associated with loving another. No matter how tempting the thought of it was.

Chapter Thirteen

Simeon stepped into his townhouse and was immediately greeted by his butler. "Evening, milord. Justice Ford and Officer Pembrooke are in your study."

"How long have they been waiting?"

"More than an hour."

Extending his top hat to him, Simeon said, "As usual, if you hear shouting coming from my study, please do not be overly concerned."

"I never am, milord," his butler replied, his lips twitching.

Simeon proceeded to his study and saw Justice Ford, the Bow Street magistrate, sitting in an armchair with a snifter in his hand. Pembrooke was sitting across from him with a frown on his face.

As he walked further into the room, the tall, aged Justice Ford huffed. "It's about time, Wentworth."

"I had a previous engagement," he stated, seeing no reason to expand on it.

Shifting in his seat, Pembrooke remarked, "No doubt it was with the beautiful Miss Pearson."

"If you must know, I had a meeting with Lord Downshire," he said, walking over to the drink cart. He decided to omit that he'd spent well over an hour with Miss Pearson in the gardens.

Justice Ford took a sip of his drink. "Lord Revett has demanded I issue a warrant for Miss Pearson's arrest."

"What?" Simeon roared. "Why would the House Secretary be interested in arresting Miss Pearson?"

"Technically, it's for a Mr. David Blackmore, but we both know who that truly is, don't we?" Justice Ford asked, raising his snifter towards him.

"How did you discover her identity?" he inquired.

"I have informants all over London, and a well-positioned one inside The Morning Post," the magistrate said. "It's only a matter of time before Lord Revett discovers her identity, as well."

Pouring two snifters of brandy, Simeon inquired, "Again, why does the House Secretary want Mr. Blackmore arrested?"

"Apparently, Mr. Blackmore submitted an article to The Morning Post, and it was picked up by the newspaper. It's running in tomorrow's papers, and it clearly details the atrocities the constables committed during the demonstration," the magistrate explained. "Furthermore, it paints Justice Keats in a bad light as the magistrate who issued the warrant for Hatcher's arrest, which we have since learned was under Lord Revett's direction."

Simeon put the lid back onto the decanter. "That still doesn't explain the call for her arrest."

"The article will no doubt rally support for the Anti-Corn Law rebels, and Lord Revett is attempting to squash the growing movement. The Tories don't want any more riots and civil unrest over the Corn Laws."

"Perhaps, then, they should recognize that the Corn Laws are hurting our people." Picking up the two snifters, Simeon walked over and extended one towards Pembrooke. "Besides, Lord Downshire would never allow his ward to be arrested."

"True, but Lord Revett doesn't know that Mr. David Blackmore is a pseudonym for Miss Pearson," Justice Ford confirmed. "At least, not yet."

Sitting down next to Pembrooke, he asked, "Is that why you're here? To inform me of the warrant?"

"No," Justice Ford said, placing his snifter on a table. "I've just come from meeting with an informant, and he's informed me that the Anti-Corn Law rebels are rapidly growing in numbers. The people are stirring because of the barbaric treatment at the last peaceful demonstration."

"As well as they should," Simeon remarked. "The constables treated the people unfairly."

"It's rumored that the Anti-Corn Law rebels are going to rally again, but this time, at Grange Gardens," the magistrate said.

Pembrooke sipped his drink. "I am not overly concerned. Grange Gardens, much like Ranelagh, is a luxurious pleasure garden and has always offered a myriad of entertainments in the form of musicales, fireworks, and balloon rides. Most people cannot afford the ticket prices to enter the gardens."

"I don't believe the Anti-Corn Law rebels intend to pay to gain entrance," Justice Ford drawled. "Most likely, they will descend upon the venue and fill the extensive walks, private arbors, and Chinese pavilions. They're trying to rally support for their cause, and they will overwhelm the pleasure garden."

Knitting his brow, Simeon commented, "Riots are occurring all over Britain in response to the passing of the Corn Laws. Why is Lord Revett targeting the Anti-Corn Law rebels?"

"Because they're more organized than the other groups," the magistrate explained. "They're also arguing for Parliamentary reform. Their numbers are vastly growing, and that is disconcerting to Parliament."

"They should be more concerned that people are starving because of the high cost of grain, famine, and chronic unemployment," Pembrooke muttered.

Justice Ford gave Pembrooke a stern look. "Need I remind you that we are officers of the law? We uphold the laws, regardless of our personal convictions."

"Understood, sir," Pembrooke said.

"I disagree," Simeon proclaimed, placing his empty snifter on the table.

"You what?" Justice Ford shouted.

Ignoring the magistrate's heated gaze, he pressed forward with his thought. "I'm beginning to see things differently, and I refuse to proceed blindly anymore. I have sat in the House of Lords and have heard both sides of the arguments. The Corn Laws only benefit the landowners, and not the people. I intend to become more vocal on the matter in Parliament."

"Are you quitting as a Bow Street Runner?" the magistrate asked.

"I intend to work this case."

"But after that?"

Running his hand over his chin thoughtfully, Simeon answered,

"I haven't thought it through completely yet. However, my priorities are beginning to shift."

"Is it because of the beautiful Miss Pearson?" Pembrooke asked innocently.

"Perhaps, but not in the way you're thinking," he answered honestly. "Miss Pearson and I are just friends, but she has offered me a unique perspective of my burdens."

Lowering his drink to his lap, Pembrooke inquired, "Why is Miss Pearson your friend, but I am not? We've worked together for nearly five years."

"Because I like Miss Pearson," he paused, "and I barely tolerate you."

Pembrooke chuckled. "Well said, Wentworth."

"You two are fools," Justice Ford said. "May we focus on the case?" When they both nodded, he continued. "We need to keep Miss Pearson safe until this warrant goes away."

"Agreed. Lord Downshire intends to move her to an undisclosed location," he shared.

"Good," the magistrate responded with a bob of his head. "And I want you both at Grange Gardens to help keep the peace during the rally." His eyes narrowed. "Do not engage the people unless they give you probable cause. We don't want another riot on our hands."

"Just to clarify," Pembrooke hesitated, smiling, "you would like me to work with Wentworth as partners on this case."

Justice Ford gave him an annoyed look. "Didn't I just say that?"

"I just wanted to hear it out loud," Pembrooke replied, giving Simeon a smug smile.

Simeon grunted. "I work better alone."

"That's rubbish," the magistrate contended. "Regardless, we need to keep a close eye on the Anti-Corn Law rebels and an even closer eye on Justice Keats and his barbaric constables."

"Understood," Simeon replied. "I wouldn't put it past them to do something underhanded again to stop the rally."

"Indeed." Justice Ford rose. "Now if you will excuse me, I'm afraid I have another pressing matter I must contend with." He tipped his head. "Evening, gentlemen."

After the magistrate left the room, Pembrooke turned towards

Simeon. "Would you care to join me at White's for supper and some drinks?"

"Thank you, but no." Simeon rose and walked over to his desk.

"You always say no," Pembrooke said. "It would be fun."

Looking down at the ledger and paperwork waiting for him on his desk, Simeon tapped his finger on top of the closed ledger. He was debating. He hadn't been to White's in years. But he had a lot of work to catch up on.

The image of Emma came to his mind. He would much rather spend the time with the charming Miss Pearson, but that was impossible. Perhaps he could do something that would please her.

"Why are you grinning like a bloody fool?" Pembrooke commented.

Wiping the grin off his face, Simeon glanced up from his books. "I have a letter I need to write."

"A letter?" Pembrooke asked, awkwardly standing. "And who is this letter to?"

"My family."

The sun was still low in the sky as Simeon rode in his coach towards Grange Gardens near Chester Square. He yawned as he leaned his head back against the plush bench. He'd spent most of the evening drafting a letter to his parents. Eventually, he wrote a simple, but sincere letter. He truly wanted to make amends with his parents, and he hoped they were receptive to the idea, as well.

The thought of telling Emma about posting the letter made him smile. Why did the mere thought of seeing her smile cause his heart to soar? She was quickly filling a void in his heart; a void he'd thought was impenetrable.

Is that wise, he wondered. Would his heart ever recover if Emma didn't feel the same about him? He already knew the answer. No. Perhaps it would be best if he cut ties with Emma now. It would be much easier.

The coach came to a stop, and he lifted the curtain covering the window. He peered out and saw men and women flocking towards Grange Gardens. There were so many protestors that they practically encircled the coach, hampering any chance of forward progression. Putting his hand through the open window, he unlatched the door.

"I'll walk the rest of the way," he announced, stepping down onto the worn cobblestone.

The driver tipped his head in acknowledgement. "Very good, milord. I shall wait for you out front."

Joining the hordes of protestors as they walked towards the gardens, he was grateful that he'd chosen to wear a brown waistcoat over a worn, white shirt and boots that had holes along the top, allowing him to blend in. He approached the iron gates of the pleasure gardens and saw that patrons were pushing through the ticket gate, ignoring the pleas of the workers to pay the two shillings and sixpence entrance fee. A fee that would be too great for most of these patrons.

Simeon filed through the gates and was stunned to find the garden was already filled to capacity. Based upon the appearances of the protestors, it was clear that they came from all walks of life. Some were sharply dressed in riding jackets, whereas others were dressed in dirtied shirts with rolled-up sleeves. But they were all here with one purpose in mind, to voice their disapproval of the Corn Laws.

Simeon's eyes scanned over the gardens, briefly admiring the Rocco style. They featured a Chinese Pavilion, as well as several walks and a lake. A tethered, red-striped, oval balloon, with an attached wicker basket, was being showcased near the front of the north lawn. It was roughly seventy feet high and forty feet in diameter. The balloon's wicker basket hovered barely over the lawn. It was a spectacular sight to behold, and people were lined up to admire it.

As he waded through the hordes of people, he heard his name being shouted over the din. "Martin!"

Turning, Simeon saw Pembrooke pushing through the crowd to meet up with him. He waited until Pembrooke came closer before saying, "Any signs of sabotage?"

Pembrooke shook his head. "None. I have searched the surrounding area and didn't find anything Lord Revett might use to dissuade the protestors."

Laura Beers

Simeon's eyes scanned the overcrowded lawn. Many of the protestors were forced inside of the Chinese Pavilion because the pathways were filled.

"Where are the constables?" he asked.

"I have no doubt that they're here, but they have yet to make themselves known."

Speaking loudly to be heard over the crowd, Simeon asked, "There are thousands of people here to protest the Corn Laws, so why hasn't the militia been called out?"

"Indeed. Why do you suppose that is?"

"We're missing a piece of the puzzle here." Simeon frowned. "Spread out. Analyze everything."

For the next short while, Simeon looked under every hedge bush, in every grove, and he even entered the Chinese Pavilion. However, nothing seemed out of place or suspicious. Could Lord Revett truly be allowing these protestors to meet uncontested to voice their displeasure of the Corn Laws? His instinct told him no.

He made his way back towards the north lawn and looked over at the tethered balloon. It was floating in the sky because it was filled with hydrogen gas. A terrible realization occurred to him. Hydrogen is flammable. Could that be Revett's plan? No, not even the cruelest person would turn a balloon into a bomb.

Pushing his way through the crowds, he finally reached the front of the lawn where people were shielding their eyes as they looked up to admire the balloon. Simeon's eyes scanned it, but nothing appeared out of place, until he stepped closer to the wicker basket and saw four barrels, tied with rope. His heart dropped. Barrels with rope were used to store gunpowder. This balloon was a bomb!

"Everyone move back!" he shouted at the crowd. "It's a bomb!"

A few of the women gasped, but a bulky man quickly stepped forward and corrected him. "It isn't a bomb. It's a balloon held up by hydrogen."

Simeon placed his hand on the side of the basket. "There are barrels of gunpowder in the basket. One spark will ignite this balloon into a bomb of epic proportions."

The bulky man shook his head. "The barrels are used to store equipment, nothing more."

159

He didn't have time for this. If a spark hit that gunpowder, it would kill everyone in the immediate area. Thousands would be killed.

Straightening himself to his full height, he declared, "I assure you that I know what I am speaking of. I am a Bow Street Runner."

The man stepped closer to him, and his eyes were filled with disdain. "Why should we take the word of a Bow Street Runner? You are against our cause. For all we know, this could be a trick to break up our protest."

"No, I assure you that I support your cause," he replied as all eyes landed on him. "Will you take the word of a viscount?"

"It depends," the man said cautiously.

"My name is Lord Wentworth, and I plan to fight for your rights in Parliament. The Corn Laws punish the poor and defenseless."

"If what you are saying is true, then why did you allow it to pass?" the man exclaimed, earning cheers from people behind him.

"I am just one man against hundreds in Parliament. But I vow to take a more active role in the House of Lords," he proclaimed. "However, now is not the time to debate it. We must evacuate Grange Gardens... *now!*"

The bulky man bobbed his head. "I'm going to hold you to your word, Lord Wentworth." He turned to the protestors and shouted, "We found a bomb! Get out!"

Panic set in on the group as people started running towards the entrance gate. As the area around the balloon started to dissipate, Simeon could see Constable Stone in the cover of the trees about thirty yards off with a flaming arrow.

If Stone caused the gunpowder to go off, it would still kill hundreds of people still waiting to evacuate. He pulled out his pistol but realized if he tried to shoot him this close to the gunpowder, it might ignite it as well.

He watched helplessly as Stone released the flaming arrow, but to his relief, it sailed past the balloon's basket. He broke into a run, hoping to stop Stone from releasing another arrow. Unfortunately, by the time he reached the man, another arrow was nocked in the string, and he had it pulled back.

Simeon brought up his pistol and pointed it at him. "Put down the arrow," he ordered.

Stone laughed cruelly. "You won't shoot me."

"I daresay you are underestimating me."

"Not as long as I have this arrow nocked," he stated. "My next arrow will hit the basket and all these pitiful protestors will be killed. The Anti-Corn Law rebels will be no more."

Keeping his pistol trained on Stone's cold heart, Simeon attempted to reason with him again. "You're wrong. The voice of the people will be made known. You cannot silence them with an act of violence."

"You're such a disappointment as a Bow Street Runner," Stone growled. "You're supposed to uphold the law, not argue against it."

His lips parted in disbelief at the hypocrisy of that statement. "Are you mad? You intend to blow up innocent men and women because they are protesting a law that's causing them to starve?"

"I'm doing what I'm ordered to do," Stone exclaimed. "I am squashing this rebellion."

Simeon shook his head. "It's not a rebellion. It's the start of something great."

"You're deceiving yourself, Runner," Stone scoffed.

Putting his hands up, Simeon shouted, "There is no reason to release that arrow! The rally is over! The people are fleeing as we speak."

Stone's eyes shifted towards the exit where hundreds were still anxiously attempting to exit the iron gates.

"Who ordered you to do this?" Simeon demanded.

In response, Stone gave him a sadistic smile as he released the arrow.

Turning his head, Simeon saw the flaming arrow hit the wicker basket. "What have you done?" he exclaimed. "You will kill hundreds, if not thousands!"

Stone's voice was hard, unyielding. "Now it's your turn."

Simeon turned around to see that Stone was now holding a pistol in his hand, and it was aimed at his chest.

Chapter Fourteen

Emma had just stepped into the dining room when she heard Luke shout, "Well done, Emma! Your article made The Morning Post."

"Congratulations," Rachel said at the same moment.

Her steps faltered. "It did?"

"And these two letters were delivered this morning for you," Luke said, extending the missives to her.

Emma eagerly accepted the letters and sat down next to Rachel.

As she tore open the first envelope from the editor at the newspaper, Rachel reached over and placed her hand on her sleeve. "We're so proud of you. I knew the paper would accept your article."

"I had my doubts," she replied honestly.

"You should never doubt yourself, Emma. You are far too clever for your own good," Luke remarked from the head of the table.

"Thank you," she murmured as she removed the letter and a five-pound note.

Taking a moment to read the missive, she couldn't help but let out a squeal of excitement. She brought her gaze back up to Luke and Rachel.

"The editor was so impressed with my article that he has asked me to write three subsequent articles on the Anti-Corn Law rebels," she reported. "He's even offered to pay me £5 per article." She brought the letter to her chest. "Can you imagine £5 an article?"

"That's an impressive sum," Luke replied. "The editor might even be willing to pay more per article. Would you like me to negotiate a higher price for you?"

A laugh escaped her lips. "No, I consider £5 to be more than an adequate sum."

"As do I," Rachel said.

Feeling overwhelmed with joy, Emma brought the letter and placed it on the table. "The editor also informed me that they received a tip about a rally for the Anti-Corn Law rebels at Grange Gardens this morning." She looked over at Luke. "May I attend, since it's only a few blocks away?"

"Absolutely not," he replied decisively. "A rally is not appropriate for…"

"…for a young woman such as myself," she said, finishing his thought for him. "I understand."

"What's in the other note?" Rachel asked, glancing at the other white envelope on the table.

"In all the excitement, I almost forgot about the other letter," Emma remarked, picking it up and tearing the top of the envelope off.

She unfolded the one piece of paper and started reading it, her joy being replaced by horror with each word. It wasn't a missive; it was a threat from Peter. More accurately, a very detailed set of threats.

"Whatever is wrong, my dear?" Rachel asked, her voice sounding very far away. "You're growing increasingly pale."

She heard Luke push back his chair, and the next moment, he ripped the letter from her clenched hand. He read:

"You are not as safe as you think you are. I see you reading in your bedchamber, and I have watched you sleep from your window. You belong to me, and I will punish you for…"

His voice trailed off, but he continued reading silently.

Luke turned towards a footman and shouted, "Go and retrieve the bloody constable. *Now!*" He turned to another footman. "I want my coach prepared and waiting out front. *Move!*"

Emma's hand was still shaking as she reached for her teacup. "Why is Peter tormenting me?"

Slipping the note into his jacket pocket, Luke declared, "We are leaving for Eliza's townhouse *immediately*. She will keep you safe."

"How is that possible? She is increasing with child!" she asked in dismay.

It was obvious that Eliza was involved in the Crown's affairs, but how could a pregnant marchioness keep her safe?

Luke pulled back her chair. "If not Eliza, then I can assure you that Benedict, Adrien, Jonathon, and Larson can keep you safe. They will protect you against Peter."

Turning to look up at him, Emma said, "But I don't want to put anyone else at risk."

Rachel smiled reassuringly at her. "Don't fret. The most important thing is keeping you safe now."

"Perhaps it would be best if we sent a missive to Simeon…"

Luke spoke over her. "Absolutely not. I will personally escort you to Eliza's townhouse. She was expecting you later today, anyway."

Emma nibbled her bottom lip. "Would it be possible to send Simeon a note to let him know I'm safe?"

"Emma," Luke huffed, "Simeon won't be able to protect you like the men in the Beckett family can. I have seen these men in action."

"True, but…" Her words trailed off. Emma didn't know why she wanted to write a letter to Simeon, but she thought it would be a good idea to let him know that she was all right. At least, she hoped he cared enough to want to know that she was in a safe place.

Rachel gave her a knowing look and shifted towards Luke. "Why don't you go make the arrangements to depart? I would like a moment to speak to Emma alone."

"As you wish." Luke leaned down and kissed his wife's cheek. "But your woman talk must be brief. The only way to keep Emma safe is to deliver her to Eliza's."

Emma watched as Luke departed from the room, closing the door behind him.

"May I ask why you are so insistent on writing a note to Simeon?" Rachel asked with an uplifted brow.

She shrugged one shoulder. "I don't rightly know."

"Could it be that you have developed feelings for your protector?"

Turning her gaze towards the window, Emma said, "It's ridiculous, really. He's in love with another."

A moment of silence descended over them before Rachel asked, "Is it Martha?"

Emma nodded, reluctantly. "How did you know?"

"Martha is one of my dearest friends, and is married to my cousin," Rachel pointed out. "Besides, she is Matthew's godmother. I know of her past, including Simeon."

"Simeon said they were betrothed, but she disappeared when he went to secure a special license. He searched for her for five years," she explained. "Even if I have developed feelings for him, it wouldn't matter. Simeon's heart still mourns her loss."

Rachel leaned closer to her. "I've seen the way Simeon looks at you. It's not the way a friend looks at another."

"He says we aren't friends," she admitted softly.

"Do you believe that?"

She shook her head. "No, but he's afraid to admit it."

"It's been my experience that love can soften the hardest soul and heal the wounds of the broken heart," Rachel replied encouragingly.

"But we don't love each other," Emma argued.

Rachel gave her a smug smile. "Don't you?"

"I couldn't possibly... no, that's impossible..." Her words trailed off. "Do I?"

Before Rachel could respond, Luke pushed the door open. "It's time to depart, Emma. Your trunks are being packed, and they will be delivered later this afternoon."

Both women rose, and Rachel gave her a tight embrace. "Be safe, Emma. I will write a missive to Simeon and inform him that you're safe," Rachel said, stepping back.

"Thank you, Rachel," she murmured.

Within a few moments, Luke had whisked her away in his crested coach to Portman Square.

She glanced out the window at the four-armed footmen riding next to the coach. "Are ten footmen truly necessary to escort me to Eliza's townhouse?"

"Yes," Luke answered quickly. "Eight armed footmen and the

drivers."

"But it is only an eight-minute ride by coach…" Her voice stopped when the coach came to a jerking stop, causing her to lurch forward, and the sound of discharging pistols erupted from outside of the coach.

Luke reached under the bench and removed two pistols from an iron box. "Whatever happens Emma, you must stay in the coach." He extended her an overcoat pistol. "I understand you know how to use this?"

"I do," she replied.

"Keep it on your person," he urged.

The discharging pistols stopped, and a deafening silence followed. A moment later, the coach door was wrenched open, and Peter Lockhart appeared, pointing a pistol towards Luke's chest.

"Hello, darling. I've missed you," Peter said sweetly as his eyes shifted towards her.

"You have no right to talk to her." Luke held up the pistol and pointed it at Peter. "Put down your weapon."

Peter shrugged and lowered his weapon. "I'm more than happy to comply, but I have fifteen armed mercenaries out here that won't listen. You may want to put down *your* pistol or they'll start killing your footmen… at least, the ones that are still alive." He smirked cruelly as he tucked the pistol into the waistband of his trousers.

Taking advantage of Peter being distracted, Emma slid her pistol into the pocket of her white gown.

Luke placed his gun on the bench. "I am willing to pay whatever amount you think is fair to keep Emma safe," he proclaimed, his jaw clenched.

"You don't have to worry about Emma anymore," Peter said. "We are to be wed."

"No, we are not," she replied defiantly. "I refuse to marry you."

"You don't have a choice," Peter declared.

"Peter…" Her words stopped when Peter reached in and grabbed Luke by the lapels of his jacket, tossing him out of the coach.

"Luke!" she shouted as she climbed out of the carriage.

She'd barely set a foot on the ground when she froze at the scene in front of her, completely taken aback by the dead bodies of the liveried footmen surrounding the coach. They were sprawled out, their void eyes staring back at her. A loud grunt of pain brought her back into the present, and she turned to see two ruffians holding Luke by the arms as Peter repeatedly hit him in the face.

"Stop, Peter!" she shouted, running up to him.

To her surprise, Peter turned and slapped her hard across the face. She crumpled to the ground.

"Don't get involved in my business, woman," he snarled. "Downshire took you from me and it's time he gets what he deserves."

Placing her hand to her burning cheek, Emma shouted, "He didn't take you from me, I chose to leave!"

"Yes, and I will deal with you later," Peter remarked, removing the pistol from his waistband. "But first, I must kill him."

"No!" Emma shouted, jumping up and running to stand in front of Luke. "Don't kill him. Please!"

Peter kept the pistol pointed at her. "Step out of the way, Emma."

"Never!" She glanced over her shoulder at Luke's bruised and bloodied face, and she knew what she had to do to keep him safe. Turning back to face Peter, she declared, "I will come with you!"

"Please, Emma," Luke whispered from behind her. "Don't worry about me. Just run from here."

Ignoring his plea, Emma squared her shoulders. "If you kill Luke," she said, her voice stronger than she thought possible, "I will never stop trying to escape. I will never stop fighting you. But if you allow him to live, I will come with you... willingly."

Peter seemed to consider her response, his pistol wavering. "Do you mean that?"

"I do," she replied, nodding. "I give you my word. Please, just don't kill him."

"All right," Peter said, lowering his weapon. He pointed towards a coach in front of Luke's coach, blocking it in. "After you, my love."

Emma turned around and threw her arms around Luke's neck, ignoring the two thugs restraining him. "Thank you for everything. I love you."

"Don't do this, Emma," Luke pleaded again. "Just run. I'll be fine."

Releasing him, she stepped back. "Tell Rachel that I love her." She walked reluctantly towards the coach and accepted Peter's assistance. She glanced over her shoulder, knowing she was making the right choice. She needed to keep Luke safe. This was her fault, not his.

Once she was situated, Peter sat across from her and closed the curtain over the window. "That was most exciting, was it not, my dear?"

"I think not," Emma muttered.

The sound of the pistol discharging could be heard as the coach started moving. Her heart lurched at the noise. "NO!" she exclaimed, lunging for the carriage door.

Peter grabbed her and tossed her back against the bench.

"It's best not to witness such atrocities," Peter commented, completely unphased.

"Did they kill Luke?" she demanded, her chest heaving with anger.

"Of course," he answered as his lips twitched. "I couldn't very well leave any witnesses behind."

"But you promised!" she cried as she lunged at him.

Peter caught her arms and held her close. "Frankly, my dear, my word doesn't mean much," he crooned.

Tears streamed down her cheeks. "Why are you doing this, Peter?"

"I told you," he said, shoving her back against the bench. "You belong to me."

"Never," she responded. "I belong to no one."

He chuckled. "Your spunk is adorable, but in time, you will learn respect."

"How could you?" she sobbed. "Luke was my guardian. My friend."

"No, he kept you from me and deserved to be punished."

Wiping the tears streaming down her face, Emma lowered her gaze away from the man she once considered a friend. He had killed Luke. He had promised her that he would let Luke live, but he'd broken his promise, which meant that she was free to break hers, as well. And she would. She would never stop trying to escape Peter's evil clutches.

Simeon let out a deep sigh as he saw Stone holding a pistol at his chest. If the gunpowder was detonated from the heat of the flaming arrow, then they were still well within the blast range.

"We don't have time for this," he declared loudly as he calculated the exact time it would take to reach for the gun in the waistband of his trousers.

Stone cocked the pistol. "I assure you that I do have time to kill you."

"Possibly," he replied, "but when that wicker basket catches on fire, it will be too late for both of us."

Simeon glanced over his shoulder and saw that the fire was just starting to spread along the length of the wicker basket.

"Before you pull the trigger," he tried again, "who gave you the order to blow up Grange Gardens?"

He could see the indecision on Stone's face.

"Lord Revett told us to stop the growing skirmish," Stone finally answered, "by any means necessary."

"By killing thousands of people?" Simeon asked. "That was your plan?"

Stone sneered. "No, I'm..." His gaze shifted to over Simeon's shoulder. "What the devil is that man doing?"

Looking over his shoulder, he saw Pembrooke dumping a bucket of water onto the basket, dousing the flame. He took advantage of the distraction to remove his pistol and turned back to face Stone.

"You're under arrest," Simeon declared, pointing his pistol at Stone's chest. "Drop your weapon."

Stone's eyes narrowed as he shouted, "Never!"

The moment Stone's finger twitched on the trigger, Simeon discharged his pistol, hitting Stone in the chest. With a loud grunt, Stone toppled down to the ground.

Pembrooke ran up and stood next to him. "The fire is out. I

doused the gunpowder barrels with water as a precaution."

"Good thinking. That will prevent them from igniting," he remarked.

The roar of multiple gunshots went off in the distance.

"What the blazes was that?" Pembrooke asked.

Simeon turned his head towards the noise. "I don't know, but it sounded like it came from a few blocks away."

They took off sprinting and didn't stop until they arrived at the ghastly scene, causing their steps to falter. Bodies were strewn along the ground, and a growing crowd was on the pavement, whispering and pointing in fascination. A few men were assisting the wounded to stand as they moaned in pain.

They approached cautiously until they saw a bruised and bloodied Lord Downshire standing over two bodies with a pistol in his hand.

"What happened?" Simeon shouted as he headed towards the marquess.

Downshire tucked the pistol into his waistband and wiped the blood off his face with the sleeve of his shirt.

"These imbeciles were no match for me." He turned his head towards the coach as he cradled his left arm in his right hand. "I don't suppose you know how to drive a coach?" he asked.

"I do. I worked undercover as a driver for an earl a few years back," Simeon replied. "But first, what the devil happened here?"

A pained look came over Downshire's expression. "Peter abducted Emma."

"Lockhart did this?" Simeon roared.

"He did. We were ambushed, and Emma sacrificed herself to save me," Downshire explained, wincing. "But Lockhart had no intention of letting me live. He waited until his coach pulled away before his men tried to kill me. It bought me enough time to formulate a plan."

"Which was?"

"My plan was quite brilliant really. To overpower the men and avoid getting killed," Downshire huffed.

Simeon pointed towards Downshire's cradled left arm. "You're injured."

"It is nothing," the marquess admitted. "I'll send for a doctor later."

Glancing up the street, Simeon asked, "Which way did they go?"

"That way," Downshire said, pointing towards a side street.

Simeon turned towards Pembrooke. "You reported earlier that Lockhart's residence is unknown," he started, "but that's when we were looking in London. He probably secured a house nearby that would allow his guards to go unnoticed. My guess is in the woods."

"For what purpose?"

"He knows that by abducting Emma, and killing a marquess, he's going to get a lot of attention, and the Sheriff of London will hunt him down personally," Simeon explained. "He would want to lie low for a few weeks until it's safe to travel on the roads again."

"Agreed," Pembrooke said. "I'll look through bills of sale and see if I can find anything suspicious." He turned his gaze towards Luke. "I would be happy to call a doctor for you."

"Not necessary. I'm sure Eliza will send for one once she sees me," Downshire responded as he walked over to the coach.

Simeon followed him and climbed up onto the driver's box. "If you discover any additional information, please send it to Lord Lansdowne's residence."

"Perhaps it would be best if we reported this incident to Justice Ford before we proceed," Pembrooke suggested.

"Good idea," Simeon said, reaching for the reins. "You report this to Justice Ford, and I'll drive Downshire to his sister's house."

Without waiting for Pembrooke to say another word, he urged the horses into a run and didn't stop until they pulled up in front of Eliza's townhouse.

Two footmen exited the main door and came to secure the coach as Simeon and Downshire jumped down and ran inside.

"Eliza!" Downshire shouted, his voice echoing off the floors of the marble entrance hall. "Where in the blazes are you?"

Benedict stepped out from the drawing room with his daughter, Caroline, in his arms. "What happened to you, Luke?"

"Lockhart abducted Emma," Simeon answered.

Eliza's steady voice came from the top of the stairs. "When?"

"About twenty minutes ago," Downshire shared.

Placing her hand on her increasing stomach, Eliza turned towards a footman stationed at the bottom of the stairs and ordered, "Go inform Lord Camden that his presence is requested in our drawing room immediately."

To Simeon's surprise, the footman ran up the stairs to the second landing to do her bidding. His expression must have given away his curiosity because Eliza shared, "Adrien was gracious enough to add a door on the second landing between our two townhouses."

"Interesting," he muttered.

"Adrien is a bloody nuisance at times," Benedict said, his tone holding only mirth, "but the door has proven useful on multiple occasions."

A maid approached Benedict and announced, "It's time for her nap, milord."

Benedict kissed his daughter on the cheek and handed her off to the maid.

The maid walked Caroline up to Eliza, who had just stepped down from the last stair, and she also kissed her daughter on the cheek. "I love you," she whispered. Then her tone grew alert as she turned her gaze towards the group. "Follow me to the drawing room. We have much to discuss."

Following Eliza into the drawing room, Simeon waited until she lowered herself down onto a velvet settee before he sat across from her. Downshire walked over to the drink cart and poured himself a drink. After he downed it, he poured himself another.

Holding the glass in his hand, Downshire started, "Lockhart ambushed us, killing some of my footmen, and almost killing me. But Emma stepped in front of me and pled for my life. She sacrificed herself to save me, but Lockhart has no honor and intended to kill me all along."

The sound of pounding footsteps on the marble floor alerted them to Camden's arrival. He ran into the drawing room. "What's the emergency?" he asked in between deep breaths.

"Lockhart abducted Emma," Benedict shared.

Camden's eyes grew alert. "What's the plan?"

Simeon spoke up. "We don't know where Lockhart is."

"Since he intends to wed Emma, he could very well be traveling towards Gretna Greens," Eliza surmised.

"True, but I'm still under the mindset that Lockhart won't dare travel on the roads for fear the Sheriff of London might overtake him," Simeon shared.

Downshire brought the snifter up to his lips. "If I had known Lockhart was capable of such dreadful actions, I would never have brought my family to London for the Season. This is all my fault."

"No," Eliza said, with a shake of her head, "this is Lockhart's fault. But he made a mistake."

"What is that?" Downshire asked.

Adrien smirked. "Lockhart has no idea who he's up against."

"True," Downshire admitted. "He is no match for agents of the Crown, especially of your caliber."

Simeon cleared his throat. "And a Bow Street Runner."

"Yes... uh... you, as well," Downshire acknowledged with a look of pity.

Eliza smiled kindly at him. "We will get Emma back, Simeon. Do not fret."

Downshire glanced between Eliza and Simeon with a baffled expression on his face. "Why are you informing Simeon of that fact? You should be comforting me."

With a light laugh, Eliza replied, "You are quite oblivious to certain things, brother."

"What are you speaking of?" Downshire asked, wincing as he cradled his left arm.

"Never mind," she remarked, "you're injured."

Downshire grimaced. "It's merely a flesh wound."

"Should we call for a doctor?" Eliza asked.

"Not necessary," Downshire said. "We need to focus on the task at hand. We don't know where Lockhart took Emma."

"We do not, but Uncle Charles did send over a file this morning with some rather telling information," Benedict said, walking over to the desk and grabbing a file. "We were going to inform you of this interesting turn of events when you arrived with Emma."

"Which was?" Simeon asked.

Benedict opened the file. "A man named Daniel Booth has been depositing £75 each month into Lockhart's account on behalf of Sir

Alymer Blackmore…" He paused, looking around. "Blackmore is Emma's grandfather."

"What?" Luke roared. "Impossible. Both sets of her grandparents are deceased."

"That's what everyone believed. However, Uncle Charles sent agents to question Sir Alymer about the payments, and that's when they discovered the truth," Benedict shared.

"Why was that kept from Emma?" Adrien inquired.

"Sir Alymer informed us that Emma's mother was disowned after she chose to marry Constable Pearson, and they lost contact until Lockhart sent him a missive informing him of his daughter's death," Benedict explained. "Then, Lockhart requested on behalf of Constable Pearson that Sir Alymer pay for boarding school for Emma. In hopes of reconciling with his granddaughter, Sir Alymer sent over £75 each month to be given in support of Emma."

"If I had to guess, Constable Pearson knew nothing of those payments," Adrien commented.

"That would be my guess, as well," Benedict said. "About two months ago, Sir Alymer demanded Lockhart to produce Emma when he discovered that Constable Pearson had died two years prior. It was his intention to present Emma for the Season."

Simeon frowned. "Was Sir Alymer not aware that Emma was Lord Downshire's ward?"

"No, he was never informed," Benedict said, reading a paper. "However, that's when Lockhart informed Sir Alymer that he and Emma had eloped, and he requested her dowry."

"How much was Emma's dowry?" Adrien inquired.

"£15,000 pounds," Benedict answered.

Downshire huffed, "That's a paltry sum. I'm offering £25,000 as Emma's dowry."

"Regardless, Emma does have a living grandfather that we must consider now," Eliza commented.

"Absolutely not," Downshire said. "Emma is my ward. She belongs in *our* family."

"Don't get jealous," Eliza chastised. "Shouldn't we rejoice that there are more people to love her?"

"I suppose so," he mumbled.

Simeon rose from his chair and walked over to the window. "All this time, Lockhart has been plotting to make Emma his in order to claim her inheritance. Do you think he might kill her once she's served her purpose?"

"I don't know, but we'll save her before that happens," Adrien assured him.

"How? We don't even know where she is," Simeon said dejectedly. "We've failed to keep her safe."

Adrien headed towards the drink cart and poured two drinks. He walked back and extended a snifter towards him. "Don't give up hope. We'll get Emma back."

"I have experienced your plans firsthand," Simeon said, accepting the snifter, "and they're dreadful."

Adrien brought the snifter up to his lips. "They've always worked though, haven't they?"

"True," Simeon reluctantly agreed as he took a sip of his drink.

"You care for the girl," Adrien stated in a low tone.

He nodded. "I do."

"I suspected as much." Adrien took a sip of his drink. "But if you hurt Emma, I will personally kill you in the most excruciating way possible."

Simeon swirled the brandy in his hand. "It matters not. I said I cared for Emma, but I never said she returned my affections."

"You didn't have to," Adrien remarked. "Don't think for one moment that we weren't following you to ensure Emma was being properly protected."

"You were following me?"

Adrien shrugged. "If it helps, we never had to intervene."

Glancing over at Luke, Simeon lowered his voice. "Did Emma give any indication she may favor me?"

Adrien chuckled. "Perhaps."

"I hate waiting," Downshire growled from next to the drink cart.

"Finally, something you and I agree upon," Simeon said, bringing the snifter up to his lips.

Chapter Fifteen

The coach jerked to a stop as Emma glanced out the carriage's window to see a dilapidated cottage in the middle of the woods. The two-level cottage had a thatched roof, and the windows on the first level were boarded up.

"Welcome home, my dear," Peter said in a teasing tone.

"This is home?"

Lockhart chuckled. "It's a temporary home, just until the law stops looking for us."

"You killed the Marquess of Downshire," Emma declared, tears filling her eyes. "I cannot wait to see you hang."

An annoyed look flickered across Peter's face. "I killed Lord Downshire for *us*."

"For us?" she repeated with a look of exasperation.

"Lord Downshire had designs on you, and he would never have let you go," he explained.

Emma pressed her lips together, attempting to hold back her disdain. "Lord Downshire welcomed me into his family. He loved me and cared for me as my guardian. He had no secret agenda for me."

"You are naïve to the ways of men," Peter said, shaking his head. "Eventually, he would have made you his mistress."

"No, he was happily married to Rachel."

"Love fades," he declared dismissively.

She tilted her chin defiantly. "No, real love grows and deepens over time."

"Oh, my dear," he scoffed. "It's a good thing I came along when I did. Your head is filled with utter nonsense."

The door to the carriage opened, and Peter exited. He turned back and offered his hand. Emma glanced down at it, but she didn't accept it. She didn't want to accept any kind of help from him.

In one swift motion, Peter reached in, grabbed her arm, and yanked her out of the carriage. He waited until her feet were steady before he let go.

"I tire of your disobedience," he hissed. "You will respect me."

"Respect needs to be earned," she contended.

"As your husband…"

She swiped her hand in front of her. "I will *never* marry you."

Pulling his hand back, Peter slapped her hard across the face. "We will be wed as soon as possible."

"No," she countered, bringing her hand up to her reddening cheek. "I won't marry you."

Peter brought his hand back up to strike her again, but then it froze as his eyes scanned the thugs waiting outside of the cottage. Slowly, he brought his hand back down.

"I don't want to fight with you now, my dear," he said calmly. "Behave, and I won't have to teach you a lesson later." Grabbing her arm, he forced her towards the door. "I think it would be best if we continued this conversation in our bedchamber, don't you?"

"Our bedchamber?" she asked, her steps faltering.

"Of course. We are betrothed, after all." He gripped her arm tighter and dragged her towards the door. "Why wouldn't we share a bedchamber?"

"Please, Peter," she pleaded. "Don't do this."

"You were promised to me," Peter replied as they stepped inside the darkened cottage.

Emma wanted to cry at the pain of Peter's fingers digging into her skin, but she wouldn't give him the satisfaction of knowing he was hurting her.

"My father never promised me to you," she attempted. "At least, he never told me that."

"After you left boarding school to come take care of your father," Peter answered as he led her towards the narrow stairs, "he was in no condition to carry on a conversation with you. He was already too far gone."

"I wish I'd arrived sooner to care for him," she remarked. "On my last holiday, my father was in perfect health, but his health declined so rapidly."

"It was a crying shame, but it was for the best," Peter said.

"For the best?" she contended. "How can you say something so horrible?"

"It's merely a fact." Peter continued to lead her down the hall towards a back room. "Your father was against change."

"What kind of change are you referring to?"

He opened the door, causing the hinges to squeak in protest.

"Your land is rich with resources," he replied, pushing her through the door, "but your father refused to sell it to me. He said that it had been in your family for generations."

"Why would my father ever sell you our land?" Emma asked in disbelief as she glanced around the bedchamber with a dilapidated four-poster bed and a well-worn dressing table in the corner.

"Because, my dear, I had bought up the surrounding areas for a cheap price and sold them for a sizable profit to Rowe Chalk," he explained, releasing her arm. "They promptly created an extensive channel of chalk quarries."

Emma took a few steps backwards, creating more distance between them. "Chalk quarries?"

"Yes, but Rowe Chalk wanted your property, because it contains a hard chalk known as Totternhoe stone."

"I will never sell my land to you," she declared, swiping her hand in front of her again.

He took a step closer to her, causing her to take two steps back. "I assumed as much, but it won't make a difference once we're married. The land will become mine." He gave her a smug smile. "But you are worth so much more than the land, Emma."

"I beg your pardon?"

He widened his stance and crossed his arms over his broad chest. "Your mother was the daughter of a powerful man, but she was disowned when she ran off to marry your father."

"I wasn't aware of that," she said, confused. "My family never spoke of my mother's past."

"Your mother turned her back on her family, leaving a fortune behind."

"A fortune?" Emma frowned. "How do you know all of this?"

Peter uncrossed his arms, then shook his head as if she was a simpleton. "When your mother was sick, she asked to speak to me as her solicitor. She had a small inheritance she wanted to be willed to you."

"But I know nothing of an inheritance."

"Sadly, that money is spent," Peter revealed.

"Pardon?"

Lockhart gave her a baffled look. "After you left me, I was forced to drain the coffers while I watched over you."

"You used *my* inheritance to watch over me?"

He closed the distance between them and placed his hand on her forearm. "It doesn't matter. The money was meant for us."

"No, it was meant for *me*," she pressed, stepping away from him.

"You're wrong. Once we marry, that money would have belonged to me, anyway." He took a step closer to her. "Regardless, did you not ever consider who paid for your fancy boarding school?"

"My father paid for it," she replied, walking over to the broken window, still trying to create distance between them.

He shook his head. "Your father couldn't afford the high tuition cost."

"If my father didn't pay for my boarding school, then who did?" she asked, her voice rising.

Walking over to the bed, Peter sat down. "Your grandfather did."

"My grandparents are dead."

"Your mother's father is alive," he declared.

"My grandfather is still alive?" Emma's mouth gaped. "That's impossible."

"No, your grandfather is Sir Alymer Blackmore, and he is one of the most powerful landowners in Bath," Peter informed her. "He was devastated to hear that your mother passed away and sent money every month for your care."

"Why didn't my father say anything?" she asked, leaning back on the sill for support.

"Your father never knew," Peter said. "Your father was under the impression that his investments paid for your boarding school."

Furrowing her brows, she questioned, "I don't understand. Why the secrecy?"

"Your father hated your grandfather and refused to initiate any contact between you and him," Peter explained. "However, David met with your grandfather on a few occasions."

"David did?" How could David keep that secret from her? Her family should have told her that her grandfather was still alive.

"He did," Peter confirmed.

"I should have been told," she stated firmly.

Peter bobbed his head. "I agree. I argued that point with your father, but he refused to see reason."

"You argued with my father?"

"Indeed. Your father was a vexing man, and I found his faulty logic to be quite idiotic," Peter said, his voice rising in indignation. "He accused me of some horrible things, but he got what was coming to him in the end."

"What did he get?" she asked, suddenly more afraid than before.

He sneered. "A painful death."

Emma shook her head, trying to sort out what Peter had said, and what he didn't say. Did Peter have a hand in her father's death? But that was impossible. Her father had died from dysentery. Feeling bold, she knew there was only one way to find out. Meeting his gaze, she asked him directly, "Did you kill my father?"

Peter considered her for a moment, then revealed, "I did, but it was for us, my dear."

Her mouth dropped open. "You killed my father!" she exclaimed, her voice becoming shrill. "How could you?"

"It was easy, actually. I placed arsenic into his sugar bowl," Peter informed her, all-too-casually.

"You are a monster!" she cried as tears filled her eyes.

"Now you're just being irrational," Peter chided. "In time, you'll see I did what I had to do to keep us together."

Wrapping her arms around her waist, Emma responded, "No, I will not. You're mad."

Peter frowned. "You and I were always meant to be together, but your father told me to stay away from you..."

"I thought he gave you his blessing?" she interjected.

"He did," Peter pressed, "but we had a difference of opinion towards the end."

Finished with this horrible conversation, Emma turned her head towards the window, hoping that Simeon would find her in time. She had no doubt that he would search for her, but would it be too late?

"No one is coming to rescue you," Peter said, as if reading her thoughts, "and if they do, they will be killed by the highly-trained men that are guarding this cottage."

"I won't marry you, Peter," she insisted, her gaze meeting his. "I care for another."

Peter rose from the bed and adjusted his blue jacket. "That's a lie. I've been watching you closely, and I know you do not have a suitor."

"He's not my suitor," she contested.

"I care not," Peter said as he walked to the door and opened it. "You belong to me, and you soon will forget this other man, if you know what's good for you. I hope when I return you will be more agreeable."

The moment Peter slammed the door shut, Emma stepped over to the dressing table and looked for anything that might aid in her escape. Unfortunately, after a thorough search, she found nothing. She moved to the bed and dropped down onto it.

Think, Emma, she thought. How was she going to get herself out of this mess?

Suddenly, an idea occurred to her. She jumped up from the bed and hurried to the window. She unlatched it and pushed it open. Leaning out, she ran her hand along the uneven stones. She had no doubt that she could climb down this wall.

Emma could hear movement in the trees near the cottage, and she knew she needed to proceed cautiously. If she was caught by a guard, then Peter might tie her up… or worse. Frankly, she had no idea what Peter was capable of anymore.

Reaching into the pocket of her gown, she felt the heavy pistol weighing her dress down. She had one shot with the pistol. And she was a good shot.

Well, she had better start moving. She wasn't going to wait around and be a damsel in distress. She was going to rescue herself.

With a drink in his hand, Simeon sat in Lansdowne's drawing room. It had been several hours, and still no word on Emma's location. And it was not for a lack of trying. Every available Bow Street Runner and agent of the Crown were scouring the streets and poring through documents in an attempt to find any lead. But no lead was forthcoming.

Now he sat alone. The Beckett family had adjourned to the dining room to eat a midday meal, but he was not hungry. How could he eat at a time like this?

He brought his drink to his lips. They had to find Emma. But what if they didn't? The feeling of overwhelming panic came into his heart as he realized he was reliving his nightmare all over again. Emma had disappeared, just as Martha had. It had taken him five years to find her. No, that would not happen again. He would go to hell and back to find Emma. But where to look?

Benedict's voice broke through his musings. "I know that look. You are about to go half-cocked on us, aren't you?"

Setting his drink down, Simeon rose and turned to see Benedict leaning against the doorframe. "I'm going mad just sitting here waiting for a lead. I'm going to start searching for Emma myself."

"Pray tell, where are you going to start looking?"

"Everywhere," he announced, his voice rising.

An amused look came to Benedict's face. "At least you have a solid plan."

Simeon's shoulders slumped. "I can't lose her... not the way I lost Martha."

"You won't. We'll find Emma," Benedict said, walking further into the room.

"But what if we don't?" he asked in despair.

Sitting down onto an armchair, Benedict looked up at him. "What happened to Martha is nothing like what happened to Emma," he said calmly.

"Isn't it?"

"It is not," Benedict replied with compassion in his tone. "Martha was sold into slavery, whereas Emma was abducted by a spurned suitor. I highly doubt Peter whisked Emma away on a boat in the middle of the night to India."

Feeling dejected, Simeon sat back down on his chair. "I failed Emma, just as I failed Martha. I am lousy at keeping people safe."

"That's not accurate," Benedict assured him. "We're all to blame for Emma's abduction. Had we known what great lengths Lockhart was prepared to go to retrieve her, then we would have hidden her away much sooner."

"May I ask where this safehouse is?"

Benedict's expression grew stern. "It's a well-guarded secret."

"Understood." Simeon ran a hand through his already disheveled hair. "I'm scared," he admitted softly.

Benedict's lips twitched. "Bow Street Runners aren't supposed to be afraid of anything."

"Neither are agents of the Crown," he contended.

"Good point." Benedict leaned forward in his seat, his expression growing serious. "This time, you're not alone. You have friends that have a particular set of skills that can help retrieve Emma."

"What if we're too late?"

"We won't be," Benedict assured him. "Lockhart wants Emma alive."

"But what kind of damage could he inflict on her before we rescue her?"

Benedict considered him for a long moment. "Emma is clever and strong-willed. She won't stop fighting Lockhart."

"And if Lockhart tires of her insolence?"

Benedict frowned. "You seem to focus on the negative. Why is that?"

"How can I not? My betrothed was stolen from me, sent to a brothel, and I spent five years searching tirelessly for her, only to have her choose another," Simeon said. "Life has not been exceptionally kind to me."

"My brother was murdered by the same man who abducted Martha," Benedict shared. "He also nearly killed Eliza. But I chose not to dwell on it. Choosing despair or hate will eventually destroy you."

Simeon blinked back the tears in his eyes. "My whole world was turned upside down after Martha vanished. I lost everything. My friends, my family, and my betrothed. And when I finally found Martha, I lost her all over again. How can I not lose hope?"

"Love is tangible, as is hope," Benedict replied.

He sighed. "But what if I am not destined to have a love match? What if the problem is *me*?"

"It's abundantly clear that you care for Emma," Benedict said, watching him closely. "I'm sure even more than you're letting on. So, I must pose the question, what are your intentions towards Emma?"

"I have deep feelings for her."

"I see," Benedict muttered. "True love is rare, and people can search their entire lives to find it. But you have been blessed to have found it twice."

"No, Martha didn't choose me. She chose Emmett."

"If Martha hadn't been sold into slavery, do you believe that you two would have married?"

"Without a doubt," he rushed to answer.

"I believe fate intervened, because you weren't supposed to marry Martha," Benedict said.

"And I'm supposed to marry Emma?"

Benedict shrugged. "You tell me."

Simeon looked up at the ceiling. "Why would Emma agree to a courtship with me? She is the opposite of me in so many ways."

Chuckling, Benedict said, "My wife can speak multiple languages, best me in weapons training, and could kill me before I even blink. But she took a chance on me."

"And I've never regretted that choice," Eliza stated from the doorway.

Simeon and Benedict rose from their seats and turned to face her.

"If you two are finished being chatterboxes, Jonathon has returned, and he has a lead on Lockhart," Eliza shared.

Benedict gave him a pointed look. "Let's go save Emma, because *we* will save her."

"Allow me to go change," Eliza said, turning to leave the room.

"Absolutely not!" Benedict roared.

Eliza turned back to face him with a determined brow. "I cannot sit back and do nothing while you go rescue Emma."

"Yes, you can, and you will," Jonathon declared from behind her.

"No, I won't," Eliza challenged, turning to face him. "I am more than capable of wielding a bow in my condition."

Adrien chuckled as he approached Jonathon. "I don't know which Beckett sister is more stubborn."

"Eliza, dear..." Benedict started.

"I'll stay back in the shadows..."

Eliza's words were stilled as Benedict approached her and cupped her right cheek. "Please think of our unborn babe. Besides, I cannot risk losing you."

"I'm more than capable of protecting myself and our unborn babe," she contended.

"You are," he agreed, placing his other hand on her belly. "But you must trust that we will bring Emma back safely."

"I know you will, but..."

Benedict cut her off, his eyes never straying from her. "I love you, but sometimes you make our assignments too easy by shooting everyone."

Eliza let out a small laugh. "That's my intention."

"We'll bring Emma back," Benedict said, earning a nod from Eliza.

The look of love was undeniable as Eliza stared back at Benedict. "You must come back to me," she murmured, her voice holding a slight plea.

"Always," he replied before kissing her on the lips.

Jonathon cleared his throat. "If you two lovebirds are finished, we should probably go rescue Emma from Lockhart."

"That sounds like a reasonable plan to me," Adrien quipped from next to him.

Benedict kissed his wife again before he stepped back. "I'll see that the coach is prepared," he said, walking out into the entry hall.

"By the way, Bow Street Runners aren't completely useless," Jonathon expressed, turning his direction towards Simeon.

"Pembrooke stopped me outside with an address to a cottage that Lockhart recently rented under an assumed name."

"How did he come by that information?" Simeon asked.

Jonathon shrugged. "He didn't say, and I didn't ask." He turned on his heel and followed Benedict.

As Simeon watched Jonathon walk away, he knew he would do whatever it took to get Emma back. And then he prayed that she would agree to his courtship. But he had a sinking feeling in his stomach that he wasn't good enough for her.

Chapter Sixteen

"That plan is truly awful," Simeon declared as they stood in a field of bluebells and hazels on the outskirts of a densely woodland area.

Adrien shrugged, unperturbed. "It's worked before."

Simeon gave him a look of disbelief. "You want me to just walk up to the cottage, knock on the door and ask to speak to Lockhart."

"Yes. By doing so, you'll distract Lockhart while we take out the guards," Adrien pressed.

"That plan is suicidal."

Benedict chuckled. "We thought so as well, but it did work out splendidly. Although, Adrien was almost shot when he attempted to rescue his wife."

"No plan is without some risk." Jonathon shrugged.

Simeon frowned. "I am not going to walk up to the cottage and let Lockhart shoot me."

"Pity," Adrien joked.

"How are you agents still alive?" Simeon asked with a shake of his head.

"Agents aren't afraid to take risks, but Bow Street Runners are quite timid," Jonathon said matter-of-factly.

"You say 'timid', but I say *not* idiotic," Simeon remarked. "Your last plan got me shot."

Benedict grinned. "That's because you jumped in front of Emmett in an attempt to win Martha's affections."

He grunted. "Regardless, I propose we come up with a new plan."

"We could proceed and improvise as we go along," Adrien

suggested.

The sound of someone approaching through the trees had everyone reaching for their pistols. A lone figure emerged, but they immediately relaxed when they recognized the form of Mr. George Larson appearing between the hazel trees.

"I counted sixteen men guarding the cottage and four men inside with Lockhart," Larson informed them.

"Perfect," Adrien said. "There are five of us and twenty of the bad guys. We each get to take out four men."

"That won't be too hard," Jonathon agreed confidently.

Simeon shook his head. "Do all agents act like you?"

"Heroic?" Adrien asked.

"Fearless?" Jonathon inquired.

Benedict spoke up. "Stouthearted?"

"No, I was going to say that you all act like jackanapes," Simeon said, reaching down to adjust the pistol in his right boot.

Larson laughed. "That does describe them perfectly."

Adrien tilted his head towards Simeon. "I see you've taken my advice about carrying a pistol in your boot."

"It was sound advice," Simeon admitted.

"I am full of sterling advice," Adrien boasted.

Benedict smirked. "You are full of something."

Simeon huffed at the banter. "Do all agents tease each other unmercifully before an assignment?"

"Yes," all the men said in unison.

Turning towards Larson, he asked, "Did you see Emma in the cottage?"

Larson nodded. "I did. She was leaning out of a window on the second level on the front-facing side of the cottage."

Reaching for the pistol in his waistband, Simeon held it in his right hand as he started down the right path. "I'm going to save her," he declared.

"Hold on," Adrien said. "I'll go with you."

"We'll take the left side," Benedict stated, grabbing Jonathon's sleeve.

Mr. Larson bobbed his head. "I'll go down the middle."

Treading softly, Simeon darted between the trees and saw a

short, burly guard yawning as he leaned against a tree. He crept quietly behind the guard and hit him over the head with the side of his pistol. The guard collapsed without making a sound.

Simeon held up one finger towards Adrien, who nodded in acknowledgement. Proceeding cautiously, they spread out as they continued to look for guards. Two tall guards were walking through shrubbery, chatting, completely oblivious to the fact that they were being stalked.

Adrien and Simeon ducked behind trees and waited for them to approach. Once they were within range, they jumped out and each knocked out a guard with a single blow. A rustling in the shrubberies alerted them that someone was approaching. Two guards jumped out, armed with daggers in their hands.

Simeon jumped out of the way as a thickset guard swiped the dagger at him. He retrieved the dagger from his left boot, and lunged at the guard, slicing the man's shirt. The man scowled as he dove towards him, and Simeon stepped to the side, simultaneously jabbing the dagger into the man's side. He twisted it before yanking it out. The man cried out in pain as he collapsed to the ground. To prevent him from crying out again, potentially warning the other guards, Simeon punched the man in the jaw, knocking him unconscious.

Simeon wiped the bloodied dagger off on his trousers as he watched Adrien strike the final blow to his assailant. He tucked the dagger back into his left boot. Without saying a word, he headed deeper into the woods, hoping the cottage would be within a few yards.

A two-level structure emerged in a clearing, and Simeon saw a guard posted near the front door. Staying low, he approached the side of the cottage and pressed himself up against it. Adrien ducked low in the high brush but tossed a rock towards a tree, causing a thud. The guard retrieved his pistol and went to investigate the noise. The moment he cleared the side of the house, Simeon held his pistol in his right hand and hit the man across the face with it.

Before the man collapsed, Adrien caught him and started dragging him towards the high brush. He dropped the man and pointed towards the open window on the front-facing second level where Emma was currently climbing down.

Simeon nodded as he tucked the pistol into his waistband and went to intercept her. However, the moment she stepped onto the ground, she sprinted towards the cover of the trees, not sparing him a glance. Not wanting to give away his position by shouting at her, he started following her.

Emma was a few yards ahead of him when she darted behind a tree. He quickly followed her and was caught off guard when she jumped out and swung a thick branch at him, hitting him hard in the shoulder. He grunted as the blow knocked him to the ground.

She raised the branch up to hit him again, and he put his hands in front of him to protect himself.

"Emma, it's me. It's Simeon," he called out, mindful to keep his voice low.

"Simeon?" she asked, lowering the branch to her side. "How are you here?"

He grimaced as he rubbed his sore shoulder. "It was quite simple, although I was forced to take out a few guards."

"By yourself?"

"No, I had a little help," he admitted, rising from the ground and dusting himself off. "Benedict, Jonathon, Adrien, and Larson are with me."

Her eyes grew determined. "What's the plan?"

"Good girl." He was secretly pleased that Emma was not acting like a simpering miss. "We are going to run to safety."

She dropped the tree branch and closed the distance between them. "I'm sorry I hit you," she said, reaching out to touch his throbbing shoulder.

"I barely felt it," he lied, his voice surprisingly hoarse as he remained close.

She grinned. "Liar."

Simeon was rooted in place. Being this close to Emma was intoxicating. He could smell the rosewater in her hair and saw a patch of light freckles on the bridge of her nose. Unable to resist, he brought his hands up to gently rest on her arms, his eyes eagerly roaming her face.

"You are so beautiful, Emma," he murmured without thinking.

A blush came to her cheeks as she diverted her gaze from his.

A clearing of a throat came from behind him. "Do Bow Street Runners normally flirt with the people they are attempting to rescue at the most inopportune time?" Adrien asked.

Simeon chuckled. "Point taken." He smiled down at Emma. "Perhaps I could flirt with you at a more appropriate time?"

"I would like that very much."

As he reached for her hand, he heard a gunshot echoing through the trees near the cottage. Blast it! Benedict or Jonathon gave away their position. He knew he needed to act quickly. They started sprinting through the trees towards the coach.

He heard men shouting behind them as they continued to weave in and around trees. They needed a distraction. He stopped, released her hand, and retrieved his pistol in one synchronized move.

"Go," he urged, "run to safety. I will stop them from following us."

"No, I won't go without you," she objected, grabbing his hand.

He attempted to release her hand, but she held firm. "I need you to be safe, Emma. Trust me."

A look of indecision crossed her face before she dropped his hand and started backing up. Unfortunately, the sound of cocking pistols stopped her. He reluctantly turned around to see Lockhart and a mercenary standing next to him, both holding pistols directed at him.

"Emma, you weren't planning to leave, now were you?" Lockhart asked dryly.

"I have every intention of running far away from you," Emma declared boldly.

Lockhart waved the gun in front of him. "Then I'm afraid I will have to kill your would-be rescuer."

"No, stop!" Emma exclaimed, taking a step closer to him.

Simeon stepped in front of her, his hand tightening around the pistol at his side. "Just go, Emma. Don't worry about me."

"That's utter nonsense!" she declared. "I refuse to let anyone else die for me."

"You were always too tenderhearted for your own good." Lockhart gave him a pointed look. "Kindly drop your weapon on the ground."

Simeon slowly placed the pistol on the ground, his eyes never straying from Lockhart.

Lockhart smirked. "And the spare pistol from your boot."

Leaning down, Simeon removed the overcoat pistol from his right boot, dropping it on the ground.

"Now kick them away from you," Lockhart directed.

Simeon took his foot and slid the weapons towards Peter and his thug.

"Now, you're free to go," Lockhart announced, lowering his pistol.

Not sure what game Lockhart was playing, Simeon asserted, "I'm not going anywhere without Emma."

"Then you shall die," Lockhart replied, bringing his pistol back up.

"Stop!" Emma said, moving to stand in front of Simeon. "If you want to kill him, you'll have to kill me first."

Lockhart lowered his gun and gave Emma a condescending smile. "I have no wish to kill you, my dear. I love you."

"You don't love me," Emma huffed. "Your actions prove otherwise."

Looking bored, he responded, "Your guardian left me no choice. I've already explained that."

"Please let Simeon live," Emma pleaded.

Lockhart cocked an eyebrow at him. "Simeon, is it?"

"Yes," she confirmed, "he's my friend."

"Is this the man that you previously mentioned that you care about?"

Emma pressed her lips together as she sheepishly glanced over her shoulder at Simeon. What a mortifying thing to admit out loud, especially given the circumstances.

"It is," she answered honestly.

"And does this man return your affections?" Lockhart asked.

Unsure of how to respond, she remained silent.

To her surprise, Simeon replied in a firm but gentle tone, "He does."

Lockhart frowned. "Then we have a problem." He pointed his pistol towards Emma. "I can't possibly let him live, or you'll continue to harbor feelings for him."

Emma squared her shoulders, despite a pistol being pointed at her. "I'm not the same girl you knew growing up, Peter. I've changed."

"I can see that," Lockhart scoffed. "You've become a harlot."

She gasped. "How dare you!"

Lockhart's expression grew accusing. "The Emma that I knew growing up was innocent and kind, and she was never one to toy with a man's emotions."

"I'm still that girl," she contended. "I've never toyed with a man's emotions."

"No?" Peter questioned. "You promised yourself to me."

"I did no such thing!"

He took a commanding step towards her. "When you were ten, you told me that you wanted to marry me down by the stream."

"When I was ten?" she asked, furrowing her brow. "Please tell me that you are not in earnest."

"We made a vow to each other," he declared.

"We were children. It was a silly game."

His face grew expressionless. "To you, perhaps, but to me, it was a promise."

"Peter, I am sorry…"

"Enough!" he shouted. "It matters not. We will ride out and be wed tomorrow."

She shook her head. "No, Peter. I will not marry you."

"You would rather marry a Bow Street Runner than me?" Peter scoffed as he began to pace back and forth. "You want to struggle for the rest of your days?"

With a fleeting glance at Simeon, she replied, "Yes, with all of my heart."

"You're a fool!" Peter shouted. "You would be nothing without me."

"I beg your pardon?"

Peter stopped pacing. "It was I that contacted your grandfather after your mother's death and began receiving money for your tuition." He pointed at her. "Without your fancy boarding school, you would have been working at the shop."

"Perhaps," she responded reflectively. "But I never desired to go to boarding school."

He scoffed. "You are Sir Alymer's only grandchild, and he intends to make you his heir. When that happens, you will be worth so much more than you are now, and I intend to possess all he plans to leave you."

Emma stared at him in shock as reality set in. "Regardless, you killed my father and Luke to achieve your nefarious purposes," she asserted, her voice rising in anger.

"Luke isn't dead," Simeon whispered behind her.

A great feeling of relief washed over her. At least Luke was still alive.

"You ungrateful chit," Peter said. "I negotiated this all on your behalf."

She shook her head. "No, *you* did this for yourself. You murdered, cheated, and stole. For what?" She met his gaze unflinchingly. "I could never love you after what you have done."

Peter sneered at her. "You became awfully self-important once the Marquess of Downshire became your guardian." He took another step closer to her. "But you will always be just a constable's daughter."

Emma took a moment to consider her words. "You are right," she finally answered. "I am a constable's daughter, but I am also so much more." She tilted her chin defiantly. "I have a family, friends, and I'm stronger than you know."

"You don't have a family, they're just using you," Peter pressed.

"For what?" she declared, tossing up her hands. "I used to think I didn't deserve their love, that I was somehow unworthy of it because I never earned it. But I was wrong. They've loved me without restraint, and I *am* worthy of being loved."

"You're spouting nonsense," Peter proclaimed. "You don't belong in their world. You belong with me."

She gave him a look filled with pity. "I belong in whatever world that I want to be in. And I will carve my own path from here on out."

"You will love me," Peter growled, pointing his pistol over her shoulder at Simeon, "once this man is out of the way."

Reaching back, Emma grabbed Simeon's hand and brought it up to her pocket of her gown. She felt him fingering the pistol and removing it from her pocket.

"It has nothing to do with Simeon," Emma said calmly. "This is between you and me."

Simeon's authoritative voice came from behind her. "It's over, Lockhart. Put the pistol down and walk away with your life."

Lockhart let out a dry laugh. "You're not in a position to be giving orders."

Stepping out from behind her, Simeon brought up the pistol and pointed it at Lockhart. "I most assuredly am, since I'm a better shot than you."

Lockhart's eyes narrowed. "How many pistols did you have on your person?"

"I like being prepared," Simeon retorted.

"There are still two pistols being pointed at you," Lockhart pointed out.

"I may just be a Bow Street Runner, but I question your ability to count."

"Why do you say that?"

Simeon smirked. "Because I count four pistols being pointed at you."

"Four?" Lockhart's eyes started scanning the trees.

Simeon cocked his gun. "You didn't think I came alone, did you?" he asked, pointing at the tree to the side of Lockhart where Adrien stood with a pistol in his hand. "Also, you might want to check behind you."

Emma practically sighed in relief as she saw Benedict and Jonathon emerge from the trees behind Lockhart. It was over. Surely, Peter would lay down his weapon now that he was so vastly outnumbered.

Lockhart's thug immediately placed his pistol on the ground and put his hands up in the air. But Lockhart wasn't as bright. He cocked his pistol as he continued to point it at Simeon's chest. "You will not win," he declared. "Emma is mine."

"No," Simeon responded. "Emma belongs to no man."

Lockhart's eyes grew frantic as he shouted, "If I can't have Emma, then no one can!" He swiftly turned the pistol towards her. As his finger contracted on the trigger, gunshots erupted, echoing through the trees.

Before the acrid smoke even dissipated, she was wrapped up in Simeon's tender arms.

"It's over," he whispered into her hair. "Lockhart will never be able to hurt you again."

Being in Simeon's arms, she felt safe and protected, and dare she believe, cherished. She tightened her hold around his waist and rested her head on his chest.

Benedict's voice came from next to her. "I believe we helped aid in the rescue as well," he teased.

Emma stepped out of Simeon's arms and gave each one of her rescuers a hug.

"Thank you for saving me," she told each of them.

Adrien smiled fondly at her. "That is what family does. We protect each other."

Glancing down at Lockhart's body, Simeon remarked, "Perhaps it would be best if I escorted Emma to the coach."

"Good idea," Jonathon replied. "We'll go see if Larson needs assistance rounding up Lockhart's thugs."

Simeon offered his arm, and Emma eagerly accepted it. As they headed towards the coach, Emma felt a huge weight lift off her shoulders. Peter could never hurt her again. She was finally free of him.

"I am relieved beyond words that you are safe," Simeon declared, placing his hand over hers.

"Thank you for rescuing me."

Simeon's eyes were filled with an intensity that she did not understand.

"I will always rescue you, Emma." His words were filled with such tenderness that it left her speechless.

Maybe he did truly care for her as he had claimed to Peter. Maybe it was not just a ruse. Maybe.

Chapter Seventeen

The sun was dipping in the sky as Simeon approached the stately townhouse of Lord Revett.

"Are you sure you want to go through with this?" Benedict asked, walking next to him.

"I most assuredly do."

Adrien sighed. "Threatening the Home Secretary at his own home is a terrible plan."

Simeon grinned as he stepped onto the paved walkway. "It appears that you agents are rubbing off on me."

With a chuckle, Benedict remarked, "Perhaps you'll become an agent one of these days."

"No, thank you," he said with a smile. "Frankly, my days as a Bow Street Runner are limited. It's time that I run my company and return home to my family."

"Does Emma know you own Martin Trading Company?"

He shook his head. "Not specifically, but I have mentioned I own a merchant company."

Adrien chuckled. "A merchant company?" he repeated slowly. "Your company rivals The East India Company."

"That may be true, but I didn't want to inform Emma of my wealth."

"May I ask why?" Benedict questioned.

With a slight shrug, Simeon replied, "I suppose I wanted to see if she would accept me for who I was, not for my title, or for my money."

"And now?" Benedict asked.

A smile came to his face. "She was far more impressed that I was a Bow Street Runner than a viscount."

"That doesn't surprise me. Titles and wealth seem to mean nothing to our dear Emma," Adrien commented.

"I agree."

Walking up to the black, main entry door, Simeon pounded it with his fist, then stepped back.

The door opened, revealing a lean butler with a thin mustache. "May I help you?" he asked politely.

Extending his calling card, Simeon said, "Please inform Lord Revett that Lord Wentworth would like a moment of his time."

Benedict retrieved his own card and handed it to the butler. "As does the Marquess of Lansdowne."

The butler looked expectantly at Adrien, who reluctantly removed a card from a pocket of his waistcoat. "And the Earl of Camden."

"Yes, my lords," the butler said as he invited them into the entry foyer. "I will inform Lord Revett of your arrival."

Simeon's eyes admired the woodwork dominating the square entry hall, along with light-colored, papered walls.

The clicking of the butler's shoes informed them of his pending arrival. "Lord Revett will see you now," he informed them.

Following the butler towards the rear of the townhouse, Benedict stepped up to walk next to Simeon, muttering, "I sure hope you know what you're doing, Wentworth."

The butler stopped next to an open door and gestured towards the room, indicating they should enter.

As they entered, Lord Revett was sitting behind a large desk with stacks of papers next to him. His head was down, but he managed to say, "Please, have a seat. I'll be with you shortly."

Rather than sit, Simeon leaned against the wall near the fireplace and watched Lord Revett work. His thinning black hair was longer than what was fashionable. He had a thin mustache, and his ears were pointed. On the rare occasion he attended Parliament, he saw Lord Revett sitting in the front row, his arms folded, looking solemn. He did not appear to be a man to trifle with, but then again, neither was he.

"My apologies," Lord Revett said with a brief smile, looking up from the papers on his desk. "There isn't enough time in the day to complete all that's required of me as the Home Secretary, especially since Parliament is in session tonight." He rose from his chair and walked over to the drink cart. "How may I help you gentlemen this evening?" His tone was cheery.

"I've come to discuss the Anti-Corn Law rebels," Simeon stated.

Lord Revett bobbed his head as he poured four snifters of brandy. "I am greatly concerned about that group of radical thinkers, as well."

"What do you intend to do with them?" Simeon pressed.

"Arrest them, discredit them... the usual," Lord Revett informed them, picking up the four glasses and walking them over to a side table. He set them down and handed one to each man.

Simeon accepted a snifter and muttered, "Thank you." He took a sip of his drink. "And what about underhanded tactics?"

"I don't condone anything underhanded," Lord Revett declared, picking up his brandy.

Swirling the drink in his hand, Simeon pursed his lips. "That's interesting. Constable Stone informed me that you authorized him to blow up a balloon at the Anti-Corn Law rebels' protest in Grange Gardens."

Lord Revett huffed. "That's ludicrous. He's obviously lying."

"I'm afraid I won't be able to verify your story since he's dead," Simeon said.

Taking a sip of his drink, Lord Revett didn't respond for a moment, clearly startled by the news. "I'm sorry to hear that. How did he die?"

"I shot him as he attempted to use a flaming arrow to blow up a hydrogen balloon with a load of gunpowder in the basket," he answered dryly.

Lord Revett's face grew pale. "You shot Constable Stone?"

"Yes, but he wasn't a constable anymore. He'd been fired from that position," he shared, giving Revett a pointed look. "Were you not aware that I also work as a Bow Street Runner?"

"I was not aware of that fact," Lord Revett admitted. "Do you know why Stone would do something so vile?"

"His intentions were to kill as many Anti-Corn Law rebels as possible," Simeon replied. "As he attempted to kill me, Stone claimed he was acting under another's authority."

Lord Revett eyed him suspiciously. "You couldn't possibly think I had anything to do with that, do you?"

"I definitely do," Simeon replied.

Lord Revett frowned, lowering his glass to his lap. "What do you want, Lord Wentworth?"

"Your resignation."

With a stunned expression, Lord Revett stared at him for a long moment. "You must be joking," he finally said.

Simeon pushed away from the wall and came to sit down across from the Home Secretary. "If your nefarious plan had succeeded, that bomb would have killed thousands."

"I had nothing to do with that…" Lord Revett attempted.

Simeon cut him off. "You gave Stone *carte blanche* to stop those protestors, including mass murder."

"I did no such thing!" Lord Revett shouted, placing his drink onto the side table. "I merely asked Stone to attend the rally and to intervene only to arrest violent protestors."

"Like he did at the demonstration in Templeton Square?" Adrien asked from his chair.

Lord Revett put his hands out in front of him. "I admit that Stone's tactics did get out of hand during that one, but we have riots daily over the Corn Laws. If that demonstration had turned violent, it could have wrecked London."

"I was at that rally," Simeon informed him. "Stone struck and arrested the Marquess of Downshire's ward."

"I heard about that," Lord Revett said with an apologetic smile. "Most unfortunate."

Simeon shook his head. "No, what was most unfortunate were the people that were beaten and battered at your request."

"Again, I had nothing to do with that. But I must question what you were doing at the rally, Lord Wentworth?" Lord Revett asked.

"I was on assignment."

"With a woman?" Lord Revett pressed. "What self-respecting young woman would attend a demonstration?"

Benedict spoke up with a steely warning in his tone. "I would be very careful of how you speak about Miss Pearson."

Lord Revett swallowed slowly. "I assure you, I meant no disrespect."

"Where is Mr. Hatcher?" Adrien asked, changing the subject.

"At Newgate, I believe," Lord Revett answered.

Adrien took a sip of his drink. "I want him released."

"Absolutely not! He's the supposed leader of the Anti-Corn Law rebels," Lord Revett exclaimed.

"What is he being accused of?" Simeon asked.

Adjusting his waistcoat, Lord Revett answered, "He is causing civil unrest." He gave Simeon a pointed look. "I would hate to think you are a sympathizer of that radical group. As one who has claimed his allegiance lies with the Tory party, it would not reflect well on you."

"My allegiance is to whatever side is right on any matter, and the Tories need to repeal the Corn Laws," Simeon declared.

Lord Revett scoffed. "That will never happen. The landowners won't go for that."

"It's simple," Benedict said, speaking up. "Either you convince the landowners to repeal the Corn Laws or step down as the Home Secretary."

"Again, why would I step down? I've done nothing wrong," Lord Revett declared.

"Your orders caused nearly a hundred people to be wounded at the Templeton Square rally, and if Stone had succeeded, thousands of people could have been killed at Grange Gardens," Simeon pressed.

Lord Revett stared daggers at him. "You have no proof."

"True, but the people are outraged after the protestors were beat nearly to death at what was supposed to be a peaceful demonstration," Adrien said. "I suspect if Mr. Blackmore wrote a few more articles, and they were featured on the front page of the morning paper, the people would stir even more. More riots would break out all over Britain."

"Mr. Blackmore is a criminal," Lord Revett replied. "He is causing more civil unrest."

Simeon huffed. "No, Mr. Blackmore is writing articles that paint you in a poor light. He is writing the truth."

"Truth is in the eye of the beholder," Lord Revett quoted.

Benedict leaned back in his seat. "My father-in-law, the Duke of Remington, was quite concerned when I informed him that you gave the order to create a bomb using a balloon." His face grew expressionless. "He also withdrew his support and has asked for your resignation."

Lord Revett grew solemn. "The Duke of Remington has asked for my resignation?" he asked deliberately.

"I could talk to my father-in-law," Benedict started slowly, "but we would want a few things in return."

Pursing his lips, Lord Revett replied, "What do you want?"

"Drop the warrant for Mr. David Blackmore," Simeon replied firmly.

"Mr. Blackmore is a menace to our society and needs to be behind bars," Lord Revett pressed.

Benedict's demeanor grew stern as he forcefully declared, "Blackmore is under the Becketts' protection, and no harm is to come to him. Do I make myself clear?"

At that moment, Simeon was grateful that Benedict's anger was not directed towards him. He truly was quite frightening.

Lord Revett bobbed his head. "I understand. The charges will be dropped against Mr. Blackmore, but would it be permissible for him to stop writing articles for the newspaper?"

"No, it would not," Benedict responded.

A frown came to Lord Revett's face. "I will also release Hatcher from prison." He took a sip of his drink. "Is there anything else, or can we end this interrogation?"

Adrien piped up, "I think that will do." He glanced over at Simeon and Benedict. "Shall we?"

As they rose from their chairs, Lord Revett said, "A word to the wise, gentlemen. By allowing Hatcher and Blackmore to go free, there will be more resistance against the Corn Laws. I'm afraid you're doing more harm than good here."

"I disagree," Simeon started. "The landowners have too much power in Parliament. Eventually, the people will take back what is rightfully theirs."

"And what is that?" Lord Revett scoffed.

Simeon grew serious. "Their voice."

Emma had a bright smile on her face as she entered the dining room. Last night, she'd taken a long soak and then slept peacefully, dreaming about being wrapped up in Simeon's arms.

"You seem happy this morning," Rachel commented from her seat at the table. "Is there a particular reason?"

Walking over to the buffet table, she said, "To begin with, I'm alive, and Peter can't hurt me anymore."

Luke spoke up from the head of the table. "I am relieved, as well." He placed the newspaper on the table. "Hatcher is being released from prison today."

"Is he?" Emma asked in a surprised tone. "I thought the Crown was going to make an example of him."

"Apparently not," Luke replied.

"That's good," Emma remarked, walking over to the table and sitting down next to Rachel. She couldn't help but notice the pointed look that Luke and Rachel exchanged. "What's going on between you two?"

Luke wiped the corners of his mouth with his napkin. "Do you intend to seek out your grandfather now that you know he's alive?"

She nodded. "I do."

"Would you like me to send a missive to Sir Alymer's townhouse to inform him that you intend to call on him soon?" Luke asked. "I have made some inquiries, and his townhouse is across town."

"That would be wonderful," she replied. "Do you think he would mind if I call upon him today?"

Rachel reached out and placed her hand over hers. "Any grandfather would love to see his granddaughter, at any time."

Luke cleared his throat, and he appeared anxious. Which was odd, she thought.

"Rachel and I were talking earlier, and if you decide to live with your grandfather, we will respect your choice," he said. "Regardless, your dowry and inheritance…"

"Inheritance?" she questioned. Her inheritance had been spent by Peter.

Rachel smiled. "Luke and I have made provisions for you. We set aside £30,000 in an account for you to access on your twenty-first birthday."

Touched by their generosity, Emma found herself speechless.

Luke gave her a tentative smile. "The money is yours. We just want you to be happy, Emma."

Jumping up from her chair, she gave Rachel a quick embrace before she embraced Luke. "I'm not going anywhere. You are my family."

"You say that now, but…" Luke began.

She spoke over him. "No buts. I'm happy here, and I always will be."

"There's one other thing I want to give you," Luke said, reaching into his jacket and pulling out a gold locket. "Jonathon found this when he was searching your cottage."

"My mother's locket," she murmured as she accepted it. "I'd wondered where it had gone." She admired the locket as the memories of her mother came flooding back to her.

So distracted was she, that she didn't hear Munro knock. "Miss Pearson, where would you like all your flowers?" he asked, holding a bouquet in his hands.

"Wherever you see fit," she replied, slipping the locket into the pocket of her gown.

The butler cracked a smile. "The entire entry hall is already filled. Would you mind if we started stacking the flowers on the table, at least, until we find enough vases?"

"Please," she said in a surprised tone, walking over and accepting the bouquet from him. "Was there a card with these?"

Munro extended a card towards her before he snapped his fingers. Two footmen each brought in a stack of large bouquets in their hands and placed them onto the long table. Then again… and again. Before long, the end of the table was filled with flowers.

Turning her attention away from the extravagant number of flowers on the table, Emma unfolded the card.

A flower for every moment I thought of you last night. – Simeon.

Taking the card, she pressed it up against her chest and sighed.

"You sound content," Rachel remarked. "May I take a guess and say those flowers are from Lord Wentworth?"

"They are," she replied, smiling.

Munro stepped back into the room. "Lord Wentworth is here to see Miss Pearson. Are you available for callers?" he asked with a twinkle in his eye.

"I am," she answered, tucking the note into her pocket.

"Very good, miss," he said. "I will show him to the drawing room."

Rachel beamed over at her. "Good luck, Emma."

"Why exactly does Emma need luck to speak to Wentworth?" Luke grumbled.

Walking out into the entry hall, she stopped by a mirror and smoothed out her yellow gown with puffy sleeves. She was grateful that she'd spent extra time on her person this morning. Peggy had created an elaborate hairstyle in hopes that Simeon would call on her. She'd never felt beautiful before, but Simeon looked at her in such a way that she felt beautiful, inside and out.

Emma took a deep breath to gather courage, knowing it was silly to be nervous. Simeon had bought every flower in London for her. He had to have some deep feelings for her.

She stepped into the drawing room and saw Simeon was sharply dressed in a royal blue riding jacket, a matching waistcoat, and buff trousers. His brown hair had been brushed forward and his long sideburns were nicely trimmed. He was fidgeting with the black top hat in his hand.

His eyes lit up when he saw her. "Morning, Emma. I hope I did not call too early."

Walking further into the room, she replied in an overeager voice, "Not at all."

Simeon lifted his brow, but thankfully, he didn't address her high-pitched tone. "I was hoping to speak to you about an urgent matter?"

"Urgent? Is everything all right?" she asked, growing concerned.

"Oh, yes," he rushed to correct. "It's more private in nature."

"Private?"

Simeon ran his hand through his hair. "I rehearsed this speech about a hundred times in the carriage ride over."

"And what speech is that?"

He pointed towards the settee. "Please have a seat and allow me to explain."

Emma sat where he indicated and was pleased when he sat next to her. He angled his body to face her. "When I first met you, I found you to be irksome and meddling."

"To be clear, are you insulting me?" she asked in confusion.

"No, no… that's not my intention," he said before his shoulders slumped. "You should've heard my speech in the carriage. It was brilliant."

She smiled encouragingly. "Please proceed. I find myself to be most curious."

He rose, walked over to the table, and placed his hat on it. "Did you get my flowers?"

"Yes, I did. Did you buy out all of London?"

He grinned. "Possibly. Did they please you?"

"They did, but I would have been content with one bouquet," she replied honestly.

Simeon stood awkwardly next to the table. "I know that, but I wanted you to feel special."

"Well, it worked," she said. "Thank you."

"The warrant for Mr. David Blackmore… well, you, has been redacted, and the charges were dropped," he informed her methodically.

"What charges?"

He frowned. "Lord Revett charged Mr. Blackmore with causing civil unrest and issued a warrant for his arrest. However, it's been taken care of. You're free to continue writing articles, if you so desire."

"Oh, thank you," she replied, hoping that was not what he'd intended to speak to her about.

A silence descended over them, and an unusual feeling washed over her. She could not describe it, but she felt vulnerable as he watched her purposefully.

"Emma," he breathed as he walked over and sat down next to her. "Would you do me the honor of allowing me to court you?" When she didn't respond right away, he added, "I want to take you on carriage rides, walks through Hyde Park, and eat lemon ice at Gunter's."

Every fiber of her being wanted to scream yes, but she had a few questions of her own that needed to be answered first. "And what of Martha?"

He gave her a baffled look. "What about Martha?"

"I heard the way you spoke her name. It was almost reverently."

He let out a deep, heartfelt sigh. "Martha was my first love, but she most assuredly isn't my last."

Not sure of his meaning, she pressed on. "You mentioned you never wanted to marry. What changed your mind?"

"*You* changed my mind, Emma." He chuckled. "I am in love with you."

She stilled. "You love me?"

Reaching for her hands in her lap, he tenderly encompassed them. "You challenge me at every opportunity, are incredibly courageous, and you're the reason I've started smiling again." He brought her hands up to his lips and kissed them. "You took my impenetrable heart and pierced it with your goodness and joy. You make me want to be a better person."

"I love you, too," she said softly.

"You do?" he asked. "It's all right if you don't…"

Emma cut him off. "I'm not just saying it for the sake of it." She smiled brightly at him. "I love you, and I have for some time now."

He waggled his brow. "Is it because I am a Bow Street Runner or a viscount?"

"You could be a night soil collector for all I care," she teased. "I just love the man, and I care not for the title or position."

He kissed her hands again, his lips lingering. "That's why I love you, Emma. Most women of the ton only care for titles and wealth."

In excitement, she shared, "Luke and Rachel just informed me that I have an inheritance of £30,000, in addition to my dowry. If we're frugal, we can get a small estate, and you can continue working as a Bow Street Runner."

"You intend for us to live off your inheritance?" he asked with mirth in his voice.

"If needs be, I can work, as well," she rushed to add. "I can take in odd sewing jobs and..." Her words stopped when Simeon started laughing loudly.

Once he stopped laughing, he shared, "I'm wealthy. Perhaps not as wealthy as your guardian, but I own Martin Trading Company."

Her mouth dropped in surprise. "*You* own Martin Trading Company?"

"I thought it was fairly obvious, since my name is in the title of the company," he quipped.

Her cheeks were starting to grow warm, and she pulled back her hands to cover them. "I just assumed you worked as a Bow Street Runner because you lacked an income."

With a tender look in his eyes, Simeon said, "And that's why I chose you. You're different than all the other women in the ton."

"I know that," she murmured, diverting her eyes. "The ton will never accept me because of what I've done."

Simeon placed his finger under her chin and lifted it up. "First of all, none of that was your fault. Peter set you up to fail."

"He succeeded," she replied.

He continued watching her, his expression assessing but not without compassion. "You mean to give up then?"

"What can I do?"

Leaning closer, he didn't stop until his lips hovered over hers. "We fight."

"*We?*" she asked, liking the sound of that immensely.

"Yes, we."

Enjoying his nearness, and afraid of moving to break the spell, she replied, "What do you propose?"

"Do you trust me?" he asked, his eyes boring into hers.

"Always," she breathed.

"Then leave it up to me."

She nodded, unable to formulate a reply, even if she'd wanted to.

Simeon's lips twitched just before he pressed them against hers.

He kissed her gently, cautiously at first. He leaned slightly back, and she drew a deep, staggered breath in response. He gave her an achingly sweet smile before he kissed her again, this time deepening the kiss. His arms came up around her, and he kissed her with passionate ardor.

So lost was she in the kiss, that her mind barely registered Rachel's voice. "Luke is on his way."

Immediately, Simeon rose and stepped far away from the settee, just as Luke entered the room.

"Did he offer for you?" Luke asked in an annoyed tone.

Emma nodded. "He did."

"Did you accept?" he grunted.

"I did."

With a frustrated shake of his head, Luke replied, "Tarnation! Benedict won the bet."

"What bet?" Emma asked, her eyes seeking out Rachel.

Rachel gave her husband an exasperated look. "The men in the family had a bet going when Simeon would propose."

Growing serious, Luke asked, "Is Wentworth coercing you in any way to marry him?"

She laughed. "No, I love him."

"I assumed as much," Luke commented, placing his arm around Rachel's waist. "This is what David would have wanted for you. To be happy, and to be in a position to select your own suitor."

Simeon came to stand next to her but stopped when Luke cleared his throat rather aggressively.

"You two will not be without a chaperone until after the wedding," Luke warned.

"Leave the engagement ball to me," Rachel said in a cheerful voice.

Simeon spoke up. "I have a few thoughts on the engagement ball, as well."

"You do?" Emma asked, eyeing him suspiciously.

He winked at her. "Trust me."

Emma couldn't help but smile back at Simeon. He was going to court her! Her fairy tale dreams were finally coming true.

Chapter Eighteen

Holding Simeon's gloved hand in the moving coach, Emma couldn't help but be nervous about meeting her grandfather for the first time. After all, she had so many questions that she needed answered.

"Cheer up, my dear," her companion said, sitting across from her in the coach. "You are an engaged woman."

"My apologies, Mrs. Morton," Emma replied softly. "I am just anxious, I suppose."

"Which is perfectly natural. I would be concerned if you weren't nervous," Simeon said lightly.

Emma smiled up at him. "Thank you for agreeing to come with me."

"There is no place I'd rather be," he declared, returning her smile.

Mrs. Morton sighed. "True love. It's rather exciting, is it not?"

The carriage came to a stop in front of a three level, whitewashed townhouse in a fashionable part of town. An iron gate lined the property. A footman appeared and opened the carriage door.

As they walked up to the front door, Simeon offered one arm to her and the other to Mrs. Morton.

The door opened, and an imposing butler asked, "May I help you?"

"I am here to see Sir Alymer Blackmore," Emma announced.

The butler glanced at her in surprise. "Do you have a calling card, miss?"

"No, but you can inform him that his granddaughter has called upon him."

The butler's eyes widened as he opened the door. "Please come in, Miss Pearson." He escorted them to the drawing room. "I will inform Sir Alymer and Lady Blackmore of your arrival."

She gasped. "My grandmother is alive, as well?"

"Yes, miss," the butler answered with kind eyes. "They've been expecting you."

Mrs. Morton walked up to her and placed her hand tenderly on her arm. "I think it would be best if I wait in the entry hall."

Once her companion stepped out, Emma turned to face Simeon and looked up at him. "I have a grandfather and a grandmother."

Simeon gave her a crooked smile. "Soon, you will have my side of the family to contend with, as well. You'll have so many relations that you may grow tired of some."

"I doubt that," she replied.

The sound of clicking on the tile alerted them to someone approaching. They stepped apart, creating proper distance.

A man bearing a striking resemblance to her brother David walked into the room, followed by a petite woman with white hair pulled back in a high chignon. They stopped and stared at her.

The woman spoke first. "Emma," she said softly, her eyes filling with tears, "you look just like your mother."

"Thank you," she responded, not knowing what else to say.

Her grandmother's curious gaze landed on Simeon.

Emma stepped forward to provide the introductions. "Allow me to introduce Simeon, the Viscount of Wentworth, and my betrothed."

Her grandfather humphed. "I think not."

"Alymer… you promised," her grandmother warned under her breath.

Unsure of her grandfather's meaning, Emma was grateful when her grandmother pointed towards a maroon velvet settee. "Please sit down. I've ordered refreshment."

Simeon led her over to the settee and waited until the ladies sat down before he claimed the seat next to her.

Her grandmother beamed over at her. "I'm so happy that you called upon us. We received the missive from Lord Downshire this morning, and our hearts practically burst with joy at the news."

"Betsey is correct," her grandfather said. "We were sickened to hear of Mr. Lockhart's deceit, but we were relieved to know that he was shot while resisting arrest. Furthermore, we are most grateful that Lord Downshire took your safety seriously and hired a Bow Street Runner to guard you."

"Yes, I was rather fortunate," Emma agreed, sending Simeon a private smile.

"Please, tell me about yourself," her grandmother encouraged, looking wistfully over at her.

Emma pressed her lips together as she debated what to say. She was caught off-guard when Simeon spoke up instead. "She is well-read, clever, and is passionate about helping other people."

Sir Alymer huffed. "I understand you also enjoy drinking champagne at social gatherings, including your own ball."

Emma stiffened. "I did drink one glass that evening."

"Apparently, your body can't handle the effects of alcohol," her grandfather mused. "It would be best if you stayed away from champagne from here on."

Simeon clenched his jaw. "Lockhart hired someone to poison Emma's drink that evening. It was no fault of her own."

"We read in the morning papers about the unfortunate debutante, but we did not make the connection that it was our dear Emma. Did we, Alymer?" Betsey asked with a forced smile.

"No, we did not," he muttered.

"How did you become the ward of the Marquess of Downshire?" her grandmother inquired.

Emma felt the tension flow out of her at her grandmother's sweet tone. "David was assigned to guard Lady Downshire while she was residing in Scotland. Unfortunately, she was attacked, and David was killed."

"Good heavens, I hadn't realized he'd been murdered," Betsey proclaimed, her hand covering her mouth. "I'd only seen him on a few occasions when he was in between assignments. He stopped coming by a little over two years ago, and I feared the worst."

"David never informed me about you," Emma began hesitantly. "Do you know why that is?"

Betsey's eyes darted nervously towards Alymer, but she remained silent.

Her grandfather spoke up. "Three years ago, David discovered the truth about us, and sought us out. Unfortunately, he forbade us to establish a relationship with you."

"Did he state why?" she pressed.

Sir Alymer shrugged. "Most likely, he still held resentment about how we disowned Helena for running off with her louse of a husband. But you must understand that she had been betrothed to Viscount Rutgers at that time."

"Please say that you are not referring to my father in such a shocking manner," Emma contended.

Betsey let out a forced laugh. "Of course not. Alymer was just teasing. Weren't you dear?" she pressed, shooting him a warning look.

"I suppose," Sir Alymer said dismissively.

"You were telling us how Lord Downshire became your guardian," her grandmother prodded.

"Lord Downshire became my guardian because he and David had become friends during that time in Scotland," she explained vaguely. "David had also grown close to Rachel."

"I see," Sir Alymer murmured. "Has Lord Downshire treated you well?"

"Oh, yes!"

"Well, we will be forever grateful that he kept you away from that vile Peter Lockhart," Sir Alymer said. "When I received the missive that you two had married, I felt sick to my stomach."

"We were never married," Emma assured him.

"That's good," her grandfather said. "We'll send a carriage around to collect your trunks from Lord Downshire's estate."

"Pardon?"

Sir Alymer's face grew expressionless. "I assume that you will want to live with us from now on, since we are your only family."

"No, I prefer to stay at Lord and Lady Downshire's townhouse," Emma said politely, but firmly.

"I will grant that request… for now," her grandfather responded. "Which brings us to a ticklish matter."

"Alymer… don't," Betsey warned through clenched teeth.

Crossing his arms over his chest, her grandfather expressed, "I have no choice but to bring it up." He lifted his brow at Emma. "You are betrothed to the Earl of Gunther."

"Absolutely not," she replied forcefully. "I am marrying Simeon."

Sir Alymer shrugged. "The contract was signed years ago, which is why I was relieved to hear you didn't elope with Lockhart. That would have surely negated the contract."

Simeon started to respond, but she put her hand on his sleeve to stop him. This was her fight, not his.

"My answer is no. I am marrying Simeon."

Sir Alymer looked at her like she was a fool. "Then I will be sued for breach of contract."

"So be it," she challenged.

His eyes narrowed. "You are an impertinent little thing..."

"Have you posted the banns yet?" her grandmother asked, speaking over her husband.

Simeon cleared his throat. "Yes, we have. We are having an engagement ball next week. You will receive an invitation shortly."

"I can't wait," Betsey declared.

"The Duchess of Remington is hosting the ball," Simeon informed the group.

Emma turned her astonished gaze towards him. "Truly?"

"Truly," he repeated, nudging her shoulder with his. "The night will be full of surprises."

"I can't wait," she replied, smiling over at him.

Her grandfather's annoyed drawl broke up their private interlude. "Lord Wentworth, may I ask what your annual income is?"

Emma's mouth dropped. How could her grandfather be so bold as to ask that question?

Unperturbed, Simeon answered, "I own Martin Trading Company, and I do not lack for income."

"This could work." Sir Alymer bobbed his head in approval. "I originally made my money in trade. I had hoped for my granddaughter to marry an earl, but..."

Hearing enough, Emma rose from her chair, forcing the men to rise, as well. "I do not care for titles or wealth. I only wanted to marry a man that loved me above all else."

"Bah," her grandfather said. "You sound just like your mother and look where she ended up!"

Emma tilted her chin determinedly. "I've heard enough. I now know why my mother left and my brother never informed me of your existence. They were both trying to protect me from *you*," she proclaimed, directing her comment at her grandfather.

"How dare you!" Sir Alymer roared. "You have no right to come into my home and speak to me that way."

"Please, Alymer calm down," Betsey attempted, reaching out to touch his sleeve.

"No, she is just like our Helena," Sir Alymer spat out.

"Good!" Boldly, Emma took a step closer to her grandfather. "I don't need your money, Grandfather. Frankly, I don't need you, either." She saw his eyes grow wide. "But I'm willing to allow you to be in my life, assuming you let me live my life as I see fit."

"But we are family…"

She put her hand up to stop him. "I already have a family. Luke and Rachel, along with the rest of the Becketts, have embraced me completely into their family. They have loved and protected me, allowing me to become who I was meant to be."

"And who is that?" Betsey asked gently.

Emma smiled at her grandmother. "Anything I want to be." She turned to look back at Simeon. "I'm ready to depart."

"Must you?" her grandmother inquired.

"I must," she replied, "but I hope to see you at my engagement ball."

Betsey's gaze grew determined. "We'll be there."

"No, we…" her grandfather started to say.

"Stop!" Betsey exclaimed, rising. "You will not run Emma off like you did to our Helena. I won't let you." She pointed at Emma. "She is our only remaining grandchild, and I refuse to lose her again."

Her grandfather's eyes softened a bit, but they were still hard. "Perhaps we could start over," he proposed, "assuming she will marry the earl…"

"No! She will marry who she wants, and *you* will accept that," her grandmother declared, pointing at him. "I won't lose my granddaughter." Her eyes filled with tears.

At the sight of his wife's tears, Alymer moved to embrace her, whispering something in her ear. He turned to address Emma. "Please forgive a stubborn, old fool," he said in a tight voice.

Emma almost frowned at his forced apology, but she couldn't help but notice her grandmother was staring at her with pleading eyes. If her grandfather could meet her halfway, then she was willing to, as well.

"I accept your apology, Grandfather."

He extended his hand out to Simeon. "We shall attend your engagement ball."

"Thank you, sir," Simeon replied, shaking his hand. "That makes us very happy."

Her grandfather gave her a curt nod. "Until the ball."

"Or you are welcome to call tomorrow," Betsey suggested in a hopeful tone.

Emma smiled at her grandmother. "I would love to."

"That pleases me greatly, Emma," Betsey replied with a relieved sigh.

"It is time to depart," Simeon reminded her softly. "We must ready ourselves for the theatre tonight."

"Before you go," her grandmother said as she stepped forward and embraced her. "I'm so happy that you're here, my dear Emma. Thank you for your willingness to forgive," she whispered into her hair. Once she stepped back, Simeon placed his hand on her elbow and led her from the drawing room.

Once they were situated in the carriage, Simeon asked, "Did you get the answers you were hoping for?"

"I did," she affirmed. "My family kept me away from my grandfather to protect me. He planned to marry me off without even discussing it."

Mrs. Morton interjected, "I couldn't help overhearing that he was marrying you off to an earl. Most women of the ton would be pleased by that arrangement."

"You'll find that I am not like most women of the ton," Emma asserted.

"For which I am grateful," Simeon added, kissing her on top of her head.

She tilted her face to look up at him. "Besides, I am much more interested in marrying a Bow Street Runner than an earl."

Simeon stood in the posh entry hall of the Duke of Remington's townhouse. He was in full dress and was waiting for Emma's arrival for their engagement ball. He had offered to escort her personally to the ball, but Downshire huffed a firm refusal, stating that it was not appropriate for an engaged couple to spend so much time together.

For the past week, he had spent every moment he could with Emma. They had gone on carriage rides through Hyde Park, toured Grange Gardens, and even spent evenings at the theatre. Unfortunately, no invitations had been forthcoming for balls or social gatherings for Emma, but he, along with members of the Beckett family, had already devised a plan to help with that. He had no doubt that after tonight, the ton would accept Emma for the beautiful, unique woman that she was.

The main door was opened, revealing Mr. and Mrs. Emmett Maddix. Previously, his breath would have hitched at Martha's beauty, but he now realized that it paled in comparison to Emma's.

He tilted his head respectfully. "Mr. and Mrs. Maddix, what a pleasure to see you again."

"Mrs. Maddix?" Martha repeated. "When did you stop calling me Martha?"

Reaching out, Emmett placed a hand on his shoulder. "You took a bullet for me, Simeon. We are past formalities between us."

"Understood." He smiled.

Turning to address her husband, Martha asked, "Would you mind giving me and Simeon a moment alone, dear?"

"Of course," Emmett replied. "It will give me a chance to get a drink before this blasted affair."

Laughing, Martha teased, "I fear that Luke is starting to rub off on you." She turned to face Simeon to explain. "Emmett and Luke have become rather close, living on neighboring estates."

"Or it could be that I prefer to see my godson, Matthew, and

Luke is always loitering about," Emmett joked. "Speaking of Luke, has he arrived?"

"Not yet, but Benedict and Jonathon are in the duke's study."

With a lingering glance at Martha, Emmett said, "Don't be long, my love."

As her husband walked away, Simeon questioned, "Are you happy?"

"Blissfully, so," she replied. "And you?"

"I am so happy that my heart might burst with joy," he answered honestly.

She smiled. "I am so pleased to hear that."

"For so many years, I thought I had been searching for you, but I realized that my heart had been searching for someone entirely different."

"You were searching for Emma," Martha said knowingly.

He nodded. "I was." He shifted his gaze over her shoulder, then admitted, "After you married Emmett, I spiraled out of control. I was filled with hate and despair, but Emma changed all that."

Martha's eyes grew reflective. "When you find true love, that's what happens. The love removes all doubts and fears, allowing you to be free from the burdens of your past."

"It's true," he remarked. "I'm finally returning to the man I was before I lost you that fateful day."

"I'm glad, especially since that was a good version of you," Martha commented, smoothing out her blue gown. "Has she met your family yet?"

Glancing in the direction of the ballroom, he responded, "She'll meet them tonight."

"They'll love her."

"I know. How could they not?"

Martha grew silent as she watched him for a moment. "Our once-merged paths have veered away from each other, and we've discovered far greater happiness than we ever thought possible when we started on our journey."

He smiled. "Well said, Martha."

"Well, it would be best if I join my husband in the study before the ball starts," Martha said. "I wouldn't want him to have all the fun without me, now would I?"

Simeon watched Martha walk down the hall, and he knew without a doubt that Martha was his past, and Emma was his future.

The main doors opened again, and Emma entered with Lord and Lady Downshire. His breath hitched at the mere sight of Emma dressed in a white gown with a pink ribbon around her waist. Her hair was piled high on her head and brown curls framed her face. Good heavens, she is stunning, he thought.

"Wentworth, you need a hobby!" Downshire exclaimed. "I fear you might smother Emma with all your unwanted attention."

"It's not unwanted," Emma remarked with a coy smile. "In fact, I find I'm constantly encouraging him."

"I will personally acquire a special license, and we will get you married tomorrow," Downshire suggested.

"We shall not," Rachel stated. "Emma and I have been planning the wedding luncheon for over a week now and invitations have been sent out."

"I need a drink," Downshire mumbled as he continued to walk down the hall.

"Poor Luke. He doesn't know quite what to do with Emma being in love," Rachel teased. She followed her husband with a light laugh.

Without waiting another moment, Simeon reached for Emma's hand and started leading her towards the gardens in the back of the townhouse.

"Why are you in such a hurry?"

He grinned as he opened the door. "I wanted a moment alone before your guardian comes looking for us, and quite possibly challenges me to a duel for absconding with you."

"I doubt he'd do that," she replied, her eyes full of mirth. "More likely, he will demand that we marry in the morning by special license."

He pulled her against him. "I find that I am in favor of that."

"As am I," she murmured before their lips met.

After a few moments, Simeon broke the kiss and reached into the pocket of his jacket. "I have something for you."

"Another gift?" Emma asked with an uplifted brow. "I daresay you're spoiling me."

He pulled out a diamond bracelet and held it up. "I saw this in a shop, and I thought of you."

Emma smiled as she fingered the matching diamond necklace around her neck. "I'm beginning to suspect you think of me often when you visit shops."

"It's true," he agreed, placing the bracelet around her wrist. "I think of little else."

Wrapping her arms around his neck, Emma declared, "I wish you would stop buying me jewelry. I don't need fancy jewels or clothes. I just want a place in your heart like you have in mine."

"You already own my heart." Simeon kissed her firmly on the lips, then added, "I love you."

"And I love you."

Resting his forehead on hers, he spoke softly. "Before you came into my life, I was a shell of the man I once was. But you changed me. With you, I'm free to live again."

"Careful," Emma teased, "it almost sounds like you believe in fairy tales."

"I admit that I am becoming a believer in happily ever afters." He smirked. "And the night is still young."

She eyed him suspiciously. "You're up to something."

"You shall find out soon enough," he said mysteriously, stepping back and reaching for her hand.

As he led her into the crowded ballroom, the Duke of Wellington was announced at the far end of the room.

Emma stopped and turned to him in surprise. "The Duke of Wellington is at my ball?"

"*Our* ball," he corrected. "And, yes."

"How did you arrange that?"

He shrugged nonchalantly. "It turns out that Lord Revett is a distant cousin of the Duke of Wellington, and he owed me a favor."

Lifting her brow, she asked, "The House Speaker owed *you* a favor?"

"You could call it that."

The crowd parted as the Duke of Remington, and a tall, lean man with a pointed nose and black hair approached them. "My dear

Emma Pearson, and Lord Wentworth, allow me to introduce you to the Duke of Wellington," he invited.

Emma curtsied. "Your grace," she murmured respectfully.

"Thank you for attending our humble engagement ball," Simeon said after he bowed.

The Duke of Wellington chuckled. "There is nothing humble about a social gathering that the Duchess of Remington hosts."

"Very true," the Duke of Remington agreed.

"I'm not a man that favors balls, but I would be honored if you would save your second set of the evening for me," the Duke of Wellington requested, his eyes reflecting kindness as he watched Emma.

"I would be honored," Emma said.

His lips twitched. "Very well, then. I will be back shortly to collect my dance."

"If that doesn't change the ton's opinion of you, then we have one more trick up our sleeve," the Duke of Remington remarked, watching the Duke of Wellington walk away.

"Which is?"

The duke smiled. "Patience is not one of your virtues, is it, my dear?"

"No, it's not," she admitted, returning his smile.

The duke bowed. "If you will excuse me, the ball is about to begin."

Taking her hand, Simeon placed it into the crook of his arm. "Would you like a glass of champagne before you dance the first set with Downshire?" he joked.

"That's not amusing," she replied, bringing up her gloved hand to hide her smile.

He chuckled. "This time if you fall, I will be the one to catch you."

"My hero," she breathed.

Sir Alymer and his wife broke through the crowd and approached them. Lady Blackmore stopped in front of Emma and gushed, "You are looking radiant tonight, my dear." She turned towards her husband. "Doesn't she, Alymer?"

"Yes, she looks just like her mother did at this age," he admitted, his voice strained. "I hadn't noticed it until now."

Betsey smiled kindly at her granddaughter. "Will you be coming for tea tomorrow?" she asked in a hopeful voice.

"Yes, I intend to," Emma replied.

"It warms my heart to hear you say that," Lady Blackmore said, breathing a sigh of relief. "I have enjoyed your visits immensely."

Sir Alymer cleared his throat. "As have I," he added gruffly, and Simeon heard the emotion in his voice. "If you have no objections, I would be honored to dance a set with you." He appeared to hold his breath in anticipation of her answer.

"I would like that, Grandfather," Emma said with a smile.

With a tender smile, Sir Alymer remarked, "I'm very happy that you're in our lives, Emma. Thank you for giving this gruff man a second chance."

Emma reached out and embraced her grandfather. "That's what family does. They forgive," she stated, stepping back.

"I shall return shortly to collect my dance, young lady." Sir Alymer turned back to his wife and offered his arm. "Shall we, Betsey?"

As they watched the Blackmores disappear back into the crush, a hush came over the room, and the orchestra stopped warming up.

"Her Royal Highness, Princess Charlotte," a herald announced.

The man continued to announce her entourage, but Simeon had stopped listening. He was too busy watching Emma. She had gone perfectly still as her eyes tracked the dark-haired princess approaching them near the center of the room.

Emma dropped into a low curtsy as Simeon bowed, both waiting to be acknowledged by her highness.

"Miss Pearson, I presume?" Princess Charlotte asked, stopping in front of her.

Keeping her gaze downcast, Emma replied, "Yes, your highness."

"Please, rise." Princess Charlotte stepped closer and lowered her voice. "I came at the behest of the Marquess of Downshire. He told me of your plight, and I do not condone Society's ill treatment of you, which is why I wanted to make an appearance. Now, your engagement ball will be the social event of the Season."

Emma brought her gaze up. "Thank you, your highness," she said with a hint of awe in her voice.

"You are welcome," Princess Charlotte responded kindly. "Lord Downshire also mentioned that you write articles."

"I do."

"That is splendid, Miss Pearson. I admire a woman that takes her own initiative." Princess Charlotte turned her gaze towards him. "Lord Wentworth, I presume."

"You are correct, your highness."

"Lord Downshire informed me that you stopped a violent attack at Grange Gardens a short time ago."

"Lord Downshire is well informed," he acknowledged.

"Your country thanks you for your service."

He bowed. "It is my honor to serve my king and country."

Princess Charlotte smiled. "I believe my work here is done," she said, her eyes scanning over the crowd before returning to Emma. "You shall be the belle of the Season after tonight, my dear. Enjoy it."

Turning gracefully, Princess Charlotte departed almost as quickly as she had arrived.

Emma's eyes filled with tears as she turned to face him. "How did Luke accomplish that feat?"

"I merely suggested that he write a missive to Princess Charlotte explaining the circumstances…"

His words were stilled when she went onto her tiptoes and kissed him firmly on his lips.

"Emma," he said against her lips, "you'll cause a scene."

She lowered herself back down to her feet. "Then let them talk about how much I love you. You wonderful, wonderful man," she gushed.

The orchestra started warming up in the corner again, and Downshire emerged from the crowd to collect Emma for the first set.

As Simeon watched Emma walk away, he felt contentment in his heart. For with Emma, he had everything he had ever wanted… someone to love, and to be loved in return. What a remarkable feeling that was.

Epilogue

Keeping her expression stoic, Emma was listening as Luke shared all the details surrounding David's death. She'd finally discovered what role everyone played those fateful days on the shores of Scotland. Although, it had been worse than she imagined.

Luke's last words were, "David died as a hero."

A contemplative silence descended over the group before Rachel spoke up as she stood next to Luke near the window. "You remind me of David in so many ways. He would have been proud of the woman you've become."

Turning her gaze out the window, Emma's eyes roamed the Scottish countryside, and the impressive stud farm. They'd traveled to Scotland after their month-long wedding tour to visit Luke and Rachel. Now a married woman, she had expressed a desire to learn the full story of her brother's death. Luke and Rachel had agreed that it was time for her to know the whole truth.

"Emma, are you all right?" Simeon asked, his arm wrapping around her shoulder.

"I am," she replied. "I'm relieved to finally know the truth."

Rachel came to sit next to her on the settee. "It's not that we didn't trust you, Emma, but you must understand the great burden of knowing the full truth of David's death, and our family's greatest secrets."

"I understand, and I would never betray my family." My family, she thought. It felt good to say that aloud.

"We know that, or we wouldn't have entrusted you with the facts now," Luke said with a weak smile. "In our own way, we were trying to protect you."

She tilted her chin with determination. "No more secrets between us."

"We can partially agree to that," Rachel stated, glancing back at her husband. "But, some of the secrets are not ours to share."

Nodding, Emma replied, "That's something I can understand."

She was not a simpleton. The women of the Beckett family had more secrets than the men, but she would eventually learn them. All in good time.

"If you don't mind, I'd like to show Simeon the cave where David died," Emma announced, rising. For the two years that she'd lived in Scotland, she was never once brave enough to visit the cave. The image of David's body lying in the darkened cave was too overwhelming for her to even attempt it.

"Would you like us to go with you?" Rachel asked with concern in her voice.

Emma shook her head. "It's time I go and see it for myself."

"There's no shame in not visiting the cave, Emma," Luke remarked, his brows furrowed.

With Simeon standing next to her, Emma felt buoyed by his presence. "I find I can do anything with Simeon by my side."

Simeon offered his arm, and together they made the trek down the long, treacherous path towards the beach. As they stepped onto the sand, Emma shuddered as her eyes sought out the cave.

"We don't have to go inside," Simeon said.

Emma turned to face her husband. "I need to. I want to."

"Would you like me to carry you?"

She laughed. "I'm not a babe."

"You didn't seem to mind much last night," he replied flirtatiously.

"You, sir, are a rogue," she bantered back.

Slowly, Emma made her way towards the cave with Simeon close behind. She stopped at the entrance of the dark, damp cave and peered in. Taking a deep breath for courage, she stepped inside, half-expecting a French soldier to jump out at her.

Her eyes scanned the wall, looking for blood or any sign of struggle, but she found none. It was just a cave. She breathed a sigh of relief.

"How are you faring?" Simeon asked, reaching for her hand.

She glanced over at him. "I feared what I would see. But there is nothing to fear here."

"Nothing at all," he replied.

Taking a step further inside, she heard the sound of trickling water along the rocky walls. "This cave has no power over me anymore," she declared, her voice echoing off the walls.

Simeon stepped closer and placed his hands on her hips. "You're an amazing woman, Mrs. Martin."

She wrapped her arms around his neck. "In what way am I amazing?"

"Coming down here and showing me where your brother died. That took great courage."

"It was time," she remarked, attempting to downplay the significance of it.

"Perhaps, but I still think you are brave."

She smiled. "I fear that you are a bit biased, husband."

"That's true," he agreed, leaning in and pressing his lips against hers. After a moment, he pulled back. "What if we named our first son David, after your brother?"

"I would like that very much."

She stepped out of his arms and walked over to the uneven walls, running her hand down the cold stones. "Because of David, I am living a charmed life that I scarcely can believe is real."

"It's a life you deserve."

"I wish I could thank him," she said, sadly.

Simeon walked slowly over to her. "I'm sure David would tell you to live your life to the fullest. To smile more, laugh more, and to show kindness to others."

She laughed. "Actually, my brother would tell me to stay out of trouble."

"He sounds wise." Simeon chuckled.

At that moment, a small amount of water started flowing into the cave. Simeon scooped her up into his arms and quickly exited. They strolled up the windy path until they found a boulder to sit on and watch the tide come in. Simeon draped his arm over her shoulder and pulled her close.

"Do I make you happy, Emma?" Simeon surprised her by asking.

"Yes," she answered honestly. "I'm happier than I ever thought possible." She paused and looked over at him. "Do I make you happy?"

Tears came to Simeon's eyes as he looked down at her. "I never thought I could be this happy, as well. For so long, I was miserable, and now I am filled with such contentment. It feels quite unbelievable."

"Well then, I propose we stick together," she joked, "especially since we get along so well."

Simeon laughed. "Life with you will never be dull, my dear Emma."

Simeon's laugh was Emma's favorite sound. She would spend the rest of her days ensuring Simeon knew how blessed she was to have married him. He supported her, cherished her, and loved her in such a way that she had no doubt of his affection.

She'd been right about one thing. Two people could fall so desperately in love with each other that they could create their own happily ever after. She knew, because she was living hers.

About the Author

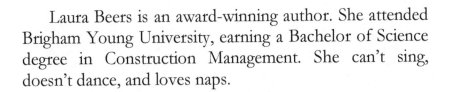

Laura Beers is an award-winning author. She attended Brigham Young University, earning a Bachelor of Science degree in Construction Management. She can't sing, doesn't dance, and loves naps.

Besides being a full-time homemaker to her three kids, she loves waterskiing, hiking, and drinking Dr. Pepper. She was born and raised in Southern California, but she now resides in South Carolina.

CPSIA information can be obtained
at www.ICGtesting.com
Printed in the USA
BVHW041051041019
560236BV00002B/104/P

9 781943 048960